No Safe Haven

LK Chapman

For my husband Ashley and son Felix, you always make me smile.

Cattleford

1

A car sped past and startled me as I hovered on the curb outside Cattleford train station. Beginning to shiver in the frosty air, I pulled my coat more tightly around my body and stared in surprise at my surroundings. The little village was so sleepy and picture perfect on this winter afternoon that it was like a Christmas model railway scene, with lights twinkling in cottage windows as the train disappeared into the distance. I should be clutching a pile of beautifully wrapped presents, not a bulging, hastily packed holdall that was fraying around the seams. But it wasn't Christmas now, it was early January, and it wasn't anything pleasant that had brought me here this day.

Sleet began to fall as I darted across the road, landing in icy splats on my sleeves and the strands of blonde hair that spilt over my shoulders from beneath my hood. I forced myself to slow down. Nobody knew I was coming here, I didn't need to run. Nevertheless, it was hard to break the habit of looking over my shoulder. Taking out my phone I quickly checked the address I was travelling to, before hastily slipping it back in my pocket as though somebody might see. Eleven Tricklebank Lane. The name was impossibly idyllic. Had I had fallen into a fairytale? The gently flowing stream I was now crossing via a pretty humped bridge was certainly nothing like the vast estuary I could just about glimpse from the kitchen window in my old flat. That river had huge gantry cranes on the opposite bank standing tall and impassive against a sky that more often than not was slate grey. This river was surrounded by nothing more forbidding than front gardens where bird feeders hung from trees and bright winter berries adorned bare branches like tiny jewels.

The sleet grew heavier and the light began to fade as I reached a sign for Tricklebank Lane. This was it. I paused and took a deep breath. What the hell was I going to say? In my frenzied flight from Habmouth I hadn't even considered how I would explain myself. Just getting away had been all I could think about.

I stopped at a sandstone cottage with ivy curling its way along the wall above the front door, beside which a ceramic sign with a picture of a hedgehog proclaimed it to be number eleven. How lucky Harriet and Jessica Dunridge were to live in a place like this. Not that Harriet would see it that way – she'd always expected the best of everything. In a way that's what I'd liked about her all those years ago. She knew what she wanted and how to go about getting it. Jessica, on the other hand, was a dreamer like me; romantic and impulsive, darting from one thing to the next without having any idea how it would work out. Or at least that's how I remembered her. I'd not seen the sisters for so long I couldn't possibly know what they were like now. Even so, it was surprising that the two women – so different in temperament – were sharing a house together. How had that come about?

It was a while before anybody answered the door. Had I definitely come to the right place? There were lights on behind the curtains, and I reached towards my pocket to check the address on my phone yet again, but my hand dropped as the door finally swung open. The woman standing there with a puzzled frown on her face wasn't instantly familiar and I stared stupidly until finally it clicked into place. Her hair was so different – no longer falling in dark, bouncy curls around her shoulders, it was now styled in a short bob, with vibrant red highlights that matched her glossy lips. She was curvier than she used to be – quite different from the girl I used to sometimes swap clothes with – and she had a real presence about her; confident and self-assured. Perhaps even a little intimidating. I blurted out her name. 'Harriet!'

She peered at me in bewilderment. 'Poppy?' she said finally, 'What are you doing here?'

'I know I should have told you I was coming,' I said, a little breathlessly, 'but I didn't know how to explain. I've got myself in a bit of a situation–'

'I did wonder why you asked for my address out of the blue,' Harriet said, 'but I didn't think you'd turn up on the doorstep! Come inside, it's freezing out there. I'll make some tea and you can warm up.'

After removing my wet boots and coat I followed her gratefully into a rustic kitchen, the cabinets painted pea green, with a brightly patterned rug on the floor. It wasn't a huge room – though it felt big to me after the tiny kitchen in my flat – and the cosy atmosphere wrapped around me like a warm embrace. My eyes kept slipping back to Harriet. What had happened in the twenty-odd years since we'd last spent any real time together? She wore no wedding ring, but hadn't I heard through the grapevine she'd got married? If she had, it must not have worked out – she was living with Jessica and not her husband.

'I'm so sorry to show up out of the blue like this–' I paused when a small boy with floppy dark hair trotted into the room, stopped in his tracks when he saw me, then turned on his heel and ran out again.

'That's Reef,' Harriet said. 'Jessica's son.'

'Reef?' I repeated, unsure whether I'd heard the name correctly.

The expression on Harriet's face left me in no doubt as to what she thought of the unusual name her sister had chosen. 'Yes,' she said, 'Jess was determined his name should be something to do with the ocean, since she met his dad by the sea.'

'I didn't know she'd had a baby.'

'Well, you know Jessica,' Harriet said. 'Full of surprises. She went away with some friends for the weekend, and Reef turned up like a belated souvenir nine months later. She seems to think it was destiny, or something.' She pulled a face.

'So her and Reef's dad, they're not together?'

'No,' she said bluntly.

I moved out of the way as Harriet called through the doorway to Reef. 'Tea time in three minutes!'

'Is Jess in?' I asked.

'Yes, she's upstairs somewhere.' Harriet handed me a mug of tea with a smile. 'Are you staying somewhere nearby then?' she asked, as her eyes drifted to my large bag in the hall.

'Um – no. Actually, I…' silence hung in the air for a moment until Harriet nodded. 'You need somewhere to stay?'

'Yes,' I admitted, embarrassed. 'Do you have a spare room? I know it's a lot to ask when I just turned up…'

A little crease appeared between Harriet's eyebrows.

'Forget I mentioned it,' I said, though my stomach tightened with anxiety. 'I'll find somewhere else. Please, don't worry. I know how weird it is asking to stay when you haven't seen me since we were teenagers.'

'It's not that I don't want to help, and we do have a spare room, it's just… well, let's sit down in the lounge and catch up for a minute. The fire's going and it's lovely and warm in there. You still look a bit chilled.'

'Poppy?' A voice on the stairs made me turn as Harriet led the way to the living room, and this face I instantly recognised. Jessica had barely changed at all. Her dark hair still fell in soft waves over her shoulders, reaching almost to the waistband of her skirt, and making a dramatic contrast to her porcelain skin and large, blue-grey eyes. She smiled widely, rushing down the stairs towards me at a pace which set her dangly silver earrings swinging chaotically. 'What are you doing here?' she asked me. 'Did you say you were coming?'

'No. I should have done, I'm sorry. It was all a bit last minute.'

Jessica bundled me into a hug and as she let me go – leaving me a little startled by the enthusiasm of her greeting – she said, 'You've got a dark cloud around you. But we can sort that out.'

I laughed uneasily. 'Yes, I suppose I do. That's how it feels.'

Now it was Jessica's turn to take in the sight of my bag in the hall. 'Are you staying?' she asked.

'I– I don't know,' I said.

'She can stay, can't she Harriet?' she said, without a hint of reservation over my sudden arrival and lack of explanation. 'She needs a friend right now, I can tell. And she looks half-starved.'

I folded my arms across myself self-consciously, and Harriet glared at Jessica.

'Well, she does,' Jessica said, before disappearing into the lounge. She emerged a few seconds later, encouraging Reef along in front of her. The small boy glanced at me shyly from dark eyes fringed with thick lashes, and I smiled at him. 'Let's get you your tea,' Jessica said to him. 'We've got a special friend with us tonight. Say hello to Poppy. She might need to sit down quietly for a bit though. She looks worn out. I think she must have had a long journey.'

'Hello,' Reef said, looking at me curiously.

'Hello Reef. It's lovely to meet you.'

Apparently now at peace with the unexpected arrival of a stranger in his house, Reef obediently trotted into the kitchen to get his dinner, and Harriet smiled at me. 'Looks like you're staying then.'

'Honestly, I don't know how to thank you.'

She waved my words away. 'Jessica's right. You do look like you've had it tough.' She gestured towards the living room and I sank down into an armchair, overwhelmed with relief. I'd got to a place where nobody could follow – not easily anyway. Finally, I was safe.

...

'So,' Jessica said, 'where do we even start? It's been forever.'

I nodded, eyes heavy with tiredness. I wanted to sleep for a week. Maybe a month. But now that Reef was in bed the two sisters had their eyes fixed on me, and I fidgeted uncomfortably on my chair, trying to force my lethargic brain to wake up.

Harriet shook her head. 'She's exhausted,' she said.

'I'm okay,' I lied.

'No, you're not. You should go upstairs. We can save catching up until tomorrow.'

Filled with gratitude as they dropped their questions, I followed Harriet upstairs and she showed me the spare room. I smiled faintly as I stepped inside, which was like going back in time. The single bed below the small window was covered with a floral bedspread, while the sloped ceiling made the room cute and cosy. There was a pine wardrobe and a chest of drawers on which stood a decorative china wash basin and jug.

'The bathroom is just next door,' Harriet said, as she walked across the room to close the frilly curtains. 'Do you want me to bring up a sandwich or something? Me and Jessica are about to make dinner but I think you'll be asleep before we're done.'

'No,' I said, 'thank you. I ate on the train.'

It wasn't true. In fact I couldn't really remember the last time I ate, but my body was so exhausted that now I was somewhere safe – somewhere I could finally switch off – I just wanted to be left in peace. Once Harriet had gone I took off my jumper and jeans and got into bed without so much as brushing my teeth or running a comb through my hair, eyes closing before my head hit the pillow.

2

'I have never known anyone sleep as long as you,' Jessica said, looking up from wiping Reef's chin as he got down from the table after his breakfast. 'Not an adult, anyway.'

'It's only eight-thirty,' I said, as my eye caught the large chicken-shaped wall clock. But she had a point. It hadn't even been eight when I'd gone to bed the night before.

'You must have really needed it,' Harriet said. 'Do you feel better now?'

I rubbed my eyes. My stomach was aching with hunger, but I couldn't start demanding food before they offered.

'There's tea in the pot,' Harriet said, as if she could hear my thoughts. 'Help yourself to toast, or cereal.'

With a surge of relief I did as she asked, forcing myself not to stuff my breakfast down, though I was so hungry it was hard to restrain myself. Reef sat on the floor playing a game on his tablet and glancing at me occasionally.

'When does he go back to school?' I asked.

'Tomorrow,' Jessica said. 'It's an inset day today.'

'How's Dominic?' Harriet asked me, as I finished my slice of toast and brushed crumbs from my lips. 'How old is he now?'

'Eighteen. He's at university.'

'Is he?' Harriet said. 'Has it really been that long?'

'You know it has,' Jessica chimed in. 'You can hardly forget Dominic was born after Poppy's waters broke in the exam hall. So you know exactly how long it's been.'

'Jess—' Harriet started to chide her.

'It's okay,' I said.

'How can water *break*?' Reef asked from beside my ankle.

'What's Dominic studying?' Harriet asked quickly.

'Botany,' I said. 'Ever since he was little he's been obsessed with plants. His room was like a jungle.'

It was an exaggeration – Dominic's houseplant ambitions had far exceeded my budget – but every birthday and Christmas I got him something to add to his collection.

'Is he enjoying it?'

'Yes, I think so. Not that I can ever find out much. He's always so busy.'

'That must be tough,' Harriet said. 'How are you finding it now he's left home?'

A wave of emotion made my throat tighten. I didn't trust myself to speak.

'I'll make you another piece of toast, if you want?' Harriet said, trying to change the subject when she saw my distress. She gave me a searching look when I didn't answer straight away and it hit me. She thought I had an eating disorder. I could hardly blame her for wondering, but there was no quick or simple way to explain to her how I'd ended up in such a state. I knew I looked thin, and ill. Some days I felt twice my thirty-four years.

'It's hard to eat when you're scared,' Jessica said.

'Scared?' Reef asked, looking up at me wide-eyed.

'I'm okay sweetheart,' I told him.

'Has Reef read his reading book a single time over Christmas?' Harriet said pointedly to Jessica. 'You should get that out of the way before he gets too absorbed in his games.'

Taking the hint, Jessica gathered up the small boy, who protested vehemently as she carted him off to the living room. Harriet placed another slice of thick buttered toast in front of me, and I spread it with jam.

'Jessica's right, isn't she? You are scared.' Harriet said gently. 'You're running from something.'

I nodded as I bit into my toast. There was no point trying to hide it.

'I know we drifted apart after you had Dominic, and I'm sorry about that. I wish I'd tried harder, but I – I guess I didn't know what to say to you.'

'I'm sorry too,' I said, and after a brief silence I added, 'it was hard for me to be around you and Jess. You were doing normal teenage stuff, and I had a newborn baby. We weren't living in the same world any more. I found it... it was just painful. I suppose *I* didn't know what to say to *you*, either.'

'You had Liam though. Did he stick by you? You said things were a bit rocky when you moved in with him and his parents, but when the two of you moved to Habmouth, I really hoped it would work out.'

I threw my toast down. The lump in my throat made it impossible to swallow. Harriet reached out and touched my arm. 'Poppy? Is this to do with Liam? Is he why you're here?'

I shook my head. Then I nodded. Then I put my face in my hands and burst into tears.

...

Harriet put her arm around my shoulders as I cried, and she spoke to me softly. 'Whatever it is, it can be fixed. Nothing is as bad as all this, no matter how it seems right now.'

I drew in several shaky breaths. She had no idea. 'It's... so bad.' I choked out.

'Well, you're safe here,' Harriet said. 'The most drama we've ever had in Cattleford is when someone nicked a couple of the "village in bloom" hanging basket displays. And the scarecrow competition can get a bit heated from time to time. I thought Mr Quail three doors down was going to punch one of the judges last year.'

I let out a shaky laugh at her words and wiped my eyes, but the tears quickly overflowed again. It was as though all the emotion from the past was trying to come out at once. Harriet rubbed my back. 'You've been holding all this in for a long time, haven't you?' she said. 'It's going to be okay now. We'll sort it out.'

My tears began to subside at her reassuring tone. 'I'm not sure... it can be sorted out.'

Harriet sat back and watched me as my tears finally dried and I took a tentative bite of my toast.

'Do you and Jessica have plans today?' I asked her eventually. 'What do you usually do in the school holidays?'

'I'll catch up on paperwork for the shop before I open up again tomorrow, and Jessica will probably take Reef to the park, or maybe swimming.'

'What shop?' I asked, realising I had no idea what the sisters did.

'It was Mum's originally,' she said. 'Bits and Bobbins – it's a fabric shop and haberdashery. That was the plan when Mum and Dad moved here – start a nice little business in a village, somewhere Jessica could get involved too. Jessica's a dressmaker. It works well, she can fit it in around Reef and she gets customers via the shop sometimes.'

'And your parents, where are they now? Does your mum still run the shop, or is it just you?'

'To begin with I had nothing to do with the shop. It was Mum and Jessica's thing. Jessica carried on living with them – she never flew the nest. Then my dad got ill and Mum had to spend more and more time looking after him. I was married at that point, and me and Ben – that's my ex husband – had moved away, but we wanted to be close to family again. I stepped in and took over Bits and Bobbins and me and Ben moved to a house in the village.'

'But now you and Jessica live here together.'

'Yes. My dad died, and then four or five years later my mum met someone else. She married him and moved to Spain, and Jessica was here in the house on her own for a bit. Then me and Ben–' her face contorted with pain. 'Well, it didn't work out. We sold our house and I moved in here with Jessica. She needed me while she was pregnant, and when Reef was first born. It wasn't an easy time for her.'

'I'm sorry. About your dad, and about you and Ben.'

Harriet nodded her thanks and stood up to clear the table, while I sat and sipped my tea slowly. My hands were still shaky and my eyes were puffy. God knows what Harriet thought of my outburst, though it appeared she'd taken it in her stride. Her unruffled, practical nature was soothing, and an unfamiliar sense of tranquillity filled me as she bustled around the warm and cosy kitchen. 'How about I help out in the shop?' I suggested. 'For free, of course, to make up for you letting me stay. Just while I get myself sorted out.'

Harriet turned. 'You're planning on staying a while, then?'

I put my hand up to my mouth. Had they only meant for me to stay one night? I could hardly remember our conversation from the evening before and now I'd put my foot right in it. 'Sorry, I–'

'It's okay,' Harriet said. 'Me and Jess realised you'd probably need more than one night, and I would appreciate an extra pair of hands in the shop. We've got someone who works Fridays and Saturdays to help me out, but having you there during the week would be good. And I'd enjoy the company.'

I tried not to show my relief too visibly. 'Thank you,' I said. 'Really, Harriet, you don't know how much this means to me.'

3

After a long soak in the bath – Harriet insisted I spend the morning relaxing – I sat on my little bed beside the window and gazed out at the view. The sister's cottage garden was a little sorry for itself in winter, dormant as the plants reserved their energy to burst into life in the year ahead, though here and there the odd cluster of berries added some cheer. Beyond the ramshackle stone wall at the bottom of the garden, leafless trees lined the edge of the stream. It was a dismal day – the sky a uniform shade of grey above the bare branches, sprays of drizzle misting the air – and yet I was still struck by the beauty of these surroundings. It was all so *gentle,* so serene. I got up and pulled on a thick jumper, before making my way downstairs.

'In this weather?' Harriet said, when I told her I was going for a walk.

'I need some fresh air, and to clear my head.'

'Me and Reef could come?' Jessica suggested. 'He's full of beans no matter what the weather. He needs to run off some energy.'

'I– sorry, Jess, normally I would, but I need to think for a little while. I want to give Dominic a call too.'

'Okay,' she said. 'I think I'll take Reef out anyway, but we'll keep out of your way. I'll take him down to the duck pond.'

I slipped out of the house while Jessica was still bundling Reef up in a coat and scarf. The weather really was horrible, the drizzle sapping the warmth from my body and misting my hair with chilly droplets. Nevertheless, I made my way to the centre of the village. No more than a small cluster of shops, the central square was empty apart from the war memorial and few vacant benches. I sat down on one and took my phone from my pocket. It was gone eleven now, so Dominic should be up. In fact, when my eyes fell on the screen I was shocked to see how many missed calls I had from him. He must have been calling while I was in the bath.

'Why haven't you been answering your phone?' Dominic said, his voice urgent. 'I've been so worried—'

'Dom, I'm sorry, I didn't—'

'Max is freaking out! He says you've blocked his number and disappeared, that he has no idea where you've gone.'

'Me and Max are over,' I said, as calmly as I could. 'It's nothing to do with him where I go or what I do.'

'I know that,' Dominic said, 'but he was good to us and he still cares about you. Couldn't you have told him you were leaving? Or me, at least? And why have you blocked him?'

'I don't owe him any explanation!' I said, more sharply than I intended. 'Sorry, Dom,' I said quickly. 'I should have told you what was going on, I don't know why I didn't.' I did know, of course. If I'd told him I was planning to leave he would have been worried, and he'd have confided in Max. 'I just need some space. I'm perfectly safe, you can tell Max not to worry, and you don't need to be concerned either. I will be changing my number soon though, and when I do, please don't tell Max my new one. I want a fresh start, and Max can't be a part of that. I need a clean break, and I think he does too, he just hasn't realised it yet.'

There was a short silence. 'So you're really okay?'

'Yes. I'm okay. I'm safe.'

I brushed away the drizzle that was settling on my face. What was wrong with my brain nowadays? I should have called Dominic before I went to sleep and told him that I'd left. Of course Max would go straight to Dominic and start worrying him once he realised I'd got away. But I'd barely been able to keep my eyes open. My body just needed to stop.

'Mum, where are you?' he asked me. 'Where are you staying?'

'I'm safe. That's all you need to know.'

'Are you sure you're safe?'

'Yes, I'm sure.'

'What about money?' Dominic asked.

'Shouldn't it be me asking *you* these questions? You're supposed to be the penniless student.'

Dominic let out a laugh. 'Hardly,' he said. 'Between my student loan, my restaurant job and the money Max gave me I've got more cash than I could have dreamed of back when we–' he stopped abruptly, sparing me the memory, and I looked up at the sound of voices. A family were walking across the square, a couple of small dogs running along in front of them. They smiled at me and said hello, and I was startled for a moment, then I smiled back, a little guardedly.

'You don't need to worry about me,' Dominic continued, 'although…' he paused and I steeled myself. I knew what was coming. 'I wanted to talk to you about that phone call.'

I closed my eyes briefly, glad when I opened them that the family had disappeared around the corner.

'Why were you asking me those questions?' Dominic pressed me. 'I thought you said we should never mention that night, and yet you–'

'And we *shouldn't* talk about it,' I said. 'I wasn't thinking straight before, and I'm so sorry I scared you. I got paranoid, that's all, but it's fine now. I know it's hard, but you need to try and forget it. We can't change what happened.'

'I'll never forget it,' he said quietly, and for a moment I couldn't trust myself to speak. I glanced up at the shop opposite me, trying to calm myself. It was closed – as all the shops were, apart from the small supermarket and the pharmacy – but this shop caught my eye as it was so pretty with its powder pink paintwork, while the window display was a riot of colour. My eyes drifted to the name painted in sprawling, curly script above the door: *Bits and Bobbins.* This was Harriet's shop! How wonderful to work somewhere so cheerful.

'Mum?'

'I'm sorry,' I said. I didn't know what else I could say to him. 'Just keep reminding yourself that it wasn't your fault. If it was anyone's fault it was mine, okay?'

'No, it was Liam's.'

I shivered involuntarily. The bench was damp, and rainwater was beginning to soak into my jeans, but I wasn't in a hurry to get up and start walking again. 'You can't stay angry at your dad forever,' I told him.

'That man is *not* my dad.'

'Dominic, listen to me. Who's to blame for any of it doesn't matter any more. And I know my actions probably make no sense to you, but once I've had a bit of time to make plans I will explain why I had to leave, okay? I will make it right. I promise.'

There was a burst of laughter and shouting down the phone and Dominic said flatly, 'We were about to go out for breakfast.'

'It's nearly lunchtime.'

'Not when you don't go to bed until three a.m. the night before.'

'You go, then,' I said, relieved that he was managing to enjoy himself despite everything. 'Go and have fun.'

'Mum… I'm worried about you,' he said. 'Are you *sure* you're okay? I can send you money, I can come and see you, you don't have to pretend you're all right.'

'I'm not your responsibility, *you're* mine,' I said, ashamed by his offer.

'You know I don't mean it like that. We've always looked after each other. Through everything.'

There was another burst of laughter, and his friends yelling his name, and Dominic sighed.

'Go,' I said. 'We can talk another time. All you need to know is that I'm okay. I'm safe. And I love you.' I paused. 'It will be okay. I promise.'

As Dominic ended the call I dug my nails into my palms until my eyes stung with tears. I had to make things right, even though it felt impossible. I couldn't let my son down, not again.

…

'So, that's it,' Harriet said, 'I think you've seen it all.'

I nodded, slightly sad the tour of Bits and Bobbins was over. I'd enjoyed losing myself in the brightly coloured rolls of fabric towards the back of the store – gazing at the patterns and stroking the rolls of cloth had made me feel cosy and safe like an animal in a little nest. We now stood in a corner surrounded by bright ribbons and thread in every imaginable colour, and Harriet eyed me quizzically.

'It's a lovely little place,' I said. 'Does it get busy?'

'People drive here from all around,' she said, 'there's nowhere else like it nearby. It's still not exactly bustling – not often anyway – but it's steady. We've got quite a few regulars. It's enough for me and Jess to get by, especially with her dressmaking too.'

'What do you need me to do?'

'Well, I want to have a tidy up and reorganise the store room but it's awkward when I'm on my own. I thought now would be a good time, with you here to help.'

'Okay,' I said, 'just tell me what to do and I'll do it.'

We worked companionably until lunchtime, Harriet darting off to serve the odd customer who came in, while I tackled the disorder that had crept into the store room. She didn't try to press me on what had brought me to her door two days before and I didn't volunteer any information, but at half past twelve she wrote a note saying the shop was closed for lunch and stuck it on the door.

'We'll go to the pub for lunch,' she said. 'If you want to?'

I nodded, and we pulled on our coats, though the pub wasn't far. On the corner of the square, The Rose and Thistle appeared for all the world like it had risen up from the earth with its old stone walls strewn with ivy and a higgledy-piggledy assortment of windows which looked like somebody had thrown them at the wall then fitted them where they landed.

I ate warily, sure that Harriet was going to start grilling me any second. Although it was the middle of the day it was dull and dark outside, and despite our table being beside the window it could almost have been evening. The food was delicious though, and gradually my guard began to come down.

'Did you manage to talk to Dominic yesterday?' Harriet asked me.

'Yes, briefly.'

'Does he know where you are?'

I hesitated. 'No,' I said, 'not exactly. He knows I'm okay, though.'

Harriet nodded as she finished her plate of ham, egg and chips and pushed it aside. 'Poppy, I can see you don't really want to talk about whatever it is that's happened…'

If she was waiting for me to speak, she would be disappointed. My throat closed up, and I jabbed helplessly at the remains of my lasagne.

'Maybe you could start at the beginning?' Harriet suggested. 'The last time we saw each other you were about to move to Habmouth with Liam. What happened after that? Did things go wrong between you?'

Her words opened up a great, yawning canyon in my mind, as though I was looking down on the last eighteen years from a great height. I couldn't fall back in, not when I'd worked so hard to claw my way out.

Before I could speak, there was a tap on the window. Jessica was outside, a hat with an excessively large, multicoloured bobble perched on her head, while her dark hair tumbled over her shoulders. She disappeared as she made her way to the door, and once inside she pulled up a chair and placed a bulging shopping bag on the floor.

'I thought you must be in here when I saw the sign on the shop,' she said. 'I've been getting food for Reef's birthday party tomorrow.'

I smiled. Reef had been talking about little else that morning before school. 'Why don't I pick him up later?' I suggested. 'It will give you more time to get organised. That's if Harriet can spare me from the shop,' I added.

'Could you?' Jessica said. 'That would really help me out. I had two brides come round for dress fittings this morning before I managed to get out of the door to get this food. I've not even bought Reef's presents yet! Having his birthday so soon after Christmas, it's chaos.'

'Well, you definitely need the afternoon to yourself then,' I said, imagining Reef's face if he didn't get all the various extra bits of train set that he insisted he needed. The house was littered with wooden track and little trains, which drove Harriet to distraction, though Jessica was apparently unconcerned by the mess, content to kick things out of the way when necessary.

Jessica rushed off to take the party food back to the house, while Harriet and I, slightly reluctantly, left the cosy pub to make our way back to Bits and Bobbins.

'Whatever it is,' Harriet said to me as she unlocked the door, 'it won't seem as bad once you've shared it, I promise you. I don't want to pry, but maybe a new perspective on things could help you plan your next steps.'

My stomach clenched. *Your next steps.* Harriet was wondering when I was going to leave. 'I– I think I'm still trying to process it all myself, to be honest,' I said.

I was relieved to be away from Harriet's questions at school pick-up time, and once I'd collected Reef I sat with him in the corner of the living room, helping him build his train set. Initially unsure about being left with me, he was now perfectly happy, attaching bits of track together and running his beloved trains around it. Harriet was startled when she came home from the shop to find me and Reef sat in the kitchen tucking into jacket potatoes, and she glanced around to see where Jessica was.

'There's two more potatoes in the oven for you and Jess,' I told her.

Harriet frowned. 'Is she still not back, then? I thought she'd be with you.'

'She said she got caught up. I'm sure she'll be back soon.'

Harriet looked at her watch, and then went over to the oven to check on the potatoes. 'She probably went to the big shopping centre in Bracton. It takes a little while to drive there.'

Jessica didn't arrive for another half an hour, when she burst through the door with bulging shopping bags. 'Got a few other things,' she said to me as she rushed down the hall, trying to keep the bags from Reef's sight.

'Good,' I said, 'I'm glad I could help out.' She beamed at me and dashed up the stairs, for all the world like a teenager who had been allowed out to meet their friends when they were supposed to be grounded. Harriet's face was set in a look of disapproval, but she made no comment. Once Jessica had deposited the shopping in her room and come back to hug Reef she'd lost none of her exuberance, and started chattering away to him animatedly.

'It's late,' Harriet said, 'he should be getting to bed.'

Jessica glanced at the clock, then she chased Reef up the stairs to the bathroom with much screaming and excitement from them both.

Harriet shook her head, and muttered something about hoping Jessica hadn't spent too much money.

'It seemed like she needed it,' I said, 'she obviously really enjoyed herself.'

'She's…' Harriet paused. 'She's not that sensible with money,' she said. 'Or anything, really.'

'Well, I can relate to that,' I said, before I could stop myself.

Harriet pushed a stray strand of red hair away from her eyebrow as she looked at me. 'Is it something to do with money? Is that why you're running?'

My skin prickled. Why the hell had I said anything about it? Apart from anything else, Harriet would realise that if I had no money I didn't have a chance of finding somewhere else to live, and would probably be keen to get rid of me before I managed to really get my feet under the table. I did have a little bit of money left, but it was hardly enough to keep me going for long, especially if pub lunches were a regular fixture for Harriet.

Upstairs there was a burst of laugher and splashing from the bathroom. 'Jess is in a good mood,' I said.

'She gets like this,' Harriet said, 'she's as excited about things as Reef when she gets going.'

'I think it's nice.'

Harriet drummed her fingers on the kitchen counter. 'Poppy, please. You can trust me. At least tell me what happened between you and Liam when you moved to Habmouth.'

'It's ancient history.'

'Then there's no harm in digging it up,' she said.

I considered her reasoning. Talking about what had happened all those years ago was painful, but she was right, it couldn't harm me. The thing was, perhaps it wasn't so ancient. After all, hadn't what happened back then sowed the seeds for everything that came after? And in the past few years I'd certainly reaped what Liam had sown, in one poisonous harvest after another.

Habmouth

4

Weak sunlight spilled through the clouds, warming our chilly faces. The estuary was a dirty brown, the tide was out and birds had come to feast on the creatures in the mud. Dominic trotted along the path by my side, a three year old barrel of energy, cheeks rosy and eyes bright.

'When's Daddy coming back?' he asked me.

I hated this question. Stuffing my hands deep inside my pockets I turned my face away from him, and an icy wind blew strands of hair across my eyes. *When's Daddy coming back?* In some ways I was surprised Dominic even knew who Daddy was, since Liam spent so little time in the flat with us.

'He'll come back when he's ready,' I said. It was the best answer I could give. Four nights was the longest Liam had ever gone missing. Every night I expected to hear his key in the lock and for him to come stumbling in and pile into bed with me expecting a quick fumble in the dark. 'Why can't you just grow up?' I screamed at him the last time he arrived back from his disappearing act. He said I was boring and no fun any more.

I turned and scooped Dominic up into my arms, where he squirmed and struggled until I put him down again. He was getting heavy now. His coat was too small. And his shoes.

Why didn't Liam understand that I was lonely? Achingly, crushingly lonely. He could go out drinking after work with whoever he was friends with now, but I didn't know anybody in Habmouth. I'd tried once or twice to go along to things with Dominic but the fact that all the other mums were at least ten years older than me left me feeling isolated and vaguely embarrassed, as if I had no right to be there. Not that anyone had ever been unkind, but the discomfort was too much, so me and Dominic kept mostly to ourselves since we moved. I could kick myself for being taken in by it all. I'd followed Liam here like an idiot when his uncle had given him a job on a building site – believing Liam when he was filled with energy and optimism – when he cast away my doubts by painting a glorious picture of how we would live and how happy we would be. 'It won't be like it is now,' he told me as we sat squashed together in the cramped bedroom in his parent's house, our eyes on Dominic's cot in the corner of the room and his toys and clothes all over the floor. 'I'll be earning proper money and we'll have our own space. And I'll sort myself out, I promise.'

I kicked out at a scrubby tuft of grass. What use were his bloody promises? They didn't put food on the table or new shoes on Dominic's feet. Sometimes it was as though the only thing I could rely on in this place was the estuary; its rise and fall, its steady inevitability. Liam was about as trustworthy as a snake, our relationship built on foundations no more stable than the mud stretching out below us that would soon be buried below the tides. I couldn't rely on him. I could only rely on myself.

…

That night, Liam did come home. Not until after I'd finished getting Dominic into bed though. God forbid Liam would be here to cook fish fingers, wipe grubby mouths, run baths or read stories. Our son was fast asleep by the time his dad burst in, with no apology and no explanation.

Although he was a couple of years older than me, Liam hadn't managed to settle into looking like an adult yet. He was tall but still lanky, as if his limbs were in permanent protest against his body. Tonight his dark hair was greasy, eyes red-rimmed with lack of sleep. Had he washed a single time since he'd gone AWOL? I wouldn't ask him where he'd been. He'd have crashed at friends' houses, sofa-surfing even though he had a home, and a family. It hurt that it was us he was getting away from, but I'd hardened myself to that.

'Is there any food?' he asked me.

'Go and look for yourself.'

He threw himself down on the sofa. 'I'm knackered,' he said.

A crazy urge to grab the lamp off the table beside him and smash it over his head nearly overwhelmed me. *He* was knackered? I had no doubt he was tired, but it was because he'd been partying for days. *I* was knackered from looking after a three year old by myself. *His* three year old.

'Dominic is fine, by the way.'

'Pops—'

'I don't like being called that.'

He put his head in his hands. 'Why can't you just give me a break?' he said. 'Whenever I'm here you go on and on at me—'

'Maybe you should leave again, then!' I screamed at him, as a red mist descended. 'You're no use to me! Just go away. Leave me alone. Leave me alone!'

I sank down to my knees against the wall, and eventually he got up from the sofa and came to kneel down beside me. 'I'm sorry,' he whispered, kissing my hair. 'I know how shit I am at this—'

'You promised,' I said. 'You promised it would be different here.'

He tried to lift my chin with his hand, and I pressed it harder into my knees. 'I love you,' he whispered.

Gradually, I raised my head and let my eyes meet his. 'I won't disappear again,' he said. 'It was a pretty shit weekend, anyway. I just didn't want to come home and have you disappointed with me.'

I gave him a shove. 'That makes no sense,' I said, my anger rising, but he grabbed me and kissed me. 'I hate you,' I told him when our lips parted.

'I know,' he said. But when he kissed me again, I kissed him back.

Cattleford

5

Jessica looked up from where she sat on the floral wool rug that covered the living room floor. Surrounded by rolls of wrapping paper and presents, her preparations for Reef's birthday were in full swing. 'I can't imagine how it must have felt,' she said. 'Only being nineteen and living somewhere you don't know with a small child and no help.'

I sighed. I'd decided I would speak to both of the sisters together once Reef was in bed, and they'd listened in silence as I began explaining what had happened between me and Liam, but what I'd said so far was the easy bit. There was a lot worse to come.

'Liam's parents visited occasionally, to give me a bit of support,' I told them, 'but it was always awkward. They felt bad for how Liam was behaving.'

'He didn't manage to grow up then?' Harriet said, sipping her mug of tea.

'No,' I said quietly. I looked down at all the presents Jessica had bought for Reef. Far more than I had ever been able to afford for Dominic, but I suspected she'd gone a little overboard in her excitement. 'Do you want me to help you wrap some of these?' I asked her.

She nodded gratefully and I sat down on the floor beside her, pulling a big book about trains towards me. It was nice Jessica got so much joy from being with Reef, and he was a lovely little boy. Quite serious, but full of fun too and always ready for a cuddle with his mum or Auntie Harri.

Harriet watched me over the brim of her mug and I mulled over her comments about Liam's lack of maturity. My own parents were always so strict and critical that meeting Liam and seeing the way he lived – how he did whatever he wanted whenever he wanted – the way he was so light-hearted about life, had drawn me to him with a force bordering on obsession. I was smitten with him, in love beyond all reason and all logic. I didn't see a single one of his flaws, though with hindsight they must have been glaring. 'He wasn't ready to be a dad,' I told her.

'Well, he was only eighteen when Dominic was born,' Jessica said.

'And Poppy was only sixteen,' Harriet shot back, her voice hot with emotion, 'and no matter how young he was, he brought a child into the world and he should have taken responsibility for it.'

'Didn't your mum and dad help?' Jessica asked.

I shook my head. From my parents' point of view they probably would say they had been helping, but their constant interfering, criticism and barely concealed disappointment in me had felt like anything but. 'Being around my parents wasn't good for me or Dom. That's why I moved in with Liam and his family before we left for Habmouth. I tried to have as little contact with my parents as possible after that. Then we stopped talking altogether.'

'They always were unreasonable,' Harriet said bluntly. 'I don't blame you Poppy.'

I sighed as I finished wrapping the first parcel and pulled a jigsaw towards me.

'I always thought it was so romantic, how you and Liam ran away to start a new life together,' Jessica said, and Harriet gave her a withering look. 'What?' Jessica said. 'It was. Even if it didn't work out.'

'We didn't run away. Everyone knew where we were going.'

'Still,' Jessica said thoughtfully.

'How long were you together in Habmouth?' Harriet asked me.

'We stuck it out for eighteen months or so,' I said. 'Then one day he came home, and…' my fingers fumbled with the wrapping paper. Liam's face filled my mind – that disturbed light in his eyes – the way he'd laughed so strangely, spouting nonsense while I tried to persuade him to go. Dominic had woken up and wandered in, standing in the doorway unnoticed by us until the glass had shattered and he'd screamed. His sobs in the semi-darkness echoed in my mind, and I could still remember the fat tears rolling down his cheeks.

Harriet got up from her armchair and crouched by my side, her hand on my shoulder.

'It's okay,' I said. 'I'm all right.'

'What did he do?'

'Well, he'd obviously taken something. He was being weird and he was scaring me. I told him to go away and to come back when he'd sobered up, but he wouldn't leave. So we started arguing. Normally when we got mad at each other it didn't get too crazy – we'd just shout for a few minutes and that would be the end of it. But that night he didn't know when to stop. I was begging him to go. I told him to sleep it off at one of his friend's houses and we could talk sensibly in the morning, but he picked up a glass and threw it at me. It hit the wall above my head, and the glass rained down on me. We hadn't realised that Dominic had got up and was standing in the doorway watching the whole thing, and when he started to cry I couldn't hold him to comfort him because I was covered in glass.'

Jessica had stopped wrapping and was watching me, her blue-grey eyes wide. 'Does Dominic remember that?'

'I don't really know.'

'Were you hurt?' Harriet asked.

'Not really. I had some small cuts but I was mostly just in shock. He'd never done anything like that before. And he was aiming at *me* – I was lucky the glass only hit the wall.'

'Please tell me that you kicked him out after that,' she said.

'I didn't need to. He chose to leave. He looked at me and Dominic, saw how upset we were and walked out.'

Managing to finish wrapping the jigsaw, I placed it on top of the pile of presents as Jessica started work on the final one. I stayed on the floor, stretching my legs out in front of me as I rested my back on the sofa. A fire was crackling away in the log burner, and I was filled with such a strong desire to stay here forever that it took my breath away.

'Good riddance,' Harriet said. 'You deserve better than him.'

'The thing was, for a long time I hoped he'd come back,' I said. 'I know that makes me sound weak, but Liam and I got together when I was only fifteen. He was my family – he'd always accepted me just the way I was. And when things were good with him, they could be so good. I was scared to be left completely on my own. I didn't want to go crawling back to my parents, so I stayed in Habmouth and kept hoping Liam would come back, but one week went by, then two, then a month. I couldn't stay in the flat without Liam's money coming in. I was going to try to get a council flat but Liam's parents said they would help me out with money for a little while. They wanted me to stay in the same place in case Liam decided to come home. He'd broken all contact with me, and them, but we thought he might try to find me again when he was ready. They paid a few months rent on the flat for me, and once Dominic started school I got a job and could pay my own way, just about. It was tough, but we got by. I just took life one day at a time.'

'And then?' Jessica said, tucking her long hair behind her ear as she fixed her eyes on me again.

I didn't answer straight away. It felt wrong to gloss over all those years and so many struggles. I'd had to change job several times – somehow I had a knack for finding work that wasn't stable or permanent. I was forced to leave the flat I'd shared with Liam when the rent went up, and I began a slog of moving around Habmouth – changing home, changing job – that went on for years. There were other relationships, but none lasted longer than a few months. Liam had cast too long a shadow for me to truly let anyone in. But I'd had Dominic, and that was everything. That made my life worthwhile. Eventually, once Dominic was older, I completed a bookkeeping course and found myself a new, stable job working in payroll. I'd thought everything would be okay then, that my life would finally settle down.

Both the sisters were watching me, waiting. One of the logs in the log burner made a loud pop that startled me out of my silence. 'Then,' I said heavily, 'then Liam came back.'

Habmouth

6

'What are you doing?' I asked Dominic, finding him sat at his desk wielding a knife and a pair of kitchen tongs, performing some kind of operation on a cactus. He paused the how-to video he was watching and turned to me, brushing his slightly-too-long dark hair from his eyebrows. 'I'm taking a cutting,' he said, as if it was the most obvious thing in the world.

'Are you sure that's going to work?' I asked sceptically. The cactus consisted of many small mounds, covered in yellow-brown spikes, and he was trying to remove an entire one of its lumps.

'Yes,' he said.

I sat down on the end of his bed, and he resumed the video. I watched him work in fascination, and once he'd removed the section he placed it on the window sill with the kitchen tongs.

'Aren't you going to put it in a pot?'

'It needs to heal over first,' he said, turning to me, and I smiled at the enthusiasm in his eyes. 'Cactus cuttings are different to other plants,' he continued. 'You can have this one, if you want – it'll be happy in your room.'

'Thank you,' I said. 'I'd like that.'

He turned back to hunch over his cactus. When he was tending to his plants serenity came over him and it was a joy to watch. His window sill was crowded with pots of cacti and succulents, his room being on the sunny side of our flat, while the dark north-facing windows in our kitchen and bathroom were full of ferns and other shady plants.

'So, about your birthday–'

'I told you I don't need anything big,' he said.

'You're really happy just to have some friends round for pizza?'

'And a pitcher plant.'

'Yes, and the pitcher plant.' I paused. 'I'll take you out somewhere as well, if you like? Just me and you.'

'Okay,' he said.

I got up, and on a whim I went over and put my arms around him. 'I'm so proud of you,' I told him, and although he tried to wriggle free – being a teenager he had to at least make a show of not wanting hugs from me – I could tell he didn't mind really. 'I'll make dinner,' I said, but as I got to the door Dominic took me aback by saying, 'Mum, I think someone is watching me.'

'What do you mean?' I said, turning to look at him. His eyes were clouded now, his brow slightly furrowed.

'There's a man I've seen a few times. Twice round here, and once near school.'

Cold dread settled around my heart as my mind raced to a hundred awful possibilities. 'Has he tried to talk to you?'

'No.'

I sat back down on the bed, and looked at Dominic closely. 'I'll phone the school and tell them. And I'll walk you to the bus stop in the morning. If we see him again, I'll call the police.'

'Mum!' Dominic protested.

'I'm not letting some weirdo–'

'I don't think he's a weirdo,' Dominic said. 'I think it might be Dad.'

...

Something was up. I sensed it the second I stepped onto the walkway that led to our front door on the second floor of the block of flats. The feeling deepened as I walked, dodging the odd airer where laundry was drying, rusting old bicycles that weren't even worth stealing, and the occasional pot with a struggling plant inside. The atmosphere was different today. Something had disturbed it, I could feel it in the pit of my stomach. I started to unlock the front door but it swung open, and laughter reached me from the living room. Not the laughter of Dom and his friends. It was Dom and a man. I ran down the hall and burst into the living room, hands tightening into fists at the scene before me. Dominic and Liam, both turning towards me guiltily. In the middle of the floor, ridiculously out of place on our disgusting hard-wearing blue carpet, squatted a brand new Playstation, still in its box.

'Mum…' Dominic started, but at my silence he faltered. Horror and shock washed through me. How dare he? How *dare* he?

'Mum?' Dominic said again.

'What is that?' I asked, gesturing at the box.

'It's a—'

'I know what it is,' I snapped at Dominic, before my eyes rested on Liam. 'Why is it here?' I asked him, my voice like glass.

'Poppy, let me explain.'

'No,' I said. I bent down and picked up Liam's gift. 'Dominic, you stay in here,' I told him, and I fixed my eyes on Liam. 'Outside,' I said.

Liam obediently followed me out of the room, while Dominic ignored my words and tagged along behind us, protesting that he'd invited his dad back to the flat, that it wasn't Dad's fault, that I should give him a chance. Once we'd stepped out onto the walkway I put the box down on the floor, shut the front door to stop Dominic following us and faced Liam, who'd backed away towards the peeling blue railings. Neither of us spoke. I stared at him, and he stared right back. My body had turned molten, boiling with emotions yet somehow rigid with rage, fear, I didn't even know what. I opened my mouth to speak, but instead of words I made a low growl of anger, turning into a cry as I beat my hands against his chest.

'I know you're angry,' Liam said, when I burned myself out with a final scream of frustration.

'You have no idea!' I yelled at him. 'Get away from here, and take your bribe with you!' I kicked the box across to him, and he ignored it.

'It's not a bribe. It's an early birthday present for Dom.'

'Dom doesn't play videogames,' I shouted at him. 'He's never shown the slightest—'

'Of course he does. He plays them at his friend's houses. He said there was no point in mentioning anything to you about it because you don't haven't any spare cash to start buying games consoles and he doesn't want you to feel bad. He said you're saving up the deposit for a flat of your own, or something? He says you've got a new job. He seemed proud of you.'

I took a step back. Had Dominic really told him all of that? I sagged against the wall.

Liam smiled at me, and reached out his hand. 'You look just the same.'

'You don't,' I told him, my voice strained. He didn't. He'd lost his gangly look, filling out and growing into his body. His dark hair was short and tidy now, not the bird's nest it had been when he was twenty-one and he left us. His eyes didn't twinkle quite the same, there was hardness there, as though the toughness of life had beaten him down.

'Let Dominic keep the Playstation,' Liam said. 'It's for his fourteenth birthday.'

'Do you have something for his fourth birthday?' I asked him. 'His fifth, sixth, seventh, eighth…' my voice was rising.

'Poppy—'

'Did you even *buy* this?' I asked him, jabbing my finger towards the box. 'Or did it fall off the back of a lorry?'

'You have every right to hate me.'

'Me and Dom don't need you. And we certainly don't need ridiculous gifts. If someone round here realises we've got that bloody thing in our flat it'll get nicked within a week.'

'I thought you were moving soon.'

'Yes, soon. Once I've got some more savings. Not that it's got anything to do with you.'

'Come on, Poppy. Dom's not a little kid any more, let him have it.' He grinned. 'At least you know where he is if he's in the flat playing on this. It's better than being out on the street doing God knows what.'

'Because you'd know all about that, wouldn't you?' I said. 'But he's not like you, Liam. Not in any way. Dominic doesn't *want* to be out on the street doing God knows what.'

'Get real, Poppy, he's a teenager.'

'Get *real?* You want to know what's real? You threw a glass at me while Dominic was watching. That was real. Or were you too high to remember?'

'I remember,' he said.

'Oh, and then you left us for the next ten years.'

'Didn't my parents help you?'

'Yes, to begin with. But I'm not their responsibility. And they've got other grandkids now. Your nieces and nephews. Or didn't you know that?'

Behind me the front door burst open, and Dominic tumbled out, his eyes burning with fury. 'Stop being so mean to him!' he yelled at me. 'He wants to make up for the time he was away. He deserves a second chance, doesn't he?'

Liam shook his head. 'It's up to your mum,' he said, and I had to stop myself from strangling him for making me look like the bad guy. 'If she doesn't want–'

'What I don't want is for you to tear my son's heart out the way you tore mine,' I said viciously. I wanted my words to hurt him.

'He's *my* dad,' Dominic said, picking up the Playstation and hugging it to his chest. 'And I want to see him.'

Cattleford

7

'I can't believe he did that,' Harriet said. 'He put you in a horrible position. He should have come to you first.'

I pulled myself up from the floor now that I'd finished helping Jessica with Reef's presents, plonking down on the sofa opposite the log burner. Jessica did the same, sitting with her legs crossed up on the sofa, hair falling over her face in a way that made her look childlike.

'Well, I had no choice but to let him see Dom,' I said heavily. 'It scared me, because Dom was giddy with excitement about his dad. He said Liam was fun, and cool, which I guess he thought I wasn't.' I sighed. 'He was at such a tricky age; it was like he was searching for something. He was trying to figure out who he was and how he fitted into the world. I knew he'd started to think more about where he'd come from, even before Liam showed up.'

'Everyone needs to know where they came from,' Jessica said softly.

'What will you tell Reef when he asks?' I said.

Jessica tucked her hair behind her ear and looked at me thoughtfully. 'That he was a gift from the ocean,' she said, apparently with complete sincerity.

Unsure how to respond to that, I cast my mind back to how it had been when Liam first showed up. I'd been wary, even once I'd agreed to him and Dom seeing each other a few times a week. Mine and Dominic's existence had always been precarious, and I didn't want anything to derail our plans of finally moving to a home of our own. But the pair of them wore me down. Using exactly the same tactics he had in the past, Liam wove me a tale of how great his life was now. He flattered me, saying I'd done an amazing job with Dominic. He said how sorry he was. He brought round pizza and made us laugh, until he was at the flat more often than he wasn't.

One night, when Dominic was round at a friend's house, he kissed me. Pulling away angrily, I told him he had no right, and that I thought he should go, but a deep ache had begun inside me and I grabbed his wrist as he started to stand. We stared at each other for a moment, as if we were sizing each other up. He was wondering if I was going to kiss him or hit him, and I was wondering the same, because no matter the good times Dominic and I had been having with him, he'd still wounded me in a way that had never healed. Our kiss ended up somewhere between violence and tenderness, there was a viciousness to it to start with, as if I was simultaneously trying to pull him close and push him away. It was a scorching hot day and our sweat mingled as we kissed, the salty taste of it in my mouth. He tore at my dress, before pushing my thighs apart so he could bury his face between them.

By the time we woke the next morning in my bed, tangled in a sweaty, sticky heap, I could hardly claim I didn't want to let him back in to my life. The days that followed were like a dream, filled with laughter as we enjoyed being a family, and once night fell and me and Liam were alone in my room, we were possessed by a desperate, grasping passion where we practically ripped each other apart with the force of our attraction, the merest touch setting us both on fire.

Of course, I gave the sisters the sanitised version of events. After all, it could really be summed up in a simple statement. 'I fell in love with him again,' I told them.

'Oh, Poppy,' Harriet said.

'If anything, my feelings were even more intense than the first time around.' I shook my head. 'I don't know how he does it to me. I don't know why no one else can even come close.'

'He's the love of your life,' Jessica said simply. 'There's just one that can be that intense, I think.'

'I take it it didn't work out?' Harriet asked me.

'I thought it was going to. I really, really did.' I took a deep breath. The betrayal was so unexpected, and so horrific. Jessica put her hand over mine and gave it a squeeze. 'What did he do?' she breathed.

'He left,' I said. 'I woke one morning to find him gone.'

'I'm so sorry,' Jessica said.

'But he hadn't just left us. He'd taken something with him. I didn't notice straight away, not until the next day, I think.'

'Didn't notice what?'

How could I say the words? I didn't want to remember. But the sisters were both staring at me, and I had to speak. 'He'd stolen from me. My bank account was empty, all my savings were gone. And he'd maxed out my credit card.'

This revelation was met with shocked silence, while the sisters' faces showed their anger, and their sadness for me. Jessica threw her arms around me, while Harriet said, 'Men are all the same. They just use you to get what they want, then they throw you aside.'

'Dominic isn't like that,' I said into Jessica's shoulder. 'I've made sure of that.'

Jessica released me from her embrace. 'Don't worry about her,' she said, 'Harriet's a natural pessimist when it comes to men. What did you do, though, Poppy? About the money? Did you go to the police?'

'No.'

'Why not?' Harriet said. 'He stole from you.'

'Because I didn't want Dominic to know. I couldn't have Dominic know.'

'But how did you live? What did you do?'

I sat back against the sofa and closed my eyes for a second. *How did you live?* Could I find the words to explain all that had followed? They wouldn't know what it was like to be so desperate, so afraid, and just so *tired* that you could be drawn into making the kind of awful decisions I had made. But I'd have to try. I owed them an explanation.

Habmouth

8

Sighing inwardly, I picked up my tea bag from the morning which I'd left drying while I was at work, and dropped it into a mug. I left them to dry out where I didn't think Dominic would notice them – I had to protect him from how bad the money situation really was. I'd become pretty used to it – the hunger. After a while, it didn't hurt so much. Eating anything substantial made it worse, as my stomach would remember what it was like to be full, and demand it again later that day, or the next morning. But even if I got used to the raw sensation of hunger it still affected me in other ways, sapping my concentration and leaving me tired and drained, like I was permanently coming down with something.

Footsteps along the walkway outside made me duck down so that I couldn't be spotted through the window. *Please go past, please go past. Please be someone else.* At the knock on the door my chest tightened, but I forced myself to stand up tall. I wouldn't let him see that he scared me. In fact, I would stand my ground. I couldn't give him what I didn't have, and he'd have to deal with it.

'I know you're in there,' his weaselly voice came loud and clear.

Of course he did. He'd hang around outside, watching for me. I tried not to go out, but I had to go to work, and by now Kevin – which I was quite sure was not his real name – was well aware of my routine. He hammered on the door again. I forgot I was holding a mug of tea, and my fingers opened letting the mug smash to the floor, the precious liquid lost as it coated the ugly kitchen lino. I swore under my breath, staring at the mess until yet another knock forced me to move. Not answering the door wasn't really an option.

...

That night I simultaneously longed for Dom to get home – to know he was safe – and dreaded it. He spent many of his evenings now with friends, and his Saturdays working at a garden centre, and I was glad he was happy and enjoying life. As much as I worried for him when he wasn't in the house, I didn't want him to know what I was scared of. I told him to never linger, to come straight home after college or from his friend's houses. I hoped he just thought I was being a normal, overprotective parent and not that anything more sinister was going on.

There was really no getting around the situation tonight. As soon as he walked into the living room, he would realise. Sure enough, 'Mum, where's the TV? And the Playstation?'

I finished cleaning up the tea from the kitchen floor and went to join him. 'It broke,' I said, 'it's being repaired.'

'They both broke?'

I blinked. What was I thinking? I'd never convince Dominic with such a stupid lie as that.

Dominic looked at me closely. 'How bad is it?' he asked me.

I gave a false laugh, and reached out for him, and immediately regretted it as my sleeve pulled up revealing the bruises on my wrist. 'You're hurt,' he said.

I wrenched my sleeve back down. 'I just hurt my wrist at work today.'

'Mum, please!' Dominic said, 'stop treating me like a little kid! Somebody has grabbed your arm hard enough to leave marks on it!'

'It's nothing for you to worry about,' I said, cursing myself for letting him see the bruises. I *had* stood up to Kevin, and the man he'd brought with him for backup. My show of rebellion had earned me a punch in the stomach along with the bruises on my wrist.

'I saw all the bills,' Dominic said, 'I found them last night. I've been thinking about it all day.'

'You… you found them all?' I made my way over to the sofa, and he sat down beside me.

'I'm so worried,' he said, and his voice caught. 'I thought you had an eating disorder when you keep making excuses for skipping meals…'

'No!' I said, 'no, Dom, I don't–'

'I know that now! You don't eat because you can't afford to feed us both, don't you, Mum? It's why we can't have the heating on, and you walk to work even when it's pouring with rain, because you can't pay the bus fare.'

Abruptly, I got up from the sofa and strode towards the kitchen, almost colliding with Dominic's pitcher plant where it hung from the ceiling, those creepy insect-catching protuberances hanging down ominously. 'What do you want for tea?' I asked him. 'We've got some pasta.'

'Mum, you need to get help! Let me give you my wages from the garden centre. I know it's not much, but it's a start. And there's a food bank not far from college. I don't think they ask any questions, I could drop in there tomorrow–'

'No.'

'*Yes*,' he insisted. He followed me to the kitchen and stood in front of me, his eyes dark and troubled. 'You haven't been the same ever since Dad left. And I was horrible to you about it back then, I know I was.'

'It's okay,' I said faintly. I let him blame me about Liam. I let him think I must have driven his dad away, because if he was angry at me he could yell and shout at me and let the anger out. If his anger had turned to Liam, there would be no way to vent it. It would burn away inside him, hurting him, and he'd only been fourteen – too young to deal with such a deep betrayal. But that was over two years ago and he was different now. When I talked to him, I was often taken aback by how much he'd grown up.

'You have to eat, Mum,' he said softly. 'You're going to get ill.'

I turned away. I didn't want to cry in front of him, but he touched my shoulder and I couldn't help but let out a sob.

'I'll go to the food bank tomorrow and see how it works,' he said.

'No,' I said again. 'That's not your responsibility. I got us into this mess. *I'll* go to the food bank when I get a chance.'

'You're at work all day.'

'I–' I shook my head. 'Dom, honestly, it's not as bad as it seems…' I started, but I couldn't bring myself to finish such a barefaced lie.

'Please, just go and sit down,' he told me. 'I'll make us both some food. And you have to eat it.'

I was so shaken up by my confrontation with Kevin that I did as he asked. I forced down the pasta coated in tinned tomatoes, although it wasn't easy with my stomach unused to large meals, but Dominic's eyes were on me and I knew he wouldn't let me stop.

'Who took our stuff?' he said, once he'd taken my plate away and sat beside me again. 'And who hurt your arm?'

I didn't reply.

'Someone you owe money to.' Dominic stated.

I wanted to deny it, but what was the point? He deserved honesty. 'Yes,' I said simply.

'How much money do you owe?'

I almost laughed.

'I found your credit card bills, so I already know it's a lot.' He was quiet for a moment. 'Did bailiffs come? They can't hurt you, can they?' he said, his voice gaining emotion. 'You should go to the police about those bruises. People can't come here and *attack* you. If they come back, don't let them in unless I'm here.'

My heart ached at his sincerity and his anger, and how he wanted to protect me. 'It wasn't a bailiff.'

'Who, then?'

'Just somebody who offered to help me out. I said I'd pay him back but I haven't, not all of it anyway, and he just wants his money, understandably.'

'Mum,' Dominic said, his face white, 'tell me you haven't.'

Cattleford

9

'A loan shark,' Harriet said, as she sat back down after putting another log in the log burner. 'What were you thinking?'

Jessica squeezed my hand and glared at Harriet. 'It's not her fault.'

'No, but… surely you knew how risky it was? There must have been *something* else you could have done.'

'The thing is,' I said, but I faltered. How would I get them to understand? 'I was in such a state when Liam left,' I explained. 'He'd conned me. He bought his way in with a few gifts and cheap words, and took everything I had. But also–'

'You loved him,' Jessica said.

'I couldn't think straight. I did get help from his parents to pay the first couple of month's rent, plus a bit extra for food. I didn't tell them what Liam had done, I just came out with some story about being between jobs and they didn't ask too many questions. But I couldn't keep going back to them, and Liam had left me in so much debt. I thought I could sort it out myself if I was careful. I got another credit card and cut back on spending as much as I could, thinking I'd be able to pay off the credit cards eventually and get myself sorted again. But bills kept on coming.' I clenched and unclenched my hands in my lap. 'It spiralled so quickly. I kept telling myself I could get on top of things, I started getting payday loans, but I was just getting loans to pay off loans. Soon no one would even lend to me any more. I was barely sleeping, and my brain didn't work properly. I couldn't concentrate or make decisions. I had splitting headaches every day and I felt ill all the time. I was so thin and stressed that my periods stopped, and I remember being pleased because I didn't have to spend money on pads.' I covered my face with my hands and then let them fall into my lap. 'I was ashamed. I was just so ashamed,' I breathed. 'And frightened. One day I broke down to one of our neighbours, and she said she knew somebody who could help me out.'

Jessica had put her hands up to her mouth, eyes huge. 'I can hardly listen,' she said.

'You don't have to. Me and Harri can talk somewhere else…'

'Don't even think about it,' she said. 'Of course I'll hear you out. And you're safe now. We won't let anyone hurt you here.'

'I know you're probably thinking I'm completely naive–'

'Of course we're not!' Jessica protested.

'I wasn't rational any more,' I continued, 'I was drowning and I'd grab onto anything to save myself, I didn't think about what could happen in the future, it was just about getting through another day. So I met this man at my flat, and he was so friendly. It felt like he really understood, and that he would make it all go away. I wanted to hear that so badly. He said he needed to take something as security. He wanted my passport but I managed to lie and convince him I didn't have one. The only valuable thing I owned was some old jewellery my grandma gave me back when I was still living with my parents. I have no idea what it was worth, probably not much. In fact I'd forgotten I had it until he asked about jewellery, otherwise I'd have already sold it months before. I felt sick when I went to get it and handed it over to him.'

'My God, Poppy.'

I couldn't speak any more, and both sisters put their arms around me.

…

I was glad the next morning to be immersed in normality again. Reef got up early, squealing with excitement at the pile of presents. Wrapping paper flew everywhere and Jessica encouraged him excitedly while Harriet tried to keep track of the gifts that had come from other friends and relatives, muttering about the need for thank you cards and how Jessica never remembered that kind of thing.

'You don't have a plan, do you?' Jessica whispered to me when Harriet left the room and Reef played with his gifts. 'You don't know what to do after you leave here.'

'Is it that obvious?'

'To me it is. I think Harri knows too.'

I nodded. I could hardly deny it.

Jessica gave my arm a squeeze. 'I don't mind what you did since Liam left you, or why you're here,' Jessica said. 'I like you. Reef likes you. It's good for the shop now you can help out. As far as I'm concerned you can stay as long as you want.'

'Does Harriet mind why I'm here?' I'd heard the sister's voices after I'd gone to bed the night before, no doubt discussing what I'd told them.

'I feel like my ears are burning,' a voice in the doorway said. Harriet stood there watching us, her dark eyes troubled, though a bright smile lit up her face when Reef ran over to her, chattering excitedly about his presents.

'We were just talking about what I told you last night.'

Harriet nodded, and caught Jessica's eye. 'Reef's not even in his uniform yet,' she said.

'Oh, he can go in late to school,' Jessica said airily.

'No, he can't. The new term has only just started; he needs to be there so he doesn't get behind.'

'It's his birthday,' Jessica said, her voice firm. 'I'll take him in an hour.'

Harriet didn't reply to this, though her expression was stony.

'She does like to get involved,' Jessica said to me when Harriet left to go and have a shower, an edge to her voice. 'He's *my* son.'

Immediately the words were out of her mouth, her face changed. 'Sorry, Poppy. I shouldn't have said that. She does so much to help me, and when Reef was tiny I couldn't have coped without her.'

She busied herself tidying the breakfast table, and I crouched down to gather up some of the discarded wrapping paper that littered the floor. The sisters' relationship was really none of my business. More concerning was that Jessica hadn't had a chance to tell me what Harriet thought of our conversation the night before. I had a feeling her thoughts about it were different to Jessica's.

Bits and Bobbins was surprisingly busy that morning, and Harriet and I were practically rushed off our feet until noon. Finally the shop quietened down, and Harriet occupied herself tidying a big basket of wool that had endured quite a rummaging that morning.

'It can't have been easy for you,' she said, 'to tell us everything last night.'

'It wasn't, but you have a right to know who you've got staying in your house.' These words turned to ashes in my mouth. Harriet might believe I'd told them everything, but they didn't know the half of it.

Harriet finished arranging the basket and faced me squarely. In her black trousers and bright red shirt, she looked formidable this morning. Since I'd arrived I'd only seen her in head-to-toe black, and the splash of colour today made a striking contrast. Maybe she wanted to look more colourful for Reef's birthday – she was going to help out at his party in the afternoon while I manned the shop alone.

Harriet sighed and then began to speak. 'Poppy, look, I was going to wait until later to say this, but it's probably better I tell you now.'

It was clear what was coming. 'I'll pack my stuff up,' I said, 'I'll leave once Reef has gone to bed.'

10

'You don't have to go tonight,' Harriet said quickly. 'You can have a few more days, to give you a chance to make plans. The thing is, what you told us took me by surprise. If it was just me and Jess it would be different, but we have a young child in the house. If some criminal is going to come looking for you…' she paused. 'Is he looking for you?'

I couldn't meet her eye. Kevin wasn't looking for me. But the man who *was* looking for me was hardly any better.

'Why don't you take the afternoon off until I have to leave for Reef's party? You can call around some letting agents, see if they have anything.'

'Letting agents will credit check me.'

'Oh, I see,' she said, turning to fiddle with the wool basket again. 'There must be something–'

'It's not your problem,' I said.

'I feel awful turning you out,' she said, 'I really don't want to. If there was any other way… it's just with Reef, we have to be careful.'

'There's no need to apologise. In your shoes I would do exactly the same. You can't put Reef at any risk and I wouldn't expect you to.'

…

Once Reef's friends had gone home with party bags clutched in sticky fingers I helped the sisters tidy up and then I went upstairs early to try to get some sleep. There was a soft knock on the door, and once I'd quickly pulled on the baggy t-shirt I wore in bed, I opened it to find Jessica. She gave me a smile. 'Thank you so much for looking after the shop for Harriet,' she said.

'It's no problem.'

She hovered in the doorway twirling her hair around her fingers as if she wanted to say more and couldn't decide if she should.

'Harriet has told me that I need to leave,' I said.

'Yes, I know. I told her I disagree.'

'She's right though, Jess. I'm not angry with her. I'm grateful you let me stay here for even one night.'

Jessica came in and sat on my bed, so I sat down beside her. Her eyes were more grey than their usual blue; troubled and hard to read.

'I can't imagine having to run away from here,' Jessica said. 'You had to run away from your home, and you chose *us* to help you. I feel like we're letting you down.'

'You're not letting me down. This is my mess, not yours.'

Jessica sighed. 'I did something really bad once,' she said, 'and hurt people that I care about. So I know what it's like to regret things you've done. But the situation you ended up in wasn't even your fault. It was Liam's. And I got a second chance, so I think you should too.'

'Jess,' Harriet's voice in the hall was sharp, 'I'm sure Poppy just wants to get some sleep.'

Jessica jumped like a small child who had been caught out of bed at night. 'Yes, okay,' she snapped at Harriet.

I frowned as Jessica left. What had she been talking about? Perhaps it was something to do with Reef's dad – after all, she'd never said much about him. Nothing that made any sense, anyway. But who was I to judge? She said that what had happened was Liam's fault, but I couldn't blame Liam for *all* the mess I got myself into. Jessica's secrets couldn't be any worse than mine.

The days until my deadline to leave passed alarmingly quickly. I tried to find a room somewhere nearby with a landlord who wouldn't ask too many questions, but without luck. Jessica suggested I move in with Dominic in his university halls, and though initially the idea seemed utterly ludicrous – not to mention almost certainly not allowed – I began to wonder whether it might work, temporarily at least. But going to Dominic wasn't a solution. I would be found there.

Finally, the day arrived that I had to go and I went up to my bedroom to pack. I'd heard there might be a room available to rent in a shared house in the next town, and if I could persuade Harriet to pay me for a few hours here and there in the shop while I found something more permanent I would hopefully be able to make ends meet. But just as I was reaching up to get my bag down from the top of the wardrobe, Harriet burst in. 'I gathered up things I could find downst–' she started, and then stopped abruptly. I quickly dropped my arms and tried to pull the front of my jumper back down, but it was too late. Harriet's eyes snapped away from my stomach to my face. 'Why didn't you tell us?'

I smoothed my baggy jumper over my bump. 'It makes no difference,' I said.

Harriet stared at me as if I'd grown a second head as well as a bump. 'It makes *all* the difference,' she breathed. 'Have you even found somewhere to go?'

'I think I can get a room in a shared house.'

'Poppy, wait a second,' she said, patting the bed as she sat down herself. I plonked down beside her.

'I'm not going to let you go and stay with a bunch of strang-ers.'

'I can handle it.'

'Then why are you shaking?'

I clutched my hands together in annoyance that they had given me away. 'You said yourself, Reef has to be safe.'

'But what about your baby?' she said, and then her voice turned officious. 'You can't leave like this. You're in no fit state to go anywhere on your own.'

'I'm all right, Harri. I can sort things out. I'll be settled before the baby–' my voice cracked, and she put her hand over mine. 'I looked after Jessica when she was pregnant, and when Reef was a newborn. She really struggled with the whole thing – not that I'm saying you will – but she was on her own and she wasn't sure where she was going with her life. *I* carried the burden for her, and I can do it for you, too.'

Jessica's words from the night of Reef's party popped into my head. *I did something bad once.*

'No wonder you've been so exhausted,' she said. 'How many months are you?'

'About four and a half, I think.'

To my surprise, she reached out and touched my hair. 'Let me help you,' she said. 'Stay here with us. You don't need to worry about a thing. Just get some sleep, and focus on looking after yourself.'

After a few minutes I lay down gratefully on the bed while she stayed sitting beside me. 'Whose is the baby?' she asked me softly. 'It's not the man you borrowed from, is it? He didn't–'

'No,' I said, my voice almost a whisper. I was giddy with relief. I didn't have to leave!

'What happened then, Poppy? What did he do when you couldn't pay the money back? Or did you find a way?'

I let out a long breath. I owed her the truth – a little more of it at least.

Habmouth

11

I screamed at the sight of the photo, legs buckling, and although I clapped my hand tight across my mouth sounds kept escaping from me. Quickly, I forced myself to regain control, but looking again at the photo brought on a fresh wave of horror and panic and my hands shook so violently that the photo of Dominic blurred before my eyes.

Pay up.

Those were the words below the photo of Dominic lying on the ground, unconscious, bloodied and bruised. I had to call an ambulance, and the police, but where was he? He'd said he was going out to his friend James's house and it was late now, so he must have been walking back home. Bile rose in my throat and I ran to the kitchen sink, retching uselessly until a thin trickle came up from my empty stomach. 'Think!' I said out loud to myself. 'Think, think, think!' I punctuated every word by hitting my palm against my forehead, anger and fear surging through me. How had I let things go so far? Dominic needed help, but if I involved the police, Kevin, or his cronies would come after me. If I called an ambulance, the police would likely get involved. But that wasn't important right now. All that mattered was making sure Dominic was okay.

I ran back to the living room and scooped my phone up from the sofa just as it began to ring. Dominic! His voice was thick and confused, 'Mum?' he said.

'Dominic! Where are you? Please tell me where you are.'

'Car… car park.'

'Are you okay?' I asked stupidly, 'Dom—'

'No police,' he croaked out. 'They said—'

'Yes, I understand,' I said, my voice frantic. 'I'm coming to get you. Tell me where you are! Were you walking back from

James's? Did you go down Holbrook Road? Or Yew Hill? Are you near the dry cleaners?'

'Betting shops,' Dominic said, 'I can see—'

It fell into place. I knew where he was. A car park, half abandoned, off of a street not more than five minutes walk away. I ran down the hall, stumbling as I shoved my feet into my trainers, before tearing out of the front door. 'I'm coming,' I told him. 'I'm coming Dom, and you're going to be okay. Don't be frightened. I'll be there soon.'

...

To my immense relief, Dominic's injuries looked worse than they really were. In fact, he was sitting up by the time I got to him, though his face was pale and his brown eyes glassy with shock. I threw my arms around him, then let go when he winced. 'I'm still calling an ambulance,' I told him firmly, but he grabbed my hand as I reached for my phone. 'No,' he said. 'Don't call anyone.'

His eyes were so full of fear that I stopped, and he got to his feet unsteadily. 'See,' he said, 'I can stand up. I'm fine.'

'You are not fine.'

'You can't call anyone.'

He was so adamant that I relented, and he let me put my arm around him to help him as he took a few unsteady steps, but soon he was able to walk on his own. Arriving back at the flat he sat listlessly on the sofa while I cleaned the cuts on his face. I fetched a pack of biscuits I had stashed away and made him eat three, though the colour still didn't return to his face.

'I'm so sorry,' I told him, my voice choked with emotion. 'I'm so sorry. This is all my fault.'

I waited for him to say something. Anything.

'What happened?' I asked him.

'I was walking home and two of them dragged me off the path and into the car park. They said you had to pay them.'

I tried to take his hand, but he pulled it away. 'Why do we owe so much money?' he asked. 'You have a good job! We barely own anything, we don't go anywhere, *you* don't even eat! What did you spend all the money on?'

'I just made some stupid decisions, that's all. You know me,' I said, trying not to upset him further. 'I'm not clever like you.'

'Your job is sorting out money!' he said.

'Doesn't mean I'm not a bloody idiot when I'm not at work.'

'Stop talking to me like I'm a little kid!' he exploded. 'I thought they were going to kill me! Then they started going on about money, and I realised it was *you*. It was – it was *your* fault!' he said, his voice breaking.

'If I could go back I would do everything differently, Dom,' I said, my voice high and desperate. 'I will never, ever forgive myself for this happening to you. Never.'

'So tell me why!' he said. 'Why is our life like this? What did you do with all the money?'

'I just… I just bought stuff–' I said, struggling to think of an answer.

'What *stuff*? We have no stuff!'

'I–'

'Are you gambling, or something? Did you give it to somebody? Were you scammed? Tell me Mum. Just tell me!'

'I– I just–'

He got up from the sofa and started striding towards the door. 'You don't trust me,' he said. 'I'm old enough to take a beating for you but not old enough to know why. This is… this is bullshit Mum!'

I reached out to him, trying to seize on some explanation, some new lie. But I couldn't do it. I was too tired to keep on taking the blame. I couldn't be the wall between him and Liam any more.

He shook his head. 'Fine,' he said, 'if that's how it is.'

'It was your dad,' I said, my voice barely above a whisper.

'Dad?' He turned, eyes full of questions. He clearly had no idea.

'He stole all our money. All my savings. He maxed out the credit card. And then he left.'

'But…' he frowned as he tried desperately to understand. 'He bought me a Playstation–'

'He would have got it off some dodgy mate. I don't believe for a second he bought it in a shop.'

He stared at me in silence, until finally he said, 'I don't understand.'

'Neither do I. But I think he must have been in trouble. He must have been desperate–'

'He wouldn't do this to us. We're his family.'

'I'm sorry, Dominic, but he did. You wanted me to tell you the truth, and this is the truth. I wish it wasn't. I'm still trying to understand myself, I still wonder what could possibly have driven him to it, but the truth is we'll probably never know why.'

'I don't believe you!' he said, but his eyes were shiny. What I'd said had struck home.

He turned again, and though I tried to call him back as he walked away, he disappeared into his room and slammed the door behind him.

Cattleford

12

'Dominic must have found that hard,' Harriet said.

Sat up on the bed, resting my back against the wall, I listened to rain pattering against the window; a soothing, rhythmic sound. No matter how painful the memories were it was cathartic to let it out. For somebody to hear and to make me feel for once like I wasn't losing my mind.

The door gently creaked open and Jessica came inside, wrapped in a bright pink dressing gown with her hair tied in a pony-tail. 'Sorry,' she said. 'I didn't want to barge in in the middle of all that.'

She shut the door behind her, before sitting down on the sheepskin rug beside my bed and nestling her head against Harriet's legs. How much had she heard? She can't have been there when Harriet realised I was pregnant, or I'm sure she would have said something. I found myself in no rush to tell her about that bit, and apparently neither was Harriet.

'Dom couldn't accept it when I first said it was his dad,' I continued, casting my mind back to the aftermath of the conversation. 'It was too much to take in. But by the next evening he'd had a chance to think it through, and he knew I was telling the truth. He was crushed.'

I crossed my legs, and pulled the floral curtain aside to look at the rain, but I couldn't see anything beyond the glass. I wasn't used to living somewhere so dark. We were at the end of the row of houses on Tricklebank Lane with only the stream and trees beyond, so there was nothing to illuminate the darkness. I let the curtain fall.

'Come on,' Harriet said to Jessica, 'let's give Poppy some space.'

...

'I can't believe it!' Jessica said, bursting into my room the next morning. 'You're a dark horse Poppy!'

'Harriet told you, then? About the baby?'

'She did. And she told me she said you can stay. Harriet would never turn you out now. She loves babies.'

I laughed. 'So it's just about the baby is it? Not me?'

'She never wanted you to go, she just felt she had to for Reef.'

'Reef is still here, last time I checked.'

Jessica watched me curiously as I finished brushing my hair in front of the ornately framed mirror hanging on the wall, clashing rather gloriously with the pink-and-white striped wallpaper behind it.

'Does Dominic know you're pregnant?' she asked me.

'No,' I said. I wanted to elaborate, but I couldn't. They didn't know it all, not yet.

She jumped when Reef called, 'Mummy, I can't find my pants!' at the top of his little reedy voice.

'You've got all of this to look forward to again,' she said, beaming at me, before rushing from the room. I put my hair-brush down with a sigh as memories flashed through my mind of walking near the estuary with Dominic when he was little. Watching him run, sitting with him on a rock when he demanded snacks and we talked about the shapes the clouds made. But Dominic was an adult now. How could I possibly have found myself right back at the start, teetering on the brink of watching another child grow from a baby to an adult?

…

'A boy!' Jessica squealed, clapping her hands together in excitement. 'Oh, Harriet would have loved to see this!'

Harriet had been desperate to come to my scan, but it clashed with other plans she had made and Jessica talked her out of rearranging. I was glad I had one of the sisters with me. *You've been through it all before,* I reminded myself, but that was half the problem. Yes, I loved Dominic more than life itself, but it had been hard doing it all on my own. What would I do longer term when I had this baby? How would I live? I couldn't rely on Harriet and Jessica's charity for the next eighteen years.

'We could go shopping,' Jessica suggested as we left the hospital. 'Buy a few baby bits. I would give you Reef's old clothes, but I sold nearly all of them, I just kept one little outfit so I can remind myself how small he used to be. '

I was about to say no, but I reconsidered. I had a little bit of cash. I could get some basics, nothing fancy. It would be nicer to do it with Jess than on my own. She drove us to the shops, and with her enthusiastic encouragement I ended up stocking up on half my own body weight of tiny clothes, muslins, bibs and blankets, and then we retreated to a coffee shop.

'I remember Harriet taking me shopping when I was pregnant with Reef,' Jessica said, as I rearranged the shopping bags piled beside our table to let a couple of mums with pushchairs pass by. 'I had no idea what I even needed.'

I settled back on my slouchy armchair and watched people bustling by outside the window while I enjoyed this moment of respite. My feet were aching and I was glad to get out of the busy shopping centre and sit down. 'It's great she's so hands-on,' I said carefully. I had witnessed other little clashes they'd had over small details of Reef's upbringing; Jessica's laissez faire approach at odds with Harriet's tendency to control and organise. 'Was she hoping to start a family with Ben?' I asked.

Jessica put her cup down a little too hard on its saucer.

'Sorry, I didn't mean to pry. I know she doesn't like talking about Ben and the divorce.'

She was silent for a moment. 'She desperately wanted to have children,' she said at length, 'but it didn't happen naturally, and then their marriage fell apart.'

'That's such a shame.'

'I've tried to get her dating again,' Jessica continued, 'I said she doesn't have to be alone forever just because of him, but she doesn't want to date. I don't think she wants another man. Just a baby.'

She stopped and put her hand up to her mouth as if she'd said something wrong.

'So… does Reef's dad not know about Reef at all?' I asked, unsure what to make of her behaviour.

'He wasn't interested in Reef at all.'

'I thought you met him on a weekend away and couldn't contact him again?'

Jessica took a quick sip of her hazelnut latte. 'Yes, well. Exactly.'

I frowned. None of this was making sense, but then that was par for the course with Jessica. If I wanted a straight answer, Harriet was the sister to go to.

'Will you tell Dominic he's going to have a little brother now?' she asked me.

'No, not yet. It's not something I want to spring on him in a phone conversation. I should tell him in person.' I leaned forward a little, I had to seize the moment. 'Jess, what you said to me once about having done something bad, was it to do with Reef's d–'

She looked at her watch. 'We need to go and pick Reef up!' she said, 'I didn't realise how long we'd been.'

She leapt to her feet, and I followed her out of the cafe, glancing at the time myself. It wasn't *that* late. Jessica just wanted the questions to end.

13

'It's incredible, isn't it?' Harriet said as she handed back my scan photo, a little reluctantly. 'To have a tiny life growing inside you.'

'He's certainly using up space that used to be bladder,' I said.

'I think Poppy feels daunted by doing it again,' Jessica said offhandedly, as she stood in the corner of the kitchen unloading the washing machine, before opening out the airer ready to hang out Reef's school uniform and little clothes to dry.

'Sorry,' Harriet said to me quietly, 'Jess does come out with things bluntly sometimes–'

'*Jess* thinks it's much quicker and easier if everyone just says what they feel,' Jessica said. 'You know what I was like after Reef was born. Pretending I was okay wouldn't have achieved anything, would it? I had post natal depression and I needed support. If Poppy is worried she can say so, we're hardly going to judge her.'

'I'm all right, honestly,' I said. 'Maybe a little daunted, that's all.'

'Well, Poppy has our support,' Harriet said to Jessica, seemingly unaware that I had spoken. 'If she needs it.'

Jessica paused, a little white polo shirt hanging limply from her fingers as she frowned. 'It's Poppy's baby though, at the end of the day,' she said, somewhat cryptically.

Freezing January soon turned to a mercifully mild February, signs of life beginning to emerge in the village and in the sister's cottage garden. I could clearly feel the baby moving inside me now, and it was a relief not having to hide my bump while in the house with the sisters, though whenever I spoke to Dominic on the phone I found myself clutching my stomach protectively as though he could see me. Not that Dominic posed any threat to the baby, of course. If anything it was the knowledge of the baby that could cause a threat to him. He worried about me though, and tried harder to get me to tell him where I was.

'I'm okay,' I reassured him when he called me one sunny, but blustery, morning. 'Honestly, I am. I'm still with friends, and they are being incredibly kind. I'm safe here–'

'Are you eating?'

'Yes, I'm eating.'

'And these friends, you're sure you can trust them?'

I sighed, and as if on cue, Harriet knocked on my bedroom door and came in holding a glass of alarmingly green liquid. She set it down on top of the chest of drawers with the words, 'It's full of vitamins,' before scurrying away again.

'Mum?' Dominic insisted.

'Yes. Yes, I can trust them. What about you? Are you having fun?'

I tried my best to listen, but my eyes kept slipping back to the glass. It was little things. Suggestions here, advice there, glasses of oddly coloured juice, an exercise ball, soft toys and little baby outfits that Harriet claimed she had seen in a sale and didn't want me to miss out on. I picked up my special pregnancy pillow – another gift from Harriet – and cuddled it on my lap. *She's just being friendly.* Harri was excited, that was all. It was clear how much she loved Reef, even if she disagreed with Jessica's parenting methods, and the thought of a newborn in the house just made her happy.

'Mum,' Dominic said, his voice turning serious again, 'can you please just call Max? He's so worried about you.'

'He's still bothering you?'

'It's not *bother*. We're both worried. Mum, he thinks you're not okay and that's why you won't say where you are. He says you've probably got no money and that you'll have stopped eating again–'

'Then you can tell him he's wrong! I'm not a child; I don't need you two checking up on me.'

'Tell him yourself!' Dom insisted. 'Stop making me your go-between.'

I closed my eyes for a second, ashamed. 'Dominic…'

'You're not being fair on either of us. And Max knows you've changed your number and keeps asking me to tell him your new one. I don't know what to say to him. How can I explain why you won't speak to him when I don't even know myself?'

'I understand,' I said heavily. 'The position I've put you in isn't right and I'm sorry. But please just trust me a little longer. I have my reasons, and I will tell you everything when it's the right time. And look, you don't have to listen to everything Max says.'

'After what he did to help me? If it wasn't for him–'

'Yes, I know,' I said quickly, before he went into any more detail and upset himself.

'At least you could hear him out,' Dom said, 'tell him he doesn't need to worry.'

The baby kicked, and I stroked my bump. I was desperate to tell Dominic the truth, but I had two babies now – never mind that one was eighteen and one was yet to be born, they both needed me to do the right thing. And telling Dom the truth about why I was behaving the way I was would scare him half to death. I'd been the wall between him and Liam once before, protecting him from the truth. Now I'd do the same again. He couldn't know what kind of a man Max truly was, not yet. Not until I had a proper plan.

As I said goodbye to Dom, I picked up the juice Harriet had brought me and eyed it uncomfortably. I sipped it, and concluding it was not something I would want to savour, I pinched my nose and downed as much as I could in one go.

My phone vibrated, and I picked it up and read Dominic's message. *I wish you'd tell me what is going on.*

I put my phone down on the bed beside me. It wasn't like I had all the time in the world, the baby was coming in a matter of months. My past was going to catch up with me, and I needed to get ahead of it. But it was too big for me to figure out alone. I would have to tell the sisters about Max. And sooner rather than later.

Habmouth

14

'Are things okay at home, Poppy?' Max asked me.

I turned to look at him, surprised at the sudden serious turn in the conversation. I fussed around with my watch, hanging loosely from my wrist. What did he mean by asking me something like that? Though I'd grown used to Max stopping by my desk more often than was necessary – especially when my co-worker wasn't around – the conversation was usually light and trivial. Occasionally he managed to make me laugh, though God knows I had little enough to laugh about. But despite us enjoying each others' company, he was my boss and I suppose he thought my welfare was his responsibility. He sat on the edge of my desk when I didn't answer straight away, and I looked down into my lap. I didn't want to answer his question and for my facade to crumble. Work was where I could be normal. I wanted it to stay that way.

'How's Dominic?' he continued when I didn't reply.

'He's good.' I forced myself to look at him. His hazel eyes were warm, and although I found his combed back hairstyle – flecked as it was with white – a little bit silly, like he was trying to be Dominic's age, it made me smile to look at him. At least it usually did. Today I was intimidated by his immaculate suit – matching, no doubt, an immaculate life. He was neat and ordered, while my life was bleak and chaotic. I didn't want him to know how badly I'd messed up. I didn't want anyone to know. 'Max, I've got a lot to get through this morning.'

'Has Dominic started thinking about universities yet?' he said, as though he hadn't heard me. 'It must be almost time for that.'

'Yes, he's applied already.'

'What does he want to study?'

'Botany.'

'Ah, yes, you told me he likes plants – he bought you all of these on your desk didn't he?'

I glanced up at the row of green lining the back of my desk; a Chinese money plant, a snake plant, and several others whose names I'd forgotten. Dominic would know what they were all called, even their Latin names. The plants always made me smile, or at least they used to. Now thoughts of Dominic made guilt bloom in my stomach – my one job was to keep my son safe and I'd invited Kevin into our lives and got my son beaten and terrified in the process. I mentally shook myself and tried to focus on what Max was talking about. 'He didn't buy most of them,' I said, 'they're houseplants he took cuttings from or divided to make new plants, and I said I'd have them here. He's so clever with things like that.'

There was a pause as Max seemed briefly unsure what to say. 'Look, Poppy, I know you're busy and I'm sorry if I upset you, asking if you're okay. You don't have to talk to me, but if you do want to my door is always open.'

'I'm fine,' I said, my voice brittle.

He smiled as though something had just occurred to him. 'Have you taken Dominic to the botanical gardens, if he's into plants? They're not far away.'

'Not recently,' I said. An uncomfortable feeling of loss and longing crept over me as I recalled a younger Dominic racing around the glasshouses with delight, stopping from time to time to stare at some exotic specimen or another. It wasn't somewhere we'd been able to afford to visit often, but I'd tried to take him once or twice a year when he was a child. Now it would be impossible.

'I'm only asking because my sister used to love it there – she died, eight years ago now – but I go every year on her birthday. Usually with our parents, but it's getting a bit much for them now. I was wondering – maybe it's a silly idea – but would you and Dominic like to meet me there when I go this weekend? My treat.' He paused, and keen to encourage me he added, 'You'd be doing me a favour, really. I'm not looking forward to going on my own.'

Taken aback by his invitation, I stared at him stupidly. 'I can't drive,' I said finally, 'me and Dom used to take the bus, but it's not very regular–'

He waved that excuse – was it an excuse? – away. 'I'll pick you up.'

I was about to say no, but I paused. Why *was* I trying to say no? He wouldn't realise about my debt, about Kevin, about any of it, just from me going out on a day trip with him.

'I'd like that,' I said. 'But Dom is seventeen now, going out with us for the day probably won't appeal to him much, even if it is to visit the gardens.'

'I understand.'

'I will ask him though.'

The phone on my desk started to ring, and Max stood. 'Even if he doesn't want to, will you still come along?'

I nodded, reaching out to answer the phone, and Max smiled as he left. Perhaps his life wasn't so immaculate after all. I already knew he was single, but it had never occurred to me that perhaps he was lonely.

...

I drew in my breath sharply at the knock on the door. After Dom's attack I was keeping up with my payments to Kevin, but he still frightened me – and my heart leapt to find it was only Max with some pizzas. I invited him in awkwardly; uncomfortable to show him our bare flat. I'd sold anything non-essential that was worth selling, leaving what felt like a featureless husk of a home. But we'd got on so well at the botanical gardens and on a couple of dates since then that I put my misgivings aside. Why should I be ashamed of my flat? It might not exactly be beautiful – and the block that housed it had certainly seen better days – but anyone who really cared about me wouldn't be bothered about that, and Max was certainly unfazed. Dominic emerged from his bedroom, and finding Max in the hall with a stack of pizza boxes he muttered, 'So this is him, then.'

'Dom!' I said, 'don't be so rude.'

'It's okay,' Max said.

'No, it isn't,' I insisted, upset that their first meeting was already going badly. As I suspected, Dominic had not wanted to come with us to the gardens, though he'd had a wistful look on his face as he thought about the place. He'd been deeply sceptical at the idea of me having a relationship with my manager and I hated the way his eyes were so full of mistrust as he took in the sight of Max. 'Liam bribed us with pizzas too,' he muttered darkly.

'Liam is his dad,' I explained to Max quickly. 'He doesn't call him "Dad" because–'

'Because he left us when I was a little kid, came back a couple of years ago, pretended he was interested in us, then stole all our money and left us with nothing,' Dominic said bluntly.

'I'm sorry to hear that,' Max said. 'But I'm not trying to bribe anybody or take anything from you. Your mum told me you like pizza, that's all.'

'There's nothing left to take, anyway,' Dominic said. 'You couldn't pick a worse place to come looking for money.'

'Max is not here for that!' I said, 'not everyone is like your dad…' I gave up. Dominic wasn't going to take *my* word about Max's character. After all, I'd let Liam back into our lives.

We sat together in the living room in silence. Dominic had changed since being attacked and finding out what his dad had done. He'd grown harder and angrier, and I could swear even the features of his face had grown sharper and lost their softness – though perhaps that was just him growing up. Either way, it was as though something had been stolen from him – his faith in people, I suppose – and I'd give anything to bring it back.

Though he was still clearly upset, I was glad Dominic managed to eat, and I took my own first bite of pizza. The flavours exploded on my tongue, and for a while I completely forgot Max was sitting beside me as I stuffed down the food until I couldn't fit any more in. 'Sorry,' I said, when I realised he was looking at me. 'I was just–'

'Really hungry,' he said. 'There's no need to apologise.' He looked around the living room, as if trying to find something to compliment. 'That plant is... interesting,' he said as his eyes came to rest on Dominic's pitcher plant.

'I gave him that for his fourteenth,' I said. 'It eats flies.'

'What do you do in the evening?' Max asked curiously, 'only, I can't see a TV.'

'Mum's loan shark took it,' Dominic said as he finished off his pizza and placed the empty box on the coffee table.

'Dom!'

'Why are you pretending?' he said. 'Please, Mum, *please* stop trying to believe you can sort everything out. You can't sort this out. And it's not your fault. *I* accepted that stupid Playstation, I let Liam–'

'It is certainly not *your* fault!' I said, my voice rising. 'I'm the adult here, and I'm to blame, not you. Don't you ever start thinking otherwise.'

'All right,' Max said calmly. 'Let's just stop for a minute. Poppy, how bad is this? Did you really go to a loan shark?'

He paused as Dominic abruptly got to his feet. He returned from his room with the bills from the kitchen drawer and dumped them in Max's lap.

'Dom, those are private,' I said, reaching out to take them back, but Max had already unfolded one of the letters. Dominic picked up a new one from the coffee table that I hadn't noticed and thrust it towards me. When I opened it, it was immediately obvious why he was so on edge.

'We're being evicted!' he said. 'I found this when I got home from college.'

I couldn't speak. I just stared at the letter.

'Are you using our rent money to pay Kevin?'

'I–' I couldn't answer. It wasn't like I hadn't expected this. In my desperation to stop Dominic being beaten up again, nothing else mattered. The rent had been one thing I hadn't wanted to touch in the past, but nothing was sacred any more, not compared to my son's life.

'We need help, Mum! If Max is your boyfriend now, he should know about this, shouldn't he?'

Max had continued studying the stack of paperwork quietly, as both me and Dominic turned to him. 'How long has all this been going on for?' Max asked at length.

'Since Dom's dad stole the money,' I said. 'It's got worse and worse.'

He nodded. 'Well, I can pay some of these off for you. It'll get at least a few people off your back.'

'No,' I said. 'I can't be in debt to anybody else.'

'For God's sake!' Dominic exploded, '*take* his money, Mum! It's not as if he looks like he can't afford it!'

I was about to reprimand Dominic, but the look on his face stopped me in my tracks. His eyes were desperate and pleading. He was pale, and he was shaking. He wasn't being rude, he was just scared. Terrified.

'This… Kevin person Dominic mentioned,' Max said, 'I'm assuming you don't have any paperwork from him?'

I shook my head.

'How much is he saying you owe him?'

'He won't give me a number,' I said, my voice almost a whisper. 'I've paid back what I originally borrowed many times over, but because I missed some payments he starts going on about interest, and I–' I sighed. 'I don't think he's ever going to stop.'

'You don't have to give him anything,' Max said, 'you do realise that? The loan isn't legal, you can go to the police.'

'No,' I said. 'It's bigger than just Kevin. He had Dominic beaten up, I don't know how many of them there are – if someone realises I've gone to the police…'

Max was silent for a long time, 'Poppy, can I talk to you alone for a minute? There might be another way I can help.'

Cattleford

15

'Like a knight in shining armour!' Jessica breathed when I told the sisters that night about Max. 'What did he do? Did he kill Kevin for you?'

I almost spat out my mouthful of tea, and Jessica laughed. 'I *was* joking,' she said. 'He would deserve it though,' she concluded, before turning back to the instructions for the flat-pack cot that had arrived that afternoon. Bits of wood and fixings littered the floor, and Harriet had nearly hit the roof when she'd walked in and witnessed Jessica's slapdash approach to furniture assembly, insisting Jessica read the instructions from start to finish before doing anything else.

I shifted uneasily on the sofa. I wanted to help with the cot but I was feeling drained and Harriet had insisted I leave it to her and Jessica. I braced myself to explain the next part of my story. Max's other way to help had been a curse as much as a blessing, but I'd gone into it with my eyes open and it hadn't been a decision I'd taken lightly. The sisters turned to me, sensing a new mystery. 'What *did* he do, Poppy?' Harriet asked uneasily.

I took a deep breath and let it out slowly. 'He told me a way I could make money,' I said. 'Plenty of money.'

'Oh no,' Jessica said, her eyes wide as she threw her hands up to her face.

'It was nothing like what you're thinking,' I said. 'Nothing… seedy.'

'But it was something bad?'

I leant back heavily against the sofa cushions. A nagging pain had started in my back. Was I coming down with something? The drained feeling was turning into something worse, like I was just starting with a nasty case of flu. I tried to focus. Should I really tell the sisters about it? I'd be putting them in an impossible position. I couldn't expect them to keep it secret, could I? But carrying it around with me any longer was too much. I needed somebody to understand.

'It was fraud,' I said. 'The place we worked, QHM Solutions, it was a big company with hundreds of employees. Max told me that he had added a couple of extra employees – pretend ones – onto the payroll, and collected their salaries. He said I could do it too.'

Just a couple of months of collecting three salaries instead of one, maybe you could get rid of Kevin once and for all.

'So his solution to your problem was to dig yourself into an even bigger hole?' Harriet said, disgusted. 'If he actually cared about you, he would have supported you in reporting Kevin to the police. That's what you needed.'

'I know,' I said. 'I wish Max's suggestion had made me realise there was something off about him, and that I'd never even contemplated doing what he said. I wish I'd been brave enough to go to the police about Kevin myself, regardless of whether anyone was supporting me to do it. Things could have worked out so much better if I had, but I was frightened and embarrassed to talk about it. I fixated on being able to pay Kevin off without anybody else ever having to know I'd got into the situation in the first place.' I sighed. 'The fraud made me sick to my stomach. I'd been so proud to get the job, I'd had to do a bookkeeping course at the same time as working two jobs to get myself where I was, only to now abuse my position and steal from the company. But I just kept thinking that perhaps I could pay Kevin off once and for all. If I managed to get enough cash together at once, maybe he really would stop and I'd be free.'

'*Or,* he'd realise you had access to a lot of money and carry on bleeding you dry,' Harriet said darkly.

'Well, did it work?' Jessica asked. 'Did you get Kevin to stop?'

The mug of tea I was holding fell from my hand and spilt over my lap as I cried out in pain.

'Poppy?' Harriet gasped, leaping up to take away the mug and pulling off her jumper to try and soak up the hot liquid from my lap. 'It's okay,' I said, after catching my breath as the cramp subsided. 'It wasn't that hot anymore.'

Harriet's face was full of panic. 'But you were in pain! What's wrong? Where does it hurt?'

Another wave of pain had me clutching my stomach, and Harriet sprang into action. 'I'm taking you to hospital.'

'I'll be okay in a minute–' I protested.

'I don't know, Poppy,' Jessica said, looking at me closely. 'You don't look right. Let Harriet take you to get checked over. It can't do any harm, can it?'

…

'How are you feeling?' Harriet asked as she handed me a glass of water and I swallowed some antibiotics.

'Tired,' I said. 'And relieved, I guess. I wish I hadn't dragged you out to hospital, I should have waited until the morning and asked to see my midwife.'

'You were in pain, Poppy, and you were worried. And you didn't *drag* me anywhere; we both thought something was wrong. And something *was* wrong. Urinary tract infections can cause complications during pregnancy. I was looking up all the causes of abdominal pain while you were talking to the doctor. You can't be complacent about these things. The sooner it gets sorted the better.'

In fact, Harriet had been keen to stay stuck by my side the entire time I was in the hospital, but I started to find her over-bearing and insisted she should stay in the waiting area. Clearly she had spent the time absorbing all the pregnancy medical advice the internet had to offer. She was still watching me closely. 'All this dragging upsetting stuff up from the past, it's not good for you. You're making yourself ill. You should get some rest, and you don't need to come into the shop tomorrow.'

I made my way out of the kitchen, and Harriet followed me upstairs, asking if I needed anything. 'Honestly, Harri, I'm okay,' I said, trying not to let any irritation creep into my voice. *She just cares about me, that's all.* But then at the top of the stairs I swayed a little on my feet and she rushed to support me.

'You are not okay,' she stated. 'You're under too much stress. Maybe I should call your midwife tomorrow–'

'No!' I said, as I reached my limit. Would she ever stop fussing? I tried to calm down. 'I mean – I just want to go to bed. Can we talk about this in the morning?'

'You are not taking your health seriously.'

'And that's not your responsibility.'

'Nothing is more important than the baby!' Harriet exploded, her cheeks colouring. Immediately she tried to backtrack. 'I mean, you *and* the baby. You're a package – for the baby to be okay, you need to be okay.'

I took a deep breath and counted to three very slowly in my head. The last thing I needed was a full blown row. 'Thank you for tonight. I didn't mean to get irritable, but I don't feel good and I just need a bit of breathing space.'

For a second I thought she was going to argue, but instead she said, 'I'm sorry Poppy. I don't know what came over me.'

I made it into my room and sat on the bed, stretching my legs out in front of me. Harriet was in the doorway, looking so chastened that I felt a rush of sympathy for her. 'Harriet,' I said softly, before she left me. 'Jessica told me you wanted to have a baby with Ben.'

Harriet nodded, but didn't respond. 'I'll bring you up a glass of water if you want?' she said instead. 'And do you need another blanket? It feels chilly tonight.'

'The baby keeps me pretty warm,' I said. 'He's like a little radiator.'

Harriet smiled, though her eyes were troubled. My comment about her and Ben had upset her. 'Okay,' she said. 'And you just stay in bed tomorrow morning, I'll bring you breakfast and your antibiotics. No arguments.'

16

Just as Harriet had instructed, I stayed in bed the next morning. Having been shivery and feverish all night I needed the lie-in, but by the afternoon I had improved and went downstairs to look for Jessica, who I assumed would be working. Sure enough she was ensconced inside her sewing room – a large, slightly ramshackle conservatory at the back of the house, which she kept in a state of perpetual chaos, much to Harriet's irritation. The blinds were all open, flooding the space with light, and she had the radio on quietly.

'Jess?' I said softly, not wanting to make her jump as she was completely absorbed in her work.

'Oh, hello,' she said, looking up at me with concern, as if she thought I might keel over. Her face cleared as she concluded I wasn't going to. 'You look a bit better. Sorry the stuff for the cot is still all over the floor in the lounge, me and Harri will finish it later and get it all out of the way.'

'Hopefully I might be able to help you with it by then,' I said as I made my way towards her table where beautiful ivory satin was draped. 'What are you working on?'

'Taking in this dress,' she said. She held it up. 'Pretty, isn't it?'

I admired the strapless gown with its dramatic spray of diamantes. 'Did you make the whole dress?'

'No, not this one. It's from Bracton Brides. They recommend me to customers for alterations sometimes.'

I pulled up the rattan chair from the corner of the conservatory to sit down near to her, and she smiled at me. 'Do you wish you'd got married, Poppy?'

'What, to Liam?'

'Well, whoever,' she said. 'Not that there's not still plenty of time, of course.'

I pretended to be absorbed in admiring the dress. Max had in fact asked me to marry him. But I'd not got so far as dress shopping, let alone walking down the aisle.

'I would like to have a wedding – the big dress and all the rest of it,' Jessica said, 'but I don't think I would want to be married. Having someone around, getting in your face all the time. It seems… bothersome.'

'I suppose people aren't so bothersome if you love them.'

'You could well be right,' she said thoughtfully.

'And besides, Harriet is around all the time, and you are fine with that.' A searching tone crept into my voice as I said the last few words, as if I was daring Jessica to admit she wasn't fine with it, but she didn't answer me directly.

'I heard raised voices when you got back from hospital,' Jessica said. 'It woke me up.'

'Sorry.'

'I wasn't sleeping properly anyway. I was worrying you'd gone into early labour or something. Harriet told me what happened and she was grousing about you not looking after yourself properly when she was in the kitchen making you breakfast this morning.'

'She doesn't need to do all this stuff for me.'

'That's what I said. I said you're a grown woman with an eighteen year old son you brought up alone.'

'I did appreciate her taking me to hospital. And it was nice to have breakfast in bed, I have to admit. But… well–'

'It's getting a bit much.'

'She just cares about me,' I said. 'Maybe I'm not used to having people care for me. I'm worried I was horrible to her, snapping at her like I did, but she was saying she would call my midwife and that I wasn't taking things seriously…'

Nothing is more important than the baby. That was what Harriet had said. That was what had turned round and around in my head all night.

'It was a difficult situation for her when I had Reef,' Jessica said, as she absentmindedly stroked the dress on her work bench, her fingers tracing over the glittering diamantes. 'She was so keen to start a family with Ben, then their marriage broke down and all of a sudden there I was with a new, unplanned baby that I was struggling to bond with, and it wasn't a good combination of events. It must have taken everything she had to take me and Reef under her wing.'

'I just worry…' I struggled with how to sum up my feelings. 'She's getting very attached to the idea of there being a new baby in the house, and I don't want her to end up getting hurt. I will have to leave eventually. This little bubble I'm in here can't last forever.'

Jessica shrugged. 'Maybe it can,' she said. 'Why not? Just because what we've got here isn't a normal family, doesn't mean it can't work out. Reef and your baby – it's like they'll each have three mums for the price of one. Doesn't seem like a bad deal to me.'

…

In spite of Jessica's words, I stepped out of the shower a few days later to the sound of a blazing row downstairs in the kitchen. Dashing quickly to my room, I pulled on some clothes and tried to make out the words of the argument, but I couldn't. I bumped into Reef coming up the stairs as I made my way down, and his face was frightened. I gave what I hoped was a reassuring smile. 'Are your mummy and Auntie Harri arguing?'

He nodded, eyes wide, and I sat down on the stairs and pulled him close to me. 'Do they argue a lot?' I asked him softly.

'Sometimes,' he said, after thinking it through for a moment.

'Why don't I put the TV on for you? You stay in the lounge for a bit, and I'll see what's going on with Mummy and Auntie Harri, okay?'

I got into the kitchen as the argument reached a head, and Jessica screamed that she was going away for a few days and taking Reef with her.

'It's Thursday!' Harriet said, 'you can't keep dragging that poor boy out of school at the drop of a hat! He doesn't know whether he's coming or going.'

'That "poor boy,"' Jessica said. 'You mean the boy that I dedicate my whole life to? The boy I try to make sure has some fun and can escape your miserable clutches!'

'Look, let's just take a breath—' I said, though the sisters barely noticed me.

'Fine,' Harriet said, 'fine. You go then. Walk away from the life *you* have trapped me into.'

Jessica dashed out of the room, and I hovered in the doorway, unsure which sister to go to. In the end I stepped further into the kitchen. 'What was all that about?' I asked Harriet. The life Jessica had trapped Harriet into?

'I told her Reef can't have chocolate spread on toast for breakfast on a weekday.'

'That… that was it?' I asked.

'That's all I said. She blew it completely out of proportion.'

Apparently Harriet wasn't prepared to be drawn any further on the subject so I went upstairs to Jessica's bedroom, where she was haphazardly stuffing clothes into a suitcase. I wasn't sure how she could even see what she was doing in the perpetual semi-darkness of her room, which had a heavily embroidered voile curtain draped over the small north-facing window. Fairy lights twinkled around the shelves on the wall though, and every surface was cluttered with colourful ornaments, some of which caught the light and glittered enticingly. 'Jess, wait,' I said. 'Harriet said this was just because of chocolate spread—'

'Yes of course she did! Making out that I'm being hysterical. It's about… it's not just about that. She's a total…' Jessica struggled for words strong enough to sum up the situation. Finally seizing on some and punctuating them by slamming her hand against the suitcase she said, 'a total *fun sponge.*'

If Jessica hadn't looked so utterly furious I would have laughed. 'Jess, remember what you said to me, about us all being a family. A weird family, but still a family.'

'I must have been soft in the head that day,' she said. Then she let out a laugh. 'I'm sure that's what Harriet thinks of me. That I'm unhinged. An unfit mother, too wrapped up in herself to think about what's best for Reef. But it's not true. Just because I value fun and adventure, and all Harriet cares about is duty and being a martyr. You'd better watch your back, Poppy, before she gets her claws into your baby.'

With that she zipped up her suitcase and rushed off to Reef's room, and the sound of drawers being opened and slammed closed drifted down the hall. There was nothing I could do right now. They were both too angry, and the last thing I needed was to get caught in the middle. But a lot of odd things had been said. Why was Harriet trapped? Why did Jessica say that Harriet was being a martyr? I couldn't make head nor tail of it, but then it wasn't really any of my business. It was probably best if I stayed out of the way and waited for it all to blow over.

'Shall I open up the shop?' I asked Harriet when I went back downstairs.

'I can do it myself.'

'I think you need to take a moment,' I said carefully. 'I will open up. Just join me when you're ready.'

'She'll be back,' Harriet said. 'She throws a tantrum every now and again, but she needs me. She's never been much good on her own.'

17

I woke to blackness, my heart pounding. Where was I? A sense of foreboding gripped me and I opened my mouth to call out to Dominic when finally reality clicked back into place. I was at Harriet and Jessica's house. Not my old flat. Kevin wasn't coming, Max wasn't coming, Dominic was safe. A floorboard creaked in the hall, and feeling completely awake, I got out of bed and slipped out onto the landing where I nearly collided with Harriet.

'Sorry Poppy,' she said, 'did I wake you up?'

'No – I – maybe. But it doesn't matter. I was feeling unsettled anyway.' I paused for a moment then added, 'It's weird without Jessica and Reef in the house.'

'It's not the first time she's done this.'

'I gathered that.'

Harriet pulled her red dressing gown more tightly around herself and sighed. Her eyes had a puffy look and her face was drawn. Had she slept at all? It didn't look like it. 'We have a big argument sometimes and she storms off,' she said wearily, 'but she comes back again. Our personalities clash. We rub along okay together for the most part but then it blows up and it takes a day or two for the air to clear and for us to realise we need each other.'

'I was going to make a cup of tea,' I said, touching her shoulder gently. 'I don't think I'll be able to sleep again for a while. Do you want one?'

'Yes – and I'll make it,' she said. 'You go and put your feet up.'

'Harri–'

'No arguments. I'd rather be doing something. I don't want to just sit and think.'

It was easier to do as she asked, so I curled up on the living room sofa. Despite her assurances that Jessica always came back and that things would return to normal again, Harriet was clearly rattled. Had the argument been worse than usual? Or was my presence upsetting the balance? I couldn't stand the thought that I might be causing stress, when the sisters had done so much for me.

Harriet handed me a mug of tea and sat down on the arm-chair near the log burner. I wished that a fire was lit – I'd feel better watching the cheery, comforting flames. Instead I picked up the purple and white checked throw from a basket beside the sofa and snuggled myself up in it.

'Harri,' I said carefully, 'why did you say Jessica had trapped you into your life here?'

Startled, her eyes flashed with some strange emotion, but she simply shook her head. 'Oh, it was nothing. I don't know. I was just angry.'

'It sounded like more than that,' I pressed her gently.

I waited while she stared down into her mug of tea. Eventu-ally, when I was about to give up on an explanation, she said, 'I didn't think my life would be like this, that's all. Not so long ago I was married, I worked in a buzzing, busy office, and I had friends and a social life. I thought I was going to start a family.'

'You said you wanted to move back here, though.'

'Yes, when my mum and dad were here and I was hoping to get pregnant and thought I would benefit from their support. But then my dad died, my mum moved to Spain, and all of a sudden here I am looking after a business I'm not really interested in, marriage over, and instead of having my own family I'm living with Jessica and helping her raise *her* son. Yes, I love Reef, and Jessica – even though she drives me round the bend – but I don't feel like I have my own life. I'm just holding together other people's lives. I–' she quickly gulped down some tea, 'does that sound awful?'

'No, it doesn't. I completely understand.'

'I know that none of us can predict how our future will be. We make plans and then life comes and sticks a great big oar in and you just have to get on with it. But sometimes… sometimes *I* want to run away. Jessica thinks I like all of it, the responsibility of running the shop and helping with Reef and everything, but the truth is sometimes I would like to drop everything and escape the way she does.'

'Perhaps you should tell her that,' I suggested. 'Maybe it would help if she knew.'

Harriet shook her head. 'She needs to feel that I'm solid and dependable. She's more vulnerable than she seems.'

I wasn't too sure this was true, but Harriet had spent a lot more time with Jessica than I had. Perhaps there were sides to her I hadn't seen.

'I don't suppose this is how you imagined your life would be either,' Harriet said.

'No. I'm not sure I *could* have imagined what has happened to me. Sometimes the whole thing is beyond comprehension.'

'So… what did happen in the end?' Harriet asked me. 'Did you pay off Kevin with the money that you–' she stopped, clearly reluctant to say "stole."

'I tried to. But it didn't work out quite how I hoped.' I said, almost wincing at the understatement.

'What happened, then?' Harriet asked. 'You're feeling up to talking about it now, aren't you? You seem a lot better.'

'Yes,' I said heavily. 'I can talk about it.'

Habmouth

18

The inevitable sound of Kevin pounding at the door didn't even startle me. I knew it was coming, and I was prepared. I took some deep breaths. I'd rehearsed the conversation in my head a hundred times, if I wasn't able to convince him now, I never would be. All I had to do was get him to understand that although I'd used all the money I'd usually pay him to make a dent in my rent arrears – and hopefully avoid eviction – in just a few weeks I'd be able to give him far more than usual once I had the money from my fraudulent payslips. Not that I'd explain where the money was coming from, of course, but waiting just a little longer for a much bigger payment was the logical choice for him. He had to see that, surely. Then perhaps I could keep my home, *and* pay him off. I just had to hold my nerve and not let him get to me.

Once Kevin burst into the flat, slamming the door closed behind him, I tried to keep my exterior unflustered even though my pulse was racing. In his late twenties, Kevin stood nearly a foot taller than me and though he was as skinny as a rake I knew firsthand from the bruises he'd made on my wrist that he had plenty of brute strength. God knows how he'd seemed charming and understanding when he'd first spoken to me. I guess he was like Liam – he had all the chat when he was trying to win someone over, but it was hollow and meaningless.

'Are you having a fucking laugh?' he said when I tried, as calmly as possible, to outline the reasoning behind not having the money ready for him.

'I can pay far more than I usually do if you just give me a couple of weeks longer,' I said, trying to hold his gaze. I was not going to let him bully me. Not today. 'I can pay back everything in two or three months, I think, if you tell me exactly what I still owe–'

'Do you think I'm stupid?' he said, glaring at me. He was in a bad mood today. Not that he was ever exactly cheery with me, but his blue eyes had had a mean glint in them from the second he'd stepped into my flat. He was looking for confrontation. 'You're paying *now*. Otherwise, your boy is getting his head kicked in.'

'Listen to me,' I said. 'I am not lying. By the end of this month I'll have more money coming in. Far more. Give me a little longer, and this works out better for you.'

He stared at me incredulously, before grabbing me by the elbow and dragging me into the living room. Shoving me to one side, he glanced around as if looking for something, then stepped through to the kitchen.

'I don't have anything valuable,' I told him, 'there's nothing left to take.'

He opened and closed a couple of cupboards until he found the one with my glasses and mugs inside. He wasn't looking for anything to take; he was looking for something to smash. My favourite pink mug – bought back when me and Dominic had been happy and safe – smashed into pieces on the kitchen floor. '*That* is your boys head.'

I dug my nails into my palms, trying to seize on something, anything to say. 'You hurt Dominic and you get nothing,' I said wildly. Stupidly.

He strode across to me and gripped my chin in his hand. 'Oh, I'm getting something,' he said, pushing me back towards the wall. His breath was hot on my face as his hand pressed between my thighs and in a fit of rage I shoved him away and slapped him.

My hand flew to my mouth. What the hell had I done? My face exploded with pain as he punched me and I dropped to the floor, but I held my hand out to him, pleading. 'Don't hurt Dominic,' I said. 'Please.' I could taste blood in my mouth, and when I reached up to my face my fingers came away red.

'I'm not going to *hurt* him. I'm going to fucking kill him. And before he dies I'm going to tell him his mum didn't love him enough to pay what she owes.'

I struggled to my feet, grabbing at him as he started to leave. 'Stop,' I said, my voice rising hysterically. 'You can do what you want to me. Just leave Dominic alone!'

'I *want* my fucking money!' he yelled at me, shoving me so hard that I fell and found myself at his feet again. I curled up as he kicked me, until the world faded away.

...

I opened my eyes at the burst of voices. I must have blacked out for a few seconds, but Kevin was still in the flat. And so was my son.

'Dom!' I called out with all the strength I had. 'Dom, run! Run!'

My voice was broken and cracked, and I struggled to focus on the two of them. Once my vision cleared, the shock of what was in front of me made me cry out.

'Dom, no,' I sobbed. I tried to get up but the pain almost made me black out again and I slumped to the floor, eyes fixed on the pair of them. Somehow, inexplicably, Dominic was holding a kitchen knife and threatening Kevin with it.

'I said fuck off!' Dominic said, gesturing towards the front door, his voice surprisingly strong as my consciousness began to fade. 'Now!'

The front door slammed closed, the sound shocking me awake again. Dominic dropped to his knees, shaking violently, and I dragged myself across the floor to him despite the blinding pain. 'Dom?'

There were tears on his cheeks, and his face was white with shock. 'He's gone,' he said. 'I got him to leave.'

'Yes,' I breathed, my mind thick and groggy, 'yes, you did.'

'Are you okay?' he said, coming back to his senses, 'I'll call an ambulance.'

'Did Kevin say anything?' I asked him, 'before he left, did he…'

The glassy sheen of Dominic's eyes told me all I needed to know. If we stayed, we were dead. 'We need to leave,' I said, as clearly as I could. 'We can't be here. We can't ever come back here.'

Dominic stared at me. 'What have I done? What have I done? Mum–'

'Call Max,' I said. 'He needs to get us right now and take us away from here.' The pain was overwhelming, but I reached out for Dominic's hand and he held it. 'We will be okay,' I reassured him. 'Max will help us.'

Cattleford

19

On Sunday morning, when we hoped Jessica would be coming home, Harriet sat in the kitchen staring at her phone, eyes full of shock.

'Are you okay?' I asked carefully as I joined her, 'you look like you've had some bad news.'

She snapped out of her trance and put the phone down on the table, picking up her mug of coffee instead and taking a long sip. I sat opposite her. 'So?'

'It's Jess,' she said.

My heart sank. 'Is she all right?' I asked. 'Is Reef okay?'

'Yes, they're both fine. They've gone to the coast. Reef's enjoying it.'

'So, what's the but?'

'She says she met someone. A man, I mean.'

'Okay…'

'Well, she's gone completely off the deep end. She says they're going to be together, that he's asked her to come and live with him at his house the other side of the country.' Harriet's shock turned abruptly to anger. 'I don't know what goes on in her head. She acts like she doesn't have a child to think about!'

'When did she meet this man?'

'Friday.'

'So she's known him two days?'

'It's classic Jessica! She can't do things half-heartedly. If she meets someone, they're the love of her life. I could strangle her sometimes!'

'And this guy…' I said, trying to calm her down, 'he really asked her to go and live with him?

'She seems to think so. She says she's going there with Reef tomorrow.'

'Just the other day Jessica was talking about how she didn't like the idea of living with someone – having them in your face all the time.'

Harriet gave a snort of humourless laughter. 'Was she talking about me?'

'No.'

Harriet's brow furrowed. 'Jessica can be adamant how she feels about something one day, and then feel the total opposite the next. You can't guess what she'll do. But this…' her voice rose again, 'she's gone too far this time. I am going to find her and drag her back home.'

I stared at her helplessly. Her eyes were glittering with anger and she was gripping her cup so hard the ends of her fingers were white. I had to say something to diffuse the situation before Harriet rushed off and destroyed what was left of her relationship with Jessica completely. 'Well, let's just think for a moment,' I said calmly. 'She can't go anywhere tomorrow – she needs to sort something out with Reef's school first.'

'That won't stop her,' Harriet said, her face like thunder. 'And I know what kind of men she picks. She'll uproot Reef on a stupid whim and it will all end in tears within a month,' she strode across the room and picked up her car keys. 'I'm going to get her.'

'Didn't she meet Reef's dad on a weekend away to the seaside?' I asked, which stopped Harriet in her tracks. 'What does that have to do with anything?' she asked suspiciously.

'Nothing, just… there really is something about her and the sea, it seems.'

'There's certainly something about her and dodgy men. This *Tyler* that she's met, she says he's "romantic" and has a "beautiful soul". What she means is he's all charm, but deep down he'll be flaky and unreliable.'

'I don't know,' I said, 'I agree you should meet him, but perhaps we should trust her. Even if it's a mistake, sometimes we have to be allowed to make mistakes. Why don't I come with you? Perhaps it might help. But I need to grab some breakfast first.'

'Yes,' Harriet said quickly. 'Yes, of course you do. Do you want me to make a green smoothie? I've got quick at them now, and you must take your vitamin D.'

'I'll just have toast, Harri, but thank you.'

I got up to make breakfast and take the pregnancy vitamins she reminded me about daily, and the baby gave me a big kick that made me stop in my tracks.

'What's up?' Harriet said, her eyes instantly on me, 'are you okay?'

'It's just the baby kicking.' I paused, and then added, 'Feel it if you like.' I could tell she wanted to, but had held herself back from asking. She reached towards me, but let her hand drop. 'No,' she said. 'We don't have time to lose. You eat, and then we'll leave straight away. We've got to get to her before she does anything rash.'

'Harri?'

She paused on her way out of the door.

'How do you know where to find her? She didn't say where she was going, did she?'

'Oh… I found the address of the bed and breakfast in her emails.'

'Does she know that you know her password?'

'I'm not sure,' she said, as though it had never occurred to her to worry about it. 'It's not like I go snooping on her all the time. It's just a precaution. For times like this.'

She rushed off to get her coat and I stared at the empty doorway where she had just been standing. Could I really blame Jessica for running? If Harriet wanted that much control over her life the house must feel like a prison.

…

Standing at the door of an old-fashioned bed and breakfast, I glanced at Harriet, whose face had regained the furious expression she'd had earlier that morning. 'Look, are you sure about this–' I started to say as Harriet reached for the door, but the decision was taken away from us when it burst open and Jessica nearly collided with us. Behind her Reef paused and gave us a smile, a red bucket and spade dangling loosely from his hand. 'Harriet?' Jessica said. 'Poppy? What are you doing here?'

'What do you think we're doing here!' Harriet said, her face reddening. 'Your message this morning! You didn't really think I was going to ignore that, did you?'

The door opened again and a man stepped out, pausing beside Jessica. He looked from us to Jessica questioningly, before running a hand through his dishevelled brown hair and giving a wide grin. 'What can we do for you ladies?' he said.

'Is this him?' Harriet asked.

When Jessica didn't answer Harriet turned to Tyler. 'I'm Jessica's sister. And I've come to take her home.'

'Harri!' Jessica cried. 'Why do you always have to do this? Why do you always try to ruin things for me?'

Alarmed by his mother's outburst, Reef looked up at her in confusion, and I took the little boy's hand. 'Why don't I take him down to the beach?' I said. It was only the other side of the road, down some steps in the steep sea wall. Harriet nodded, and Reef and I made our way across the road, until finally the sounds of Jessica and Harriet's argument were whipped away in the breeze.

'What are they shouting about?' Reef asked me.

'They're not shouting,' I said automatically. Then I paused. 'Well, I suppose they are shouting a little. Sometimes grownups disagree with each other. They shouldn't be shouting, but they just need to talk it through, then they'll be friends again. Do you ever get cross with your friends?'

'Sometimes,' Reef conceded.

'It feels bad for a little while, doesn't it? But you make up again and everything's okay,' I reassured him. 'Like it will be with Mummy and Auntie Harri.'

'Is it because of Tyler?' Reef asked.

'Perhaps,' I said. 'Your Auntie Harri doesn't know him yet.'

'He's nice. I like him,' Reef told me. 'He said he'd teach me how to throw stones really far into the sea.'

I gazed out to the ocean, the surface of which was ruffled by choppy waves, seagulls circling above it. Why couldn't life just be simple? Everyone was always so tied up in knots, trapped by their pasts and scared of their future. I was no different.

'Were you going to throw stones this morning?' I asked Reef.

'Yeah. Before we go away.'

'Well, I can try to teach you. Although I'm probably not as good as Tyler is.'

'Auntie Harri doesn't like Mummy having new friends,' he said, as we slipped and slid our way down a bank of shingle to get closer to the ocean. 'They always have fights about it. But it's nice to have friends.'

'I think Auntie Harri just wants to make sure your mummy makes good friends,' I said, though his statement made my skin prickle. What on earth was going on between the sisters? Why didn't Jessica tell Harriet to get stuffed? In her position, that's what I would do. But to my surprise, when Jessica and Harriet finally came down to the beach where Reef had started skimming pebbles – without a huge amount of success – Tyler was nowhere to be seen, and Jessica's eyes were puffy with tears.

'I'm not saying never,' Harriet said, 'you can stay in touch with him, see how things go.'

'I don't think he's going to like that.'

'Then he isn't really right for you,' Harriet said. 'He shouldn't make you rush things. If he's serious–'

'He was serious!' Jessica said. 'We were both serious! I can't *believe* you've done this to me again! You've scared him off – no one wants anything to do with me after they've met you!'

Jessica stopped talking as she reached Reef, and her face softened.

'Is Tyler going to come and throw the stones?' Reef asked.

'I don't think so,' Jessica said. 'Not today.'

Reef ran over to Harriet, and abruptly hit her in the side with one of his little hands. 'Why do you have to make everyone go away?' he shouted in his little, angry voice. 'Why are you so mean to everybody?'

'You have no idea what I've sacrificed for you!' Harriet yelled. 'For both of you.' She faced Jessica. 'Your son just hit me,' she said.

'Good!' Jessica said. 'Well done Reef.'

Without another word Harriet turned on her heel and stormed off down the beach, while Jessica knelt beside Reef. 'You shouldn't hit people, Reef,' she said softly. 'Even if you're really cross.'

'I *am* really cross!' he said.

Jessica put her arms around him. 'I know,' she whispered. 'I know, Reef. I am too. But Auntie Harriet is usually right about things. We have to listen to her.'

Reef nodded against her shoulder, a fat tear rolling down his cheek.

20

'You *don't* have to listen to her,' I told Jessica, once Reef had calmed down and was hunting for shells along the shore, whooping when waves came to lap around his wellies. I didn't want to cause trouble, but the way Harriet had swooped in and left Jessica and Reef in tears shocked me. After she'd stormed off down the beach we'd seen no sign of her, though presumably she would turn up again eventually.

Jessica sighed, 'I do.'

'Why?'

Jessica started absent-mindedly picking up handfuls of sand and letting it run through her fingers. 'You should be careful,' she said eventually, startling me. 'She'll want your baby. I can see her plotting already.'

'What?' Had I heard her right?

'She started looking up how to adopt Reef when he was born,' Jessica continued, her voice full of spite. 'She always, *always,* wants to interfere. She still thinks he's hers, just because she had to look after him a lot when he was first born and I wasn't well.'

I was so astonished that I couldn't answer straight away, and Jessica quickly snapped out of her dark mood and said, 'Ignore me, Poppy. I'm just upset. She's done a lot for us. More than I could ever have expected. I shouldn't resent her.'

My eyes slipped towards Reef, who was splatting heaps of sea foam with his spade, delighted as it sprayed all over his wellies and trousers and I smiled, thinking of Dominic when he was that age. My smile quickly faded and I put my hands on my bump. No matter how I tried, I could feel nothing but dread about the new baby. My circumstances were far more precarious now than when I'd had Dominic at sixteen, and it had been challenging enough back then. *She'll want your baby. I can see her plotting already.* I shivered, and thought of the green smoothies, the gifts, the

91

unnecessary advice and concern. Jessica was just letting her imagination run away with her, surely. There couldn't be any truth to it.

'Jess,' I said at length.

'Mm?'

'Perhaps I should move out. It's bound to be putting more pressure on you both.'

She turned to me, an eyebrow raised. 'How would you get by?'

'I'll try and find a job. I know Harriet can't afford to employ me properly at the shop, but there must be something around–'

'Poppy, you're getting on for six months pregnant. Now isn't the time to begin a new job. And I can't imagine you're keen to start applying for benefits and having people dig around in your history when you were stealing from your old employer. So what would you do if you moved out? Where would you go, really?'

I stared at her, stunned to get such a stark reality check from the sister whose head was usually in the clouds. Of course she was right – what would I do if I left? But what she'd said about Harriet and my baby had unsettled me deeply – how could I stay in the house when Jessica had made an accusation like that?

'Can you really not go to Max?' she said, her voice having lost its bluntness now. 'It sounds like he tried to help you.'

'No,' I said flatly.

'Well, then, it doesn't seem like you've got a lot of other options,' she said. She brushed sand from her legs and stood up abruptly, her upset about Tyler seemingly having been forgotten. 'Reef, let's go and get an ice-cream,' she yelled down to her son. 'Come on,' she said, holding her hand out to help me up. 'I'll get you one too. You look like you could do with some sugar.'

'Jess,' I said, once I was on my feet. 'I'm sorry about Tyler.'

She shrugged. 'I'll do what Harriet said. Keep in touch with him. If it's meant to be it's meant to be. Love finds a way.'

Habmouth

I woke to the sound of voices outside the door, and I sat bolt upright, terrified, staring at my surroundings in total confusion. My eyes came to rest on the large picture opposite the bed – an abstract scene of blue, purple and green brushstrokes that could depict anything from wild moorland to a peaceful coastal landscape depending how you looked at it. The pieces clicked into place and I sank down gratefully into the soft sheets of the king size bed in Max's bedroom.

'Is she okay?' Dominic's voice came to me clearly through the closed door.

'Yes,' Max replied. 'She's asleep. I'm going to make her some breakfast.'

'But she slept all day yesterday. And the day before.'

I rubbed my eyes. It was true, since I'd called Max to come and rescue me and Dominic from the flat and we'd fled to his house it was like all the sleep I'd missed out on through the months of stress and fear descended on me at once and I could barely keep my eyes open.

'Your mum's been through a lot, and she's in pain from Kevin attacking her. It might take her a few days to get back on her feet. She's been running on empty for a while, and she's recovering from everything that happened.'

There was a brief silence, and I strained to hear Dominic's next words, said more quietly. 'Thank you for looking after her,' he said. 'If you hadn't been able to come and get us–'

'You don't need to thank me. I'm glad I could help.'

'I just wanted him to leave. I know how stupid it was to pull a knife on him but I thought he was going to kill her.'

Tears sprang to my eyes and I choked back a sob.

'I should have done more,' Dominic continued, 'I should have realised sooner what was happening so I could help her with money. I would have given up college and tried to get a job, I would have given her all the money I earned at the garden centre rather than saving it for university–'

'That's not what your mum wants. And you need to go in to college this morning. You can't stay here every day.'

'But—'

'I know what you're worried about. I'll drive you there and back and I'll drop you right at the door. If any of Kevin's people are looking for you they won't get a chance to go near you. And you're on revision leave soon, anyway, aren't you? You won't even have to go in except for exams and I'll take you to those.'

I put my hands over my mouth to stop myself letting out a cry of relief. Thank God we had Max. 'Your mum will be okay now,' Max reassured him. 'You don't need to stay here worrying about her. She wants you to do your exams.'

'Will you make sure she eats?'

'Yes, I'll make sure. There's no reason for her not to now. There's plenty of food here, and she knows she'll get more later, she doesn't have to try and stop herself getting hungry. But you'll have to be patient with her. She's been through a lot and she's not going to get better overnight.'

My eyes began to close, and I let myself drift away, confident that here, nothing could hurt me.

...

Over the next week I grew stronger, the bruises from Kevin's beating began to settle down, and I told Max I thought I was well enough to go back to work.

'I'm sure Kevin doesn't know where I work,' I said, 'and even if he does, we can go there and back in your car and he won't get a chance to corner me. As long as he doesn't figure out where I live. If… if me and Dom can stay here longer?'

'Of course you can. And are you sure about work? You look like you could use more rest to me,' he said.

I stretched out my legs luxuriously. Once I'd felt up to getting out of bed I'd spent lots of time on the grey velvet sofa in Max's living room, snuggled under a fleece blanket watching box sets on TV. Initially I felt that I'd died and gone to heaven, but now it was time to get up and about again. I was far stronger than

I had been, colour had returned to my cheeks, and my thoughts were clear and unmuddled.

'Once I've paid off all the credit card debts and everything, I don't want to carry on with… what we've been doing,' I told him. 'I hate stealing. When my debts are cleared, it needs to stop.'

'You don't have to decide that now.'

'I do. I'm not a thief, Max. It was only to help me survive.'

'And what about Dominic and his university fees? I've seen his student loan paperwork – do you know how much debt *he's* going to end up in? Looking at the numbers made my eyes water.'

'That's different.'

'Well, I'm going to pay some of the fees for him,' Max said. 'I'll tell him at the weekend, on his eighteenth birthday.'

'You don't have to do that,' I said in astonishment. Though, admittedly, it was hardly as if he was spending his own hard-earned money.

'I want to. He's not had an easy time of it, but he still works hard. He's ambitious, and he cares about you more than anything else. He's loyal, and he had the courage to stand up to Kevin. I've got a lot of respect for him.'

'Thank you,' I said, deeply touched by his words about my son. I reached up to his face and he kissed me gently, before I looped my arms around his neck, pulling him down onto the sofa with me. Our relationship had been so brief – and so overshadowed by my drama – that we hadn't made love before. Max hadn't even slept in the same bed as me when I'd come back to his house, he'd given me the main bedroom and slept down the hall in the spare room. But I was healing now. I wasn't addled with stress, I wasn't weak with hunger. I was alive, and I wanted him. Our morning passed in a bliss of touch, his skin warm against mine, his hands and lips tender and gentle as he opened up my body to his. It wasn't like it had been with Liam – there were no ripped clothes and no nail marks in backs, but it was warm and safe and beautiful. Pleasure bloomed in me like a rose gently opening as I gasped and wrapped my legs around his, feeling whole with him inside me.

Cattleford

21

'We should start getting ready for the baby,' Harriet announced.

'What do you mean?' I asked her, as I finished tidying away rolls of fabric. It had been a brisk morning, and my back was starting to ache. Had I ached like this when I was pregnant with Dom? I couldn't really remember, but I didn't think so.

'You've got the cot and some baby clothes, but that's not enough. You need a pushchair, a baby bouncer, a baby bath. You should get a few toys and books, too.' She took a breath before adding, 'If you're struggling for money, I can–'

'I can't ask you to do that. You already bought the cot, and you've given me so many gifts for the baby.'

'Do you have any money left? From the… you know. From what you were doing?'

'No,' I said, after a brief pause.

'You don't sound sure.'

I sighed. 'I don't have any money left from that. And even if I did, I can't build my future using it. I want to start things with this baby the right way.'

'But how are you going to do that?'

Our conversation was interrupted by the phone ringing, and while Harriet talked to her customer I continued tidying, trying to immerse myself in the myriad colours and textures of the shop. My life had never had so much colour; the flats Dominic and I shared had always been drab, and the estuary, as much as I loved it, was nearly always on the spectrum of brown to grey. Inside Bits and Bobbins it was like a rainbow had exploded, and I loved it.

I was so distracted with my thoughts that I didn't hear Harriet finish the phone call, and her voice startled me. 'If you wanted to focus on getting a different job, or doing some training or something, I can help out. You know, with the childcare.'

'What do you mean?'

'Well, you'll need something to live on,' she said quickly, 'you'll need to plan for the future. This is real, Poppy, you've only got a little bit more time and then the baby will be here. But I can help.' Her cheeks coloured a little. 'If you want me to.'

'Won't you need to run the shop?'

Harriet's cheeks reddened further, and she turned away from me. 'Ignore me,' she said, 'it was a silly idea.'

'Well you're right that I need to plan for the future,' I said.

'This stuff with me and Jess,' Harriet said at length, 'I know it probably looks like I'm a control freak.'

'It's got nothing to do with me.'

'You haven't seen Jess when she's been really struggling,' she said. 'There are times she's completely relied on me and I've had to step up whether I wanted to or not. I've made a lot of sacrifices for her, and that makes things strained sometimes.'

'Is that why you were looking into adopting Reef? When she was really struggling?'

Harriet nearly dropped the pile of knitting patterns she was restocking the shelf with and stared at me. 'Is that what she told you?'

'Yes.'

Harriet shook her head. 'She *asked* me to adopt Reef. I didn't want to do it! I only started looking when she was so low that I thought she might–' she stuffed the patterns on the shelf, '– I thought she might kill herself,' she said, her voice strained. 'And Reef needed somebody.'

'I'm sorry Harri–'

'She always makes me out to be some sort of monster!' Harriet said, her voice high, 'but if you knew what *she* had–' she stopped and shook her head. 'It doesn't matter. Look, how about we shut up the shop for half an hour and nip across to the pub for lunch. My treat.'

…

I had a feeling there was more to Harriet's offer of lunch than met the eye, and the second I finished my last mouthful and sat back in my chair she spilt out the idea she'd clearly been bursting to tell me.

'There might be another way for you to get back on track with everything,' Harriet said.

I frowned. Her voice had a wheedling tone to it that made it clear I wasn't going to like what she had to say. 'And what is that?' I asked, tearing my eyes from the window. It was so pretty outside today, the old buildings in the village square framed wonderfully by such a perfect clear blue sky. It had been rainy the day before and the puddles had frozen to ice overnight. Harriet had clutched my arm when we'd set out early in the morning to Bits and Bobbins, clearly worried I'd slip on the ice and hurt the baby.

'It's going to sound a bit mad,' she continued, 'but just bear with me Poppy. Hear me out.'

'Yes, I'll hear you out,' I said. It was hardly as if I'd thought of any good solutions myself.

'Okay. So, you wait until the baby is born. Don't tell anyone you've had it – no one knows you're pregnant anyway, apart from me and Jess. Some people may suspect at the shop but as long as you stop coming in before your bump gets really visible…'

'Harri, what on earth–'

'Just listen. You turn yourself in for the fraud, after the baby is born, and if you have to go to prison, *we* will look after the baby. Me and Jessica, until you get out again.'

I stared at her in astonishment. 'What?'

'That way, you keep the baby away from Max, if that's what's important to you, but you can also clear your name and start over. You're not going to get a massive sentence, not if you own up to it. You might not have to go to prison at all. Offer to pay back the money. I know you can't, but at least show willing. Show that you're sorry. If you did end up having to go to prison, we're your safety net. We'll keep the baby safe until you're ready to look after him again.'

I struggled to take it all in. About to say no, I caught myself. It sounded crazy, but could it work? Starting again with a clean slate, keeping myself and the baby away from Max and having a chance to rebuild my life – it certainly had an appeal to it.

'Think about it,' Harriet said.

'But what about you? It's too much, I can't ask you to–'

'You didn't ask, I offered. And it's a genuine offer.'

I found myself lost for words again as I tried to wrap my head around her scheme. 'Poppy?' she said. 'I know it's a lot. You don't have to decide right now. But I can see you're terrified of Max, even if you haven't told us why. I know you can't see any way out of this.'

'I–' I said, 'It's just… going to the police…'

'Yes, it's scary,' she said. 'Of course it is. But is it worse than being in hiding forever? Never able to get on and live your life because you're scared someone will realise what you did?'

'You don't understand,' I said, 'maybe it could work, but there's more to it. There's a lot more.'

'Then tell me. What went wrong between you and Max?'

She reached across the table towards me and I gripped her hand. Her face was kind, those dark eyes beneath her choppy red fringe searching mine, but Jessica's words rang in my ears: *She'll want your baby. I can see her plotting already.*

Habmouth

22

Dominic's reaction when I showed him the ring was not what I was hoping for. He stared at the diamond for a moment, forehead creased, and then stopped his packing for university to sit down at the desk Max had bought him to use during his exam revision. It wasn't the only thing Max had given him; there was a new bed, new curtains, and cheerful pictures hanging on the freshly painted walls. This was our home – a proper home, a place we could be safe and feel cocooned. Max had put so much effort into making me and Dominic feel welcome, even though Dominic was about to leave for university. Max's words about Dominic's room had touched me deeply; 'I want him to know he always has a home here,' he had said. 'This room is his, whenever he needs it.' Those words were what stayed in my head whenever I had to brush off some offhand hurtful remark Max made about me, and the strange distaste he seemed to have at the idea that I was okay now and didn't rely on his help and protection the way I once had.

I sat down on the bed beside Dominic's desk, waiting for him to say congratulations, or that he was happy for me.

Instead he said, 'Are you sure about this?'

'Of course I am. I wouldn't have said yes otherwise.'

He rubbed his hands against his jeans as though the thought of what he had to say to me was making his palms sweat.

'Dom,' I said, before he could speak, 'I know these past years have been hard, and unsettling…'

'Did you say yes because I'm leaving in a couple of days?'

I paused. Yes, the thought of Dominic going away to a different city was tearing my heart out. We'd always been together, and we'd always been so close. Nobody understood me better than Dom, but knowing he was about to take the first step towards the future he'd dreamed of since he was only little made any pain I felt worth it.

'Look, I know you're wary of letting anyone in after what your dad did to us,' I said, 'but we can trust Max. He's been so kind and generous to us; he even gave you all that money to help you through uni.'

'I like Max. But I don't trust money. Where's it all coming from?'

I couldn't meet his eye as he asked that. 'Well, money makes you secure,' I said quickly. 'If I've taught you anything from the mess I made of my life, I'd hope it would be that. To be careful with money, and be careful who you trust with it. Max is giving you that money because you're important to him and he believes in you.' I smiled. 'Besides, he said if you discover some new plant species one day you can name it after him.'

Dominic's face stayed serious. 'You've taught me a lot more than you think you have.'

'I can't imagine it's anything good.'

'Mum, stop it!' Dominic said, his eyes flashing with emotion. 'It's not *you* who messed things up for us. It was Liam!'

'Dom–'

'No. I hate him. I wish–' he paused, then in a rush of anger he said, 'I wish he was dead.'

There was a heavy silence, where Dominic's face showed he was trying to decide whether to retract this statement or not.

'I know you feel like you hate him,' I said carefully, 'but–'

'Why don't you? Why don't *you* hate him?'

I sighed and drew my legs up onto the bed, wrapping my arms around my knees. 'Because he's your dad,' I said softly. 'And every time you call him "Liam", it makes me feel like you're trying to deny half of who you are.'

'I am nothing like him!'

'No, you're not. But you wouldn't exist if it wasn't for him. Anyway, we're not talking about your dad. We're talking about Max. And I *am* sure. Living here, being secure and happy, I can't imagine anything better.'

It was true that the past few months had been blissful. In this lovely, comfortable home life was the easiest it had ever been. Kevin still crossed my mind from time to time and Dom and I kept a low profile, but that wasn't much of a sacrifice when being in the house was such a pleasure. But a creeping sense of doubt spread through me. It wasn't just the odd remarks Max made to me sometimes, more concerning was that whenever I said I wanted to scale back on the payroll fraud Max would try to talk me out of it, insisting that I keep the employee files paying money to us open. I still hadn't quite cleared my loans and credit card debts, but I was getting close. Max didn't seem to understand how I felt about it. He'd told me after proposing that I deserved to have a dream wedding. His voice echoed in my ears: Why did we have to compromise? Why shouldn't I have something amazing and special after a life of hardship? I hadn't agreed with him at the time and I still didn't now. I didn't need a big showy wedding, and my life hadn't been all hardship. He wouldn't accept that me and Dom had enjoyed our lives – for the most part, anyway – before Liam took our money. To Max we were victims in a tragedy, we were people who needed saving. But how could I blame him for getting the wrong idea when he'd seen us at our lowest and most desperate? Now things were better he would soon realise I was so much more than the person Liam and Kevin had briefly made me. After all, that couldn't *really* be the person he wanted me to be.

'You don't love him though, do you?' Dominic said bluntly, startling me.

I stared at him, 'You don't know that, Dominic. You don't know how I feel.'

'Well, you just said that living here and being secure is what you are looking forward to. Nothing to do with Max. And I do know how you feel, because I saw how you were with Liam. And this isn't that.'

I looked round sharply. Was that a footstep in the hall? There was only silence. No matter what Dominic said, I was doing the right thing. I didn't want to struggle any more. I wanted my life to be simple, or at least normal, and why should I feel bad for wanting that? 'Look, the way I felt about your dad–' I started explaining.

'Liam,' he insisted.

'Fine, with Liam. I loved him so much. And I suffered so much because of it. I don't ever *want* to love somebody like that again. Loving him made me into an idiot and almost ruined both our lives.'

'Isn't that what love is supposed to be? Something that makes you crazy.'

'Not if it's making you crazy over someone who is going to hurt you. I don't want that. Never again.'

Dominic got back up and started on a drawer of clothes, sorting through what he would take – not that he exactly had hundreds of outfits to choose from after our mad dash from the flat – but he chucked a couple of t-shirts that were too small into a box marked "charity".

'I care about Max,' I said. 'He makes me happy.'

'You said "care,"' Dominic said. 'You didn't say love. And that ring he gave you – it isn't you.'

I had to admit that was true. The big diamond glittering on my finger was ridiculous on me, a shiny bauble that I felt no connection to and found completely impractical. Frustration filled me and I got to my feet, wanting to be alone.

'You know I'm right,' he said. 'I'm not trying to upset you, Mum, but no matter how kind Max has been to us, you can't force yourself to feel something that you don't. And it's not fair on Max, either.'

…

That night Dominic went out for the evening with his friends – much to my concern as I was terrified he would bump into Kevin – but Max convinced me that Dominic should spend time with his friends before he left for university.

'It's one night,' he said. 'We can let him have one night. I'll cook us dinner.'

'You don't have to do that,' I said, 'at least let me help.'

He gave me a squeeze. 'You just sit down, put your feet up. I can treat the future Mrs Dorsett, can't I?'

I smiled hesitantly. The future Mrs Dorsett. I wasn't entirely comfortable with that. I was also well aware that he'd said *we* can let Dominic have one night, not *you* can let him have one night, as if he'd fully taken on the role of being a parent to my son. But did that matter? I could hardly forget how much he'd done for us, and we did all live together. Why should I be reluctant for him to think he was responsible for Dominic's welfare? Having someone else looking out for him could only be a good thing for my son. Perhaps I should broach the subject of keeping my own surname with Max, though. I'd fought so hard and for so long on my own that it felt odd for my name to become an extension of his.

'It smells delicious,' I called through to the kitchen as I listened to him clattering about busily. 'What is it?'

'It's prawn linguine. It'll only be a few more minutes. I'll pour you some wine.'

Obligingly I sat down at the glass dining table and sipped at my glass of wine, but when he carefully placed my meal down in front of me, I laughed out loud in surprise. There were no more than a few forkfuls in my bowl, while he had plenty.

'Where's the rest of it?' I asked him playfully. If it was some sort of joke, I didn't get it.

'What do you mean?' he asked as if he genuinely didn't understand. He began winding linguine around his fork, while I stared helplessly at my own meal. 'Maybe you could give me a little of yours? It smells so good, and I–'

'No.'

'I don't understand,' I said, irritated now. 'Is this some sort of joke? I'm really hungry.'

'I thought that's what you like.'

'What?' I said, as a cold feeling spread through me. The room began to blur before my eyes in my panic over his bizarre comment. Something was wrong here. Very wrong.

I shook myself. Stop overreacting! There would be some simple explanation for his behaviour. But his voice had been hard, and his eyes had lost their warmth.

He put his fork down and looked at me steadily. 'I heard your chat with Dominic.'

'I thought it was best if it came from me that we are getting married,' I explained quickly, trying to sound as innocent as possible. 'I'm sorry – did you want us to tell him together?'

'*Are* we getting married?'

'I said yes, didn't I?'

'You want to marry somebody you only "care" about, do you?'

I gave an uneasy laugh. 'Look, Dominic was worried about me, that's all. He thinks I said yes because he's about to move away, but that's not–'

'It's not because you still love Liam then?'

'No!' I said, 'I *hate* Liam. I want to bloody strangle him for what he did.'

'You didn't tell Dom you hated him.'

'It's complicated!' I cried. 'I'm not going to tell my son I hate his dad, even if he thinks it's what he wants to hear. And besides, Liam gave me Dominic, and that's the greatest gift I could ever have. But I'll never forgive him for what he did to us. Never.'

Max went back to his food, loading up a huge forkful which he chewed thoughtfully. 'I just thought I'd got it wrong. Maybe you don't *want* kindness. Maybe you want a man who's going to leave you starving and destitute. And at the mercy of charming gentlemen like your friend Kevin.'

I pushed my chair back and stood up. 'You're being ridiculous,' I said. 'I'm sorry you were upset by what you overheard, but you're blowing it completely out of proportion! Liam was my first boyfriend, it was very intense and he made a mark on me–'

'Yes, he did!' Max shouted, and I jumped, his ferocity startling me. 'He almost had you and Dom out on the street! He left you at the mercy of a bunch of criminals. *I* saved you. And yet you'll never love me like you love some scumbag who was only screwing you because he wanted to steal your money!'

'*We're* stealing money, Max!' I shot back at him, trying not to let my hurt show. 'And you don't even want to stop! You have no debts to pay; you weren't even short of money to start with!'

'I could turn you in,' he said, his voice low. 'And I could tell Dominic what you've been up to. See what sort of role model he thinks you are then.'

'Stop,' I said, as calmly as I could. 'Max, stop. You can't turn me in without incriminating yourself, and you've made your point. I can see you're hurt, but please don't get nasty.'

'Nasty? You think *this* is nasty? I picked you up out of the gutter, brought you back to my home, paid half of Dominic's university fees, and yet you don't even have the decency to love me as much as you love some little prick who got you pregnant when you were only fifteen. You're happy enough to live here though, aren't you? Sponging off of my generosity and pretending you have feelings for me. You don't want me. You just want a roof over your head and food on the table!'

I took a couple of steps back. Who was this man in front of me? Was that really all he thought of me? My conversation with Dominic flashed through my mind. He'd seen through me too. *Did* I just want a roof over my head and food on the table? *Was* I stringing Max along? I'd never meant to. It hadn't been a calculated thing. I might not be *in* love with him, but I did love him. He was my closest friend, the one person apart from Dominic who made me happy, who made me laugh and feel glad to be alive. Wasn't that enough? 'I'm sorry that what you overheard upset you,' I said carefully, trying not to let his words get to me. *It's not fair on Max.* That was what Dominic had said, and I could see why Max was hurt. But Dominic didn't understand how complicated it was and what a tangle my feelings were in. Just because it wasn't how it was with Liam, did that really mean my relationship with Max meant nothing? 'I do love you,' I continued, 'we have so much fun together, we're always laughing–'

'Are we laughing now?'

'Well, no, but—'

He swept my bowl with its small amount of remaining pasta off of the table, where it smashed on the floor, staining the shiny grey tiles a shocking red.

'A few days of going hungry and perhaps you'll remember where your loyalties lie,' he spat at me.

Cattleford

23

'So, are you still feeling okay about Harriet's offer?' Jessica asked me, looking up as I stepped out of the back door to join her in the garden. It was a bright early spring morning, and though the sun didn't have a lot of warmth to it, it was pleasant to be outside. Jessica was kneeling on the patio, next to a large raised bed. 'Harriet would say it's too early to start doing this,' she said, not bothered that I hadn't answered her question. 'She says it will just fill up with weeds and we should wait until it's a little warmer, but as soon as it's March I want to start planting things.'

'What are you going to plant?' I asked her, as I helped move the cardboard that was covering the bed to stop weeds from taking hold.

'Lettuce, radishes and Swiss chard,' she said. 'And later when Reef gets home from school we'll plant some sunflower seeds in pots.'

I glanced around the garden. It was still mostly bare of leaves and consisted of shades of brown, but some daffodil bulbs were beginning to bud, which made me smile.

'Harriet doesn't really like coming out into the garden,' Jessica said.

'Why not?'

She shrugged. 'Sometimes I think she doesn't want to move on from her misery,' she said. 'She doesn't want to see new life and hope.'

'Apart from my baby. She's excited about that.'

Jessica paused in the middle of reading the back of a seed packet. 'Yes, that's true. That's what she needs. Something to make it worth getting up in the morning.' She fixed me with a piercing gaze. 'How *are* you feeling about the plan, really?'

I sighed as I sat down on the bench near the raised bed. It was a little damp, but I got uncomfortable if I stood for too long.

Though Harriet's idea had sounded completely outlandish to begin with, I had to admit that if it worked, I would get my life back. Someone at QHM Solutions could stumble across the fraud at any moment, and even if it wasn't discovered that way, I couldn't be sure Max wouldn't turn me in; despite the fact he'd be admitting his own involvement too. Simply waiting for my crime to be discovered was excruciating, and deep down I knew it was only a matter of time until somebody realised what I'd done. I might have fled somewhere Max couldn't find me, but if the police got involved they would be able to track me down. Confessing had to be the best way of both soothing my conscience and reducing the severity of my punishment, but I couldn't turn myself in just yet. If I was pregnant when I confessed I was sure Max would find out about the baby. If I could hold my nerve and pray nobody stumbled upon the fraud before I'd given birth, perhaps I really could turn my life around with Harriet's plan. After all, I couldn't run forever. It was daunting though. There were so many unknowns. Somehow I wasn't able to sum all that up for Jessica, so in answer to her question of how I felt about the plan, I said limply, 'I don't know.'

'You don't know how you feel about it?' Jessica asked.

'No, I mean, I do know how I feel about it. Sort of.'

'And?'

'Well, it's complicated. What Harriet has suggested is a huge thing, and I'm scared. And…' I instinctively lowered my voice, even though Harriet was out at the shop, 'I keep thinking about what you said to me on the beach that day. About Harriet wanting the baby.'

'Oh, that was just the anger talking,' Jessica said, waving her hand dismissively.

'Was it?'

'Of course it was.'

'And about her wanting to adopt Reef? Did you just bring that up because you were angry? I asked Harriet about it, and she told me her version of what happened back then.'

A shadow passed over Jessica's face. 'She told you that I asked her to adopt him, didn't she?' she said.

I nodded. 'Is it true?'

'Yes, it's true,' she said. She wouldn't meet my eye, focusing instead on the back of the seed packet. 'I don't know what you must think of me. It's unnatural, isn't it? A mother wanting someone else to take her baby?'

'You weren't well, Jess, and that's not your fault. It doesn't make you unnatural, or a bad mother. Harriet told me how low you felt.'

'Even so.'

'Jessica, look at me,' I said, and she obediently raised her eyes. 'You've got nothing to be ashamed of.'

She gave a weak smile. 'You know, if you tell the police about what was happening to you – about Liam and Kevin and all of it – surely they will take pity on you. You weren't stealing out of greed, you were doing it to get by.'

'Max wasn't. He was doing it out of greed and I knew it. I helped him do it. I should have pushed harder to make him stop, but I didn't. It all got so… difficult. So ugly.'

We lapsed into silence and Jessica started to sprinkle the lettuce seeds into the raised bed. She was absorbed in her task and it was soothing to watch her. In a few weeks those little seeds would burst into life. Perhaps by the time they were fully grown lettuces my baby would be due. 'Do you want me to help?' I asked her. 'All I've been doing recently is sitting around the house. It's driving me nuts, to be honest.'

'Harriet's just trying to keep you safe by saying you shouldn't come into the shop anymore. If you want us to take care of the baby and make sure Max doesn't realise what's going on, you need as few people as possible to realise the baby is yours. Me and Harriet need to be able to say it's the baby of some relative or other. That's if it comes to that. I still think the police will go easy on you. You were the victim, as far as I'm concerned. I can't see it coming to prison.'

'Perhaps it would be better if somebody else, like my parents, looked after the baby,' I said. 'If it's necessary.'

'Would you really want that? You cut them out of your life for a reason, didn't you?' She sat down next to me on the bench, stretching out her legs as if she was admiring her bright pink wellies. 'Look, you need to just sit tight for the moment. I know it's scary, and you don't like having to hide away here every day, but if you make sure nobody realises you had a baby, then it can't get back to Max. You told Harriet he flipped out when he realised you didn't have feelings for him. You don't want someone like that having a reason to be in your life.'

I closed my eyes, the gentle rays of sun warming my face.

'Look, Poppy, it's not just Harriet who would be helping you,' Jessica continued. 'I'm here too. Let us take care of the baby if we need to. No one knows you're here, no one knows you're pregnant. It could really work.'

'The hospital and the midwives know I'm pregnant.'

'Yes, well, the midwife won't visit for long after the birth. Then you'll be left to your own devices.'

'I just don't know,' I said heavily. 'There's a million ways it could go wrong.'

'But once you've owned up you'll be free. Poppy, trust us,' she said. 'I know you've been let down by people before, but me and Harri will come through for you.'

24

I stood next to Harriet as she knocked gently on the door to Jessica's room. 'Jess?' she said, 'I've brought you some tea.'

She edged her way in to the darkened room, while I hovered on the landing outside. For the past three days, Jessica had spent as much time as she could in her bed. The dresses in her sewing room had remained untouched, and though she did her best to look after Reef, it was clear how much she was struggling. I had to pick him up from school one day, much to Harriet's annoyance now I was seven months pregnant and my bump was too big to hide.

Muffled voices drifted from the bedroom as the two sisters talked quietly, obviously not wanting me to overhear. I sighed and disappeared inside my own room. I was worried about Jessica. Her mood had changed as the spring days had lengthened, and something was clearly bothering her. Running my hand along the edge of the cot, I cast my eye over all the other things piled up on top of my chest of drawers – the baby clothes and blankets, a few toys and books. Harriet had said she would clear out the remaining things they were storing in my room so I could put everything away properly before the baby arrived – an event that had changed from being far off and distant to alarmingly soon, with only a couple of months to go.

At the sound of Harriet leaving I slipped out of my room to meet her on the landing. 'Is she okay?' I whispered. 'I mean, obviously she's not okay, but how bad is it?'

'This happens sometimes,' she said evasively. 'She just needs a bit of time to recharge. She gets overwhelmed and tired when Reef is being demanding.'

'Is that all it is?'

'Well…' she sighed. 'It's Tyler. She's been messaging him for weeks but he doesn't reply to her. I hadn't realised she still thought they were a thing. I thought she'd forgotten about it.'

I frowned as I remembered Jessica telling me that "love finds a way". Tyler obviously didn't feel the same about her as she did about him, though.

'Let me try talking to her,' I suggested.

I waited for Harriet to get to the bottom of the stairs before I made my way into Jessica's bedroom.

'Jess?' I said, looking down at her. With most of her body covered by the duvet, all I could see of her was a splash of dark hair across the pillow.

She didn't respond, and I touched her shoulder gently. 'I know it's a cliché, but it really is his loss,' I told her. 'You deserve a lot more than someone who won't even reply to a message.'

'At least Harri is happy,' Jessica said, turning so that she could face me.

'Harri is not happy. She's worried about you. Why would Harriet want you to be alone?'

'Because she is alone,' Jessica said. 'And it's my fault. She has to keep sorting out my mess rather than having a life of her own. Why would she want me to have a future when I've taken hers away?'

· · ·

I woke to loud ringing, and groggily reached across to grab my phone. Jessica. And it was three a.m.

'Jess?' I said. 'What is it? What's going on?'

'Reef is ill! He's got a fever and I don't have anything to give him. He's been crying all night–'

'What?' I said, 'Where are you? I can't hear anything–'

'I left!' she cried, 'after you and Harriet went to bed. I packed our suitcases and me and Reef crept out. But now he's ill and I don't know what to do! I don't know what to do!'

'All right,' I said, 'just try to catch your breath. Where are you?'

She blurted out an address, and I got her to repeat it as I made a note. 'How far is that?' I said. It sounded close by – she'd simply fled to the nearest bit of coastline – but I wanted to check for sure.

'Twenty minutes drive,' she said. Her voice shook. 'I'm a terrible mother. Why do I do these things? I'm so stupid, from the first moment I was cursed, from the moment I was shameless enough to sleep with–' she stopped and caught her breath. 'He needs medicine,' she said, 'bring the Calpol from the cupboard; I can't leave him to go anywhere, and I can't bear to take him out in the cold to the car, it's tipping down with rain–' she paused. 'Oh, but you can't come! You can't drive, I forgot…'

'I'll get a cab,' I said, 'stay where you are. I'll bring the Calpol. Just comfort Reef, don't worry about anything else.'

Questions swirled around in my head as I waited downstairs for the taxi. Who had Jessica been shameless enough to sleep with? It was such a bizarre statement.

Somehow Harriet had slept through me dashing around the house getting medicine and throwing on some clothes, and there was still no sign of her as I slipped out of the front door silently. Probably just as well. She would have wanted to come with me, and presumably if Jessica had wanted to see her, she would have called her instead of me.

I arrived at the caravan park Jessica had given me the address for, and looked around until I spotted her standing in an open doorway waving. I hurried across, pulling my coat tightly around me against the night time downpour. Reef was curled up on the sofa, and I felt his forehead. 'I brought the thermometer,' I said, 'and the medicine.' I handed her the bottle while I took Reef's temperature. 'It's not *too* bad,' I said, 'it's raised, but I'm sure he'll be feeling better soon.'

'There are bugs going round the school at the moment,' Jessica said, 'Reef usually doesn't catch things.'

I smiled at her. 'Look, you're not the first parent to forget to take medicine with you when you go somewhere. Things like this happen.'

She nodded, and rubbed her face. 'I'm so tired. I just had to get away from the house. I needed a change of scenery, and to get outside of my own head, but I should have been thinking about Reef.'

'Forgetting the medicine was an accident,' I said. 'You didn't even realise he was coming down with something. And a change of scenery is a good idea, though when Harriet realises you've taken Reef out of school again…'

'She doesn't know what's best for me. Or my son. Life isn't all about what grades you get and how hard you work, it's about family. It's about making memories. I don't want to give up on my life because she's given up on hers!'

Reef's eyes fluttered open, and I helped to sit him up while Jessica gave him some medicine. He took a few minutes to settle again, but soon his breathing fell into a slow and steady rhythm.

'You go to bed,' I told Jessica, 'I'll sit with Reef.' In fact, Reef was already looking a little better, his skin having lost some of its feverish sheen. 'I know it's scary when you're on your own,' I said. 'I was always on my own with Dom. It's difficult not having anybody you can turn to for back up.'

'Normally I'd have Harri.'

'But you didn't call her, you called me.'

Jessica looked at me warily, 'What I said on the phone…'

'Don't worry about that. Just get some sleep. We'll take Reef back home in the morning.'

…

The next day dawned cloudy but calm, the stormy rain from the previous night having finally cleared. I'd dipped in and out of sleep on the sofa next to Reef, and when Jessica joined me in the early morning the little boy was fast asleep.

'Poppy, I'm so sorry,' Jessica said. 'I shouldn't have called you and stressed you out, and I shouldn't have made you sit with a sick child when you're pregnant, the last thing you need is to catch whatever Reef has.'

'It's probably just a nasty cold,' I said, 'nothing more than that. Anyway, I need a wee, this baby is really giving my bladder a squeeze this morning.'

'I'll make some tea,' Jessica said.

A few minutes later I sat with her at the small table, while Reef continued sleeping. 'Jess,' I said slowly, 'Reef's dad isn't some guy you met on holiday, is he?'

Jessica shook her head, her hands clasped around her mug of tea.

'Who is he?' I asked quietly. 'And why did you say sleeping with him was "shameless."'

'I can't tell you,' she said.

'Why not? Was he married when you started seeing him? Was it an affair?'

'I wish that's all it was,' she said.

For a moment I stared at her, totally bewildered, and then an idea hit me like a bus. I knew exactly who Reef's dad was. How hadn't I seen it before?

'Jess,' I said softly, 'it wasn't…' I paused. If I was wrong, she would be horrified at my suggestion, but I was utterly convinced my instinct was right. 'It wasn't Ben, was it? Harriet's ex-husband?'

25

Jessica's eyes were wide with shock. 'How did you–'

'So it's true, then?'

She nodded.

'Jess, how… how did it end up happening?'

'I don't want to talk about it,' she said. 'It's so awful you can't believe any one would ever do it. My own *sister's* husband…'

I smiled at her kindly. 'Torturing yourself about it this much after all these years isn't helping anybody. You have to forgive yourself.'

'I can't,' she said. 'I mustn't.'

'Why not?'

'Because Harriet is still hurting. As long as she's hurting, I should be hurting too.'

'That's not true. Perhaps if you can forgive yourself it will help her to heal as well.'

Abruptly she stood up and went across to Reef, feeling his forehead before sitting down beside him with a sigh.

'Do you have any food here?' I asked her.

'No. I was going to go across to the little shop and get some croissants.' She looked at me with concern. 'You look exhausted,' she said.

'I'm okay.'

'No, you're not.' She glanced between me and her son. 'I can't believe I've done this. I let myself get so wound up about bloody Tyler that I ran away and hurt the people who actually do care about me.'

'Jess,' I said calmly, 'it's all right. Everyone is fine. Reef is catching up on his sleep, but he's not feverish now. He'll probably be completely fine by tomorrow. But you do need to message Harriet and explain where we are. She'll be getting up in a minute and she'll worry when she realises none of us are there.'

My words did the trick, as Jessica's face lost its haunted look and after messaging her sister she bustled off to get dressed and buy some croissants. By the time she got back with our breakfast Reef was beginning to wake up, and he ate a few bites of a pain au chocolat, though he didn't have much appetite. Admitting defeat Jessica tucked him up under his blanket and put on the TV, before sitting down at the table opposite me.

'It wasn't just physical,' Jessica said once she'd finished her croissant, her voice low as Reef was the other side of the room. 'Ben had this way of drawing you in.'

'I know what that's like,' I said, thinking of Liam.

'He seemed to be offering me everything I ever wanted,' she continued. 'I always had kind of a sheltered life, staying at home with my parents rather than moving out. I felt safe with them, but it got boring sometimes. I started to want adventure, and Ben fed into that – he encouraged all my wild ideas, he said we could go travelling – that I didn't need to hold myself back and be afraid. And I believed him. Now of course I know it was all empty promises to manipulate me. As soon as he found out I was pregnant he didn't want to know. He was absolutely furious when I said I would tell Harri. He told me I was deranged and childish, and that it had all been a big laugh to him. He said he only slept with me because I was there and I made it so easy. But I was in love with him. I thought we were going to be a family. As much as I knew it would hurt Harriet, my feelings for him over-whelmed me and I couldn't help myself. And he laughed at me for it.'

'What a complete pig,' I said.

'I never saw it, the contempt he had for me. He seemed so charming and funny.'

I looked over at Reef, who was completely absorbed in his cartoons.

'What happened then?'

Jessica's face grew guarded and she lowered her voice further. 'Well, I told Harriet about the baby and all hell broke loose. They got divorced, and I never saw him again.'

I drained the last of my tea, watching Jessica closely. She was agitated, running her hand through her hair over and over. 'But Harri stuck by you,' I said.

'She said Ben was the one to blame, and that he'd taken advantage of me. She was there by my side through everything – she still is – even though I can see how much it hurts her to watch Reef grow up and know who his father is.'

'And you invented the story about his dad being someone you met by the sea? You even chose the name Reef to support it?'

She sighed wistfully. 'Sometimes I almost convince myself to believe it, because it's easier if I can tell myself that's what happened.'

We fell into silence as I considered all she had said. 'I'm so sorry Jess,' I told her at last. 'For you *and* for Harriet.'

'That's why things are so weird between us. I don't blame her for getting mad at me sometimes. I'm not sure there's anyone else in the world who would put up with someone who betrayed them so badly.'

'Well, you have to hold on to people you really care about,' I said. 'Even if sometimes it hurts.'

. . .

I jumped out of my skin at the hammering on the door of the caravan, and Jessica leapt to her feet. 'I *told* her she didn't need to come here!' she said.

'You think it's Harri?'

Sure enough, once Jessica unlocked the door Harriet spilled into the caravan in a blaze of fury. 'What is wrong with you?' she shouted at Jessica. 'You scared me half to death, telling me Reef was ill, that Poppy was sat up with him half the night! Poppy is pregnant, Jess, what the hell were you thinking dragging her out of bed and exposing her to whatever it is that Reef has?'

'I'm okay,' I said. 'I know I'm pregnant but I'm not *ill*, I'm perfectly capable of helping out with things.'

'Yes, apparently more capable of helping out than Reef's own mother!' Harriet said, her cheeks the same colour as her red highlights.

'Stop shouting!' Reef cried from his spot on the sofa. Immediately Harriet rushed over to him, making a show of fussing over him. Expecting Jessica to be angry, I was surprised when she went and sat down beside Harriet, apparently having shaken off her sisters' direct attack on her parenting without comment. In fact she said softly, 'I'm sorry.'

Harriet stared at her in blank amazement. 'What?'

'I don't want to fight. I know I shouldn't have run off with Reef in the middle of the night. I was upset about Tyler and I wasn't thinking straight, but I'm thinking straight now.'

Reef snuggled up against Harriet's legs, and Jessica laid her head on Harriet's shoulder. I couldn't help but smile at the sight of the three of them. No doubt they had their struggles, but the bonds between them were strong. Strong enough to overcome some pretty daunting odds, anyway.

My phone began to ring, and seeing it was Dominic I slipped outside and made my way down through the caravans towards the path to the beach as I answered.

'Mum, you have to agree to see Max,' he said, with barely a hello. His voice was panicky, and I sat down on a low wall by the side of the path. 'Why?' I asked slowly. 'What's happened?'

'Max told me what you and him were up to with the payroll. And he said to tell you they're doing an audit at QHM Solutions.'

26

Ice settled around my heart. An audit. The payroll fraud could be uncovered! On top of that, Dominic now knew what I'd done. He knew I was a criminal.

'Dom, listen–'

'No. Listen to me, Mum, please. I always suspected there was something going on, Max just told me exactly how you did it.'

I opened my mouth to try and explain but Dom pressed on quickly. 'I don't care what you did. You don't need to try and explain it. All that matters is that Max thinks he'll be able to cover it up more thoroughly and protect you. But he needs to talk through a few things face to face. You have to see him. How bad can meeting him really be? If you talk to him and he can cover it up enough that it's not discovered in the audit, you'll be safe. You won't need to hide any more.'

I closed my eyes. Of course, Dominic would think the fraud was the only reason I was hiding. He didn't know anything about how Max had treated me since he'd realised my feelings for him weren't what he'd hoped.

'Dom, if it was possible for him to cover it up more thoroughly, why wouldn't he just have done that anyway? It's a trick to draw me out, but I can't meet with him.'

'Why not?' he said, his voice rising.

I looked down at my body. Short of wearing a tent, there was little I could do to disguise my bump anymore.

'I can't explain, Dom.'

'We used to always talk to each other,' he said. 'But if you don't trust me enough to tell me what's going on, why should *I* trust *you* any more? Max knows more about my life nowadays than you do.'

'Dom–' I said, my voice cracking, 'if you knew…'

'Then tell me! I know you and Max weren't right for each other and you broke up with him. You did the right thing, but why are you treating him so badly now? He was good to us. He took us in when we had nowhere to go. Kevin would have had us both killed.'

'I appreciate what Max did for us back then. Of course I do.'

'And as for what he did for *me*…' Dominic said, his voice choked. 'When I–'

'I know,' I said quickly, before he could say any more. 'You must try not to dwell on that. And listen to me, Dom, Max is up to his neck in the fraud. Believe me, if he could do anything more to cover it up, he will do it anyway regardless of whether he meets with me.'

My hands began to shake. If my crime was discovered before I'd managed to have the baby and confess, what would happen to me? I'd be treated far more harshly, and everyone would realise that Max was the father of my baby, including Max himself.

'I know it doesn't make a lot of sense to you right now,' I said, trying to keep my voice steady, 'but I will explain everything to you soon. Once it's safe to.'

'And what do I say to Max?'

'How often do you see him?' I asked, avoiding his question. 'Is he bothering you?'

'Bothering me? No, he *cares* about me. A lot more than you do anyway.'

My eyes filled with tears, but he flung one more barb at me. 'You know I've always said I want to change my surname once I turn eighteen, so that nothing connects me to Liam.'

'Yes, I know.'

'I was going to change it to Farrow the same as you,' he said. 'But I don't know if I can any more, not now that you've shut me out. What Max did for me that night–' I shuddered as he reminded me of it again. What had happened after my argument with Max was beyond a nightmare, and Dominic had no idea what a terrible chain of events it had set unfolding. 'Well,' Dominic continued, 'I want him to know how much I appreciate it. I'm going to change my surname to match his. I'm going to be Dominic Dorsett.'

I nearly screamed as he hung up, and when I tried to phone back he rejected the call. Dominic Dorsett? He couldn't do it. Once it was safe for me to tell him the truth he'd be cursing the new name he'd given himself as much as he hated having Liam's surname now. I hugged my phone to my chest, a low moan escaping from me. I'd have to tell him what Max was really like to stop him from changing his name. But the surname was only scratching the surface of the problem. After being so angry about Liam's betrayal Dominic had finally felt safe opening up to someone again and the person he'd chosen was Max. Going through another betrayal by another father figure would crush him completely.

'Poppy?' Harriet's voice startled me and I turned to her. 'What on earth?' she said when she saw the tears on my cheeks.

'Dominic,' I said helplessly.

'What about Dominic?'

'It's a nightmare, Harri! It's a nightmare. You don't know – you just don't know…'

'Then tell me,' she said softly. 'Come on, let's go down to the beach. The sun is starting to come out, and there's no one there this early. Jess is fine with Reef, she won't disturb us for a while. I know there's still a lot more to all this than you've said.'

Habmouth

27

Max followed me up the stairs. 'So you're going to leave are you?' he said. 'Just like that?'

'The way you spoke to me, Max. I know I've made a lot of mistakes in my life, but you do not get to talk to me the way you did.'

He grabbed my arm as we reached the top of the stairs, and for a moment I nearly lost my balance. He quickly helped me steady myself, and his face softened. 'I'm sorry,' he said. 'I know I completely lost the plot down there. It's only because I love you so much.'

'Don't give me that,' I said. 'That's not an excuse.'

'But it *is* true!' he protested. 'I never thought I was going to find someone like you, and not just you, Dom as well. I have a family of my own now and I don't want to lose you.'

I brushed past him and made my way to the bedroom. Although I'd said I had no choice but to leave, I didn't want to. I had nowhere to go and Dominic would be worried and probably decide he couldn't start university straight away. But on the other hand, Max's outburst had frightened me. Was he going to behave like that whenever things didn't go his way? I couldn't stay here, but where would I go right now? Was it sensible to drag Dominic off somewhere and unsettle him when he was just about to leave home anyway?

'Poppy,' he said gently. 'I really am sorry for how I behaved over dinner. I couldn't stand the thought that you felt more strongly about Liam than you do about me when he treated you so badly and caused you so much pain.'

I turned to him. His face had lost that strange look he'd had over dinner. This was the man I knew, his eyes pleading with me to believe him and forgive him. Hadn't Liam looked just the same when he'd come back into our lives? I'd never know for sure whether he'd been plotting to steal from us from the start, but the possibility was there; the possibility that I had been utterly taken in by a man whose only intention was to use me. If I'd got it so wrong then, how could I trust my judgement now? Max had two sides to him, that was the truth, and having a side that was capable of kindness didn't make it okay that the other was capable of terrifying me.

'Max, you implied I *liked* being left penniless after what Liam did. That I didn't want kindness.'

He placed his hand on my arm gently and I stepped away from him. 'I'll make you a proper meal now,' he said. 'I was being ridiculous and childish.'

'And saying you'd turn me in? Smashing things on the floor? Max, you are so critical of Liam – and God knows he deserves it – but the way you behaved tonight wasn't so different to him! *He* used to yell at me. He threw a glass at me once. If you are going to get angry like this how can I predict what you'll do next? I can't live like that. I'm not doing it to myself.'

There was a long silence. Max sat on the bed, staring down at the carpet between his feet, and I fidgeted with my engagement ring as I joined him.

'There's something I haven't told you about me,' he said.

'I don't know if it will make any difference now,' I said heavily. 'I can't pretend the last few minutes never happened.'

'Let me tell you anyway,' he said. 'Please.'

I didn't reply, and at length he started talking. 'I got married young,' he said. 'I was only twenty. Caitlyn was twenty-two. I was head over heels in love with her, and I was happy. I thought it would be forever.' He took a deep breath. 'We were together a few years, and then the next thing I know she's divorcing me. She said our relationship had been over for months, but it's the first I heard of it.'

'I'm sorry,' I said, 'but like I said, it doesn't–'

'Just hear me out. Please,' he said. 'It turned out she'd left me for someone else. I didn't know what to make of it all. I was so shocked and naive that I didn't put up a fight. I just said I wanted her to be happy, even though inside I was in turmoil. After it was over she blocked my number and I tried to get on with life and move on, though I really struggled. I wished I could speak to her, just one last time, to help me make sense of what had happened. Then, thirteen years later I happened upon a photo of her online with a daughter. A thirteen year old daughter, who looked so much like me there could be no doubt. She'd hidden my child from me. I've never met her, my daughter. She's in her twenties now. When I realised what Caitlyn had done, I said I'd never let the same thing happen again. I wouldn't let anyone walk all over me the way she did.'

'Max,' I said gently, 'that's horrible. I wish that hadn't happened to you.'

'I love you, Poppy,' he said. 'And Dom is like a son to me. I can't live without you. I can't.' There was a brief pause. 'I'd rather be dead,' he finished.

'Please don't say that.'

He gripped my hands, and I met his eyes, which had a strange light to them again that frightened me. 'Give me another chance,' he begged me. 'I don't care if you don't feel as strongly as I do. I mean, I do *care*, but I can live with it. You said yes when I asked you to marry me, so you must want to be here.'

'I did.'

'Did?'

'I *do*. I do want to be here.'

'There's still a but, isn't there?'

I pulled my hands away from his grip and made my voice firm. 'Max, I appreciate what you've done for us more than I can say, and believe me I want to feel as strongly about you as you do about me, but...' I took a deep breath, steeling myself to say it. I owed him the truth. It was the kindest thing to do. 'I do love you, in a way, but it's not the way you're hoping for. And I don't think it ever can be. I don't want to hurt you by staying and making you settle for second best, especially after what you've been through. I'm not the answer. I can't make what your ex-wife did to you right again. I'm sorry.'

He nodded slowly. 'I see,' he said.

'You do?'

'Yes. You wanted me when I could save you from Kevin, and help get Dom through his exams, but now you've squeezed everything useful out of me you're going to walk out and leave me.'

'It's not like that,' I said, though an uncomfortable wave of guilt washed over me. Of course it looked that way, but it hadn't been deliberate. How could I have predicted what would happen when I'd moved here after only a handful of dates with Max? We didn't know each other properly then, for all I'd known my feelings could have grown, not fizzled out the way they had.

He stood up, and pulled me to my feet too. 'Look at yourself,' he said, leading me in front of the mirror. 'When you came here you were skin and bone. And now look at you. You look healthy. You've changed completely.'

I did look. He was right; my hair was shiny, my cheeks had lost their hollow look and gained some colour, and my eyes were bright and alert. I was a person again now, not the shadow I had been. In fact, I was waiting for my periods to start again now I'd gained a bit of weight, though so far there had been nothing.

'Like I said, Max, I will never stop being grateful to you. I was in a terrible mess, I admit it. I don't think I could have got myself out of it without your help.'

'You and your son would probably be dead by now if it wasn't for me.'

I started to pace around the room. He was right, of course. But that didn't mean I was incapable of doing anything by myself ever again. I'd needed help, yes, but did that mean I owed Max for the rest of my life?

'Max, please,' I said. 'I will stay until Dominic has gone to university, but after that I'm going to have to leave. This isn't going to work, you must see that. We're only going to make each other unhappy.'

'You can't leave, Poppy,' he said. 'I won't let you.'

'You can't stop me.'

He was clearly about to argue but his phone rang and when he told me it was Dominic I frowned. Why was he calling Max? He listened carefully to what my son was telling him while I hovered about, desperately trying to make out Dominic's words. Eventually, Max told Dominic to stay out of sight and that he'd be there in a minute, and once he'd ended the call he looked at me levelly. 'I think you'll be sticking around for a bit, Poppy.'

'Why?' I asked, my voice strained. Something had happened. Something bad.

'Because Dominic has stabbed Kevin.'

28

Harriet stared at me, eyes wide. 'Surely you're not telling me… is Kevin *dead*?'

I glanced around the beach, which was still deserted. The sun had broken through the clouds, and the sea lapped lethargically against the shore. The world was still and quiet, as if everything was holding its breath. 'Yes, he's dead,' I said.

Harriet was silent, and my heart began to race. What had I done? Why on earth had I told her? She shook her head at one point, and I thought she would speak, but instead she put her hand over mine and squeezed it.

'He – Dominic – was on a night out with his friends before they all went off to different universities,' I explained. 'It was the first time I'd let him out in the evening since we moved in with Max because I was scared Kevin or one of his people would see him.'

'And is that what happened?'

I nodded. 'Dom was walking home and he came across Kevin. He said he tried to get away but Kevin started saying that he'd discovered where we were living now. He said soon I'd learn what happened to people who didn't pay their debts. Dom didn't believe that he had really found us, but then Kevin said Max's address.'

'Oh Poppy,' Harriet said.

'Kevin started telling him exactly what he was going to do to me. You can imagine the kind of stuff – he knew how to goad a boy Dominic's age about what he'd do to his mother. That's when Dominic couldn't take it anymore and stabbed him.'

Harriet was frowning. 'Why did he have a knife?'

'I asked him that. And when I thought about it carefully, I realised the answer had always been right in front of me. Dominic had threatened Kevin with a kitchen knife when he saw me being attacked in our old flat. He couldn't have come in through the living room door, past Kevin and into the kitchen to get it without being noticed. So he already had it with him. He said he's had a knife with him every day since Kevin had him beaten up because he was scared and thought it would help him defend himself...' my voice broke and I had to stop. What sort of mother was I to have put Dominic in a situation like that?

'Dominic stabbed Kevin to protect himself, and you,' Harriet said, 'and he was a child–'

'He wasn't a child,' I said, 'he was eighteen. And Kevin wasn't attacking him. It wasn't self defence.' I sighed, and my heart ached for Dominic. 'I understand exactly why he did it and I don't blame him for a second,' I went on. 'But it looks bad, Harri. It looks really bad.'

A couple walking their dog came into view, and though they were nowhere near us we waited until they completely disappeared from sight before we spoke again.

'What did Max do when Dominic called him?'

'Dominic didn't want me to know what had happened, which is why he called Max and not me. Max just used the whole thing as a way to get me to stay.' I closed my eyes briefly. I had screamed in horror and run after Max as he left the house, pleading with him to take me to my son, but he got into his car and sped off without me. I wanted to call Dom, but Max had told him to stay out of sight. If he needed to be hidden I didn't want to put him in danger by phoning him.

I dug my fingers into the sand as I recalled that night, stalking around the house in darkness, knowing that Dominic had never needed me so much in his life and yet he was putting his trust in a man who'd now shown his true colours. Eventually I messaged Dominic asking him to tell me where he was. He didn't reply, but he'd read my message, which was some small reassurance.

'I'm assuming Max and Dominic didn't go to the police,' Harriet said.

'No. Max dealt with it.'

'He dealt with it?'

'Yes.'

'Poppy, what exactly did he do?'

I let the sand slip through my fingers, and the light breeze caught it as it fell. *What exactly did Max do?* I turned to her. 'He used it to get what he wanted.'

Habmouth

I flew down the stairs at the sound of the front door closing and launched myself at Dominic, encircling him in my arms. 'I'm so sorry,' I said into his hair, 'I'm so sorry Dom, I'm so sorry.'

He let me hold him for a second and then he broke free from my embrace. 'He shouldn't have told you.'

'Of course he should!' I said, my voice high and panicky. Dominic didn't look well. His face was as white as a sheet, apart from a smear of blood on his cheek. He swayed on his feet and clutched at the wall, and me and Max both made a grab for him.

'Where… where is Kevin's body?' I asked Max shakily as I propped Dominic up. 'What have you done with it?'

'Max sorted it,' Dom said before Max could reply. 'You don't need to know details.' He sagged to the ground and I sat beside him.

'Dom, look at me,' I said, and when he didn't, I took his face between my hands and made him meet my eyes. 'This is *my* fault,' I told him. 'Do not blame yourself, not for a second. But you need to tell me what you and Max did. I need to know what's happened.'

Dom's eyes slid up to Max's, and Max shook his head at him. I leapt to my feet and grabbed Max, giving him a shake. 'Tell me what you did! Is Dom safe? What have you done with Kevin's body?'

'Kevin is in the river,' Max said. 'Given what he did to make his living, I'm sure any number of people want him dead. I don't see why anyone would suspect Dominic.' He knelt down in front of him, 'Come on son,' he said, 'let's get you upstairs and out of these clothes. Your mum will wash them, and mine too, and you can have a shower then get some sleep.'

Dominic got obediently to his feet, letting Max lead him away from me.

'Dom–' I cried.

'You shouldn't have told her,' he said again to Max, ignoring me. 'I didn't want her to know.'

…

Sitting cross-legged on the utility room floor, my back against the washing machine, I listened to the rhythmic swishing and tried not to think about the blood mixing with the water and soap suds. I'd tried several times to go and talk to Dominic in his room but he didn't want to see me, staying shut up in there with Max. Eventually, at three a.m., Max came and said curtly, 'He wants to see you.'

I rushed towards the door and Max stepped in front of me. 'He thinks I threw the knife in the river with Kevin's body,' he said. 'But I didn't. I kept it. And if you try to leave me, or if you tell Dominic I kept the knife, it will find its way to the police, along with an anonymous note suggesting exactly where they need to look for Kevin's killer.'

Horror rooted me to the spot. 'You said he's like a son to you,' I said, my voice trembling.

'And he is. I don't want to do it Poppy, but I will if I have to.' He gave me a chilling smile. 'It won't come to that though, will it? He's your flesh and blood, and I know you will do the right thing.'

29

Harriet's eyes bulged with anger. 'How dare he?' she said.

'After he said it, I rushed upstairs to check on Dominic. He was in a worse state than I could have imagined; beside himself with terror that he would be caught, and so guilty and ashamed of what he'd done. That's why he didn't want me to know – he didn't want to see a look of fear on my face. As if I'd ever be scared of him! He told me the threats Kevin had made, how he'd provoked him by going into every grisly detail of what he'd do once he found me. Dom said he just wanted it to stop, that he'd stabbed Kevin before he knew what he was doing. I kept telling him that Kevin was a monster who got a kick out of terrorising people. That anyone would have done the same as him in that situation.'

'The poor kid,' Harriet said.

'He was wracked with guilt. I was worried to death about him. I still am.' It was around that time I'd started being sick frequently, and feeling very unwell. I'd assumed it was the stress – since I'd never been so stressed in my life, not even when I was still living in the flat and fearing every knock on the door. Knocks on the door scared me far more when I thought it was the police coming for Dominic.

'He wished he'd called the police straight away,' I continued. 'And if he'd phoned me instead of Max to come and help him, maybe we would have called them. I could have said it was me who did it.'

'Poppy–'

'The truth is I ruined my son's life,' I told her. 'He acts like he's okay, and I think he's managing at university, but he'll have this hanging over him for the rest of his life. I worry he's suddenly going to have a breakdown. And now I'm torn between having him think he can't trust me, or telling him the man he thinks of as his dad used what happened to Kevin to try to force me to stay with him. How can I tell him what hell Max put me through?'

'You can't be a wall between him and Max. You tried to be a wall between him and Liam, didn't you, letting him be angry at you even though you didn't deserve it? You shouldn't put yourself through it again.'

'I won't. I will tell him the truth, but I have to do it at the right time, after I've had the baby and been to the police about the fraud.' A sudden new resolve filled me. The sister's plan, strange though it was, was really the only way. 'Max was stealing long before I joined in. He stole far more than I did, and all out of greed. Once he goes to prison, I can tell Dominic the truth and Max will be safely out of the way for at least a little while. He'll never realise I had his baby. He'll have no reason to ever try and contact me again.'

'And if Max tells the police what Dominic did to Kevin?'

Goosebumps broke out over my skin. 'He'd be mad to bring it up, he'll only get in more trouble himself. I don't think he'd do it to get revenge. Max is… he's opportunistic. He uses things to his advantage, but I'm sure he wouldn't put himself at that level of risk just to hurt me. And I –' I sighed. '–I believe he genuinely cares about Dominic. Now he's lost me anyway, he won't try to hurt him. Not when it won't get him anywhere. Besides, he can't prove it.'

'But he does have proof, doesn't he? He kept the knife.'

'Poppy, Harri!' Jessica called, startling us before we could finish our conversation. 'I've been trying to find you – you've been gone ages!'

She was making her way down the path to the beach, holding her floor length purple skirt up from the ground so she didn't trip over it. Reef was at her side, plodding along slowly, though he gave a small smile at the sight of me and Harriet.

'Reef!' Harriet said, holding her arms open as the little boy trotted towards her. 'How are you feeling?'

'Poorly,' he said, snuggling into her before they walked a little way down the beach and then plonked down on the sand. Jessica sat down beside me and gave me a searching look. 'Are you okay?'

'I had a bit of an argument on the phone with Dominic.' *Dominic Dorsett.* It sent shivers down my spine.

'Oh, I'm sorry,' Jessica said. 'I guess it's an adjustment for you both. You must miss him terribly.'

'I do.' I smiled shakily as I watched Reef, now curled up in a ball on Harriet's lap. 'He seems a little better.'

'He wanted to see Harriet,' she said, lowering her voice. 'Sometimes... sometimes I wonder if he knows deep down that I couldn't look after him when he was first born.'

'Of course he doesn't know.'

'When he's poorly he always wants her.'

'Yes, and when he wants to have fun he comes to you. Harriet takes control in a crisis, that's probably why he gravitates to her when he doesn't feel well, because she seems like she knows what to do. But if she wasn't here you'd do perfectly well on your own, you just have to believe in yourself and be confident.'

Jessica slipped her flip flops off and dug her feet in the sand. 'I suppose Dominic can tell you're lying to him,' she said perceptively.

'Yes.'

She nodded towards Harriet, 'Did you tell her that you know about me and Ben?'

'No. It didn't come up.'

'It's probably best if she knows you know. At least we can all be honest with each other then.'

'Okay.' I gazed down at Harriet and Reef, and fear gripped me afresh. What the hell was I doing, telling Harriet about Kevin and Dominic? A woman whose motivations I still didn't fully trust or understand, and I'd told her the one thing that had to stay secret! Not that she'd been all that shocked, but maybe she was hiding it well. *Or maybe she's opportunistic, like Max. If she could get me out of the way for longer, leaving the baby in her care...* No, I couldn't believe it of her. She was my friend; there was no way she'd go to the police. Yes, she'd caught me with my guard down and I'd told her more than I'd meant to, but she was clearly a far kinder and more understanding woman than people gave her credit for. After all, who else would be prepared to live with their sister after discovering she'd had an affair with your husband?

30

'Jessica told you about Ben?' Harriet said incredulously, pausing in the middle of reaching for the next plate to wash. We'd been back home for a day and it was comforting to all be together again.

'I think it's weighing heavily on her,' I said, as Harriet resumed washing up. 'She's ashamed of what she did.'

Harriet tutted and sighed as she handed me the plate to dry.

'You've done a really selfless thing, living here with her and helping look after Reef. Even staying in touch with her would be admirable in the circumstances.'

She turned to me with an odd expression on her face. 'I blame him, not her,' she said finally.

'That's what Jessica said. I told her she needs to try to forgive herself, so that she can move on and you can too.'

'What she needs to do is learn from it,' Harriet said firmly. 'This business with Tyler, it's not the first time she's let herself get entangled with someone like that. She's drawn to men who fill her head with dreams and promises that they are never going to be able to fulfil. It's like she just can't see reality.'

I finished drying the last plate and put in the cupboard. I wasn't sure what kind of reception my next question would get, but I had to ask. 'Doesn't Ben ever want to see Reef?'

'No.'

'He must have met him, surely? His own son–'

'He's never met him. He made it perfectly clear to Jessica how he felt about her pregnancy, and that was that. Quite frankly after how he reacted he doesn't deserve to see Reef.'

'But do you think he still feels the same?'

Harriet's brow furrowed and she flicked her fringe back from her eyes. 'How would I know? I haven't spoken to him for years. If he wants to see Reef, he knows where we are. I can't promise I wouldn't slam the door in his face though.' She took a breath and then looked at me, her face sympathetic. 'What exactly happened in your conversation with Dominic earlier? You told me about–' she lowered her voice, 'about Kevin, but why were you so upset?'

I sighed. Of course I hadn't forgotten what Dominic had said about the audit, and I outlined the issue to Harriet. 'To be honest, it wouldn't surprise me at all if there was no audit coming up,' I explained. 'Max could easily have made it up to scare Dominic and try and force me to agree to a meeting.'

'But if he's telling the truth?'

'Then there's nothing I can do. Me and Max already covered our tracks as much as we were able. It might be that the fraud still isn't discovered, even if there is an audit. But if it is–'

'–all our plans will be for nothing,' Harriet said, as she finished wiping the kitchen worktops and placed her pink rubber gloves down on the side of the sink.

'The crazy thing is, I think I'm too exhausted emotionally to even feel scared anymore,' I said. 'I've been scared for so long.' I busied myself taking dry clothes off of the airer in the corner of the room. Harriet had insisted that all the new clothes for the baby needed washing in sensitive laundry liquid before the baby arrived, and I was glad of the task, which had given me something to do. I should ask Harriet if I could take over doing the accounts for Bits and Bobbins since I didn't help out in person at the shop any more. It was silly her doing it all when I was sat in the house twiddling my thumbs. I became aware she was watching me, a searching expression on her face. She knew there was something else. 'Dominic wants to change his surname,' I said at length.

'Oh, that'll just be a phase,' she said dismissively as she came over to help me sort out the baby clothes. 'I wouldn't worry about that.'

'No, you don't understand. I've known for a long time he didn't want Liam's surname and that he wanted to be Farrow, like me. But he told me–' I paused. I didn't want to say the words out loud. 'He wants to have *Max's* surname. Because of how much Max helped him with the…'

'The cleanup,' Harriet said.

'Yes, exactly.'

'What cleanup?' Jessica's voice startled us, and we both turned to find her standing in the doorway. I stared at Harriet in horror. Not Jessica as well! One person knowing was bad enough. But Harriet simply said to Jess, 'Close the door and we'll all sit down.'

'I don't think this is a good idea,' I said. 'I should never have mentioned it at all, not to anyone.'

'Poppy, we're in this together,' Harriet said. 'The three of us. You need as much help as you can get to sort out this mess.'

'I–'

'Jess can handle it,' Harriet said firmly, 'and once she knows about it, you can tell us what happened next. There are several months between what you've told me and the day you turned up at our door, and I know from the state of you when you showed up here that things must have got pretty bad.'

Habmouth

31

'I can't go!' Dominic said desperately, grabbing onto my arm as if he was a child again.

My eyes met Max's and I shook my head. What were we thinking, trying to pack him off in this state? He couldn't leave for university now, not when either me or Max had needed to stay by his side continuously since he'd killed Kevin. He stayed shut up in his room, curtains drawn, eyes staring at us sightlessly. That was until terror overwhelmed him and he'd bombard us with his fears of being caught; yo-yoing between declaring he would go to the police and confess, and then coming up with outlandish plans to run away abroad so he couldn't be caught.

'You don't have to go,' I told Dominic gently as he stumbled to a halt on our way out to Max's car. 'Perhaps I could call the university and explain that you've been through a traumatic event and they could send you some work to do at home? Or it might still be possible to defer until next year if you really don't think you can cope–'

Before Dominic could respond Max snapped at me. 'Don't be so ridiculous Poppy. Saying that Dom has been through a traumatic event? What traumatic event is that then? Because when he eventually turns up don't you think somebody will ask him?'

'We would come up with something to explain it. Just look at him, Max!'

Dominic was cowering by the car, the boot still open where we had been packing his clothes and belongings, plus the various household bits and bobs we'd bought for him to use in his halls. He appeared to be on the verge of fainting, but Max took me by the elbow and led me back inside the house, closing the front door behind us. 'Don't make such bloody stupid suggestions!' he hissed at me. 'No son of mine is going to cower at home over a thug like Kevin.'

'He's not your son,' I said.

'Yet I'm the one he called when it mattered most. He didn't even want *you* to know what he'd done!' His face softened. 'Poppy, please just accept that I know what's best. University will be a distraction for him. Being here isn't doing him any good. You mean well, of course you do, but you haven't exactly done a great job over the years, have you? Dominic should never have been exposed to someone like Kevin.' He stroked my hair and my skin crawled. 'Let me talk to Dom, and we'll get this sorted out. That boy deserves a future. You don't want him to end up like you, do you?'

Furious, I shoved him away from me and made for the door, but a wave of nausea overwhelmed me and I had to run instead to the downstairs toilet. When I joined them on the drive Max had taken hold of Dominic to help him stand up straight. 'Look at me,' he said. Obligingly, Dominic raised his eyes to meet Max's.

'That bastard was going to come here and kill your mum,' Max said firmly.

'We should talk about this inside,' I said. Though their voices were hushed, it wasn't a conversation for the street.

'We're not hiding inside,' Max said, and immediately turned back to Dominic. 'Listen, son, the world is a damn sight better off without Kevin in it. You need to put it behind you. Once we drive out of Habmouth, it all stops. It's day one of your new life, okay? Say it.'

'It's day one,' Dominic repeated. His voice was stronger. He was lapping up every word Max said.

'It's day one of what?'

'My new life.'

'Exactly,' Max said. 'Now let's go.'

...

'Mum, could I talk to you for a second?'

'Of course,' I said, turning back to him. Every fibre of my being was protesting against leaving him in this strange room, in a strange city. Down the hall other parents were saying emotional goodbyes to their children and it wrenched my heart. Saying goodbye under normal circumstances was difficult enough – but how many other students would be carrying a burden like Dominic's?

Max was waiting too, hovering in the doorway. 'Can I talk to her on my own?' Dominic asked him, and reluctantly Max slipped outside. 'I'll wait by the car,' he told me.

I encased Dominic in my arms, breathing in the warm scent of his hair, though he protested. 'Mum, I'm okay,' he said as he extricated himself from my embrace. 'That's what I wanted to tell you – that you don't need to worry about me. Max is right. This is day one for me; now I'm here I can forget about Habmouth. Not all of it,' he added quickly. 'It wasn't all bad.'

I gave him a watery smile. 'No,' I said softly, 'it wasn't.'

'And this room is nicer than my bedroom in our old flat. It's bigger even than my bedroom at Max's house – look how much space I've got.' I couldn't argue with this statement – his room was very pleasant; bright and sunny, with a large desk next to his bed – but was he putting on a brave face for my benefit? Would he crumble the second I walked out of the door?

'You must call me straight away if you need to talk,' I told him. 'You've been through a lot, and it's not–' my voice cracked. 'I can't leave you here,' I said in sob. 'Not after what's happened, I can't…'

'Mum, it's okay,' Dominic told me, the old warmth back in his voice, and I looked at him in astonishment. Was he really going to be all right? He didn't look much like that boy he'd been this morning; pale and jumpy, terrified of his own shadow. Had he really managed to separate himself from what he'd done so easily – and was it really healthy to do so?

'I'm proud of you,' I told him shakily. If he said he was okay, who was I to say he wasn't? He wanted me to let him go, so that's what I would have to do. After one final hug, I turned away from him with tears in my eyes, and made my way outside to join Max.

32

I leaned back against the wall of the QHM Solutions building and took a deep breath of crisp autumn air. At the sound of voices, I moved a little further from the entrance so I could have some privacy amongst the shrubs and trees around the side of the building. There was a peaceful bench that was hardly ever used, and I had taken to sitting there on my lunch break to clear my head. I sent Dominic a text, grateful to receive a swift reply that he was okay and just on his way to his next lecture. With the exception of one or two minor wobbles, whenever I called him he sounded normal. Had he repressed what he'd done to Kevin entirely? Was that even possible? I hoped he'd found peace with it. He'd done what he'd done out sheer terror – at heart he was still the same boy who wanted to study plants so he could find new medicines in the rainforest, or solve world hunger – and I never wanted that to change.

I leant forward as a wave of nausea washed over me, and closed my eyes to focus on breathing in and out slowly.

'Poppy, you have to sort yourself out. This worrying is making you ill.' Max's voice startled me, and I straightened up quickly. Ever since the true reason behind my nausea had been confirmed by a pregnancy test, I tried to hide my sickness from Max so that he didn't cotton on to my condition. He certainly didn't appear to be suspicious; after all, I'd told him when I moved in with him that my periods had stopped during the malnutrition and stress I suffered after Liam left. Perhaps it wouldn't occur to him that I was able to get pregnant. It had taken long enough for it to occur to me. In fact, my periods had never restarted – apparently the moment my body had decided it was healthy enough to withstand a pregnancy, that was exactly what had happened to me.

He sat down on the bench beside me and put his hand on my leg. 'I don't like seeing you like this.'

'I'm fine,' I said, 'it was a busy morning, that's all. And I was thinking I should go and see Dominic again this weekend.'

'You've visited him twice in the space of a month,' Max said. 'He doesn't want his mum hanging around all the time. He's got loads of friends there already and he's going out and having fun. Just let him be.'

'I miss him.'

'Of course you do. You had him so young that you've never been an adult without having him by your side. You basically grew up with him.'

I shot Max a look. For some reason he was always making digs about me being a teenage mother, as if he thought it was yet another sign that I was weak and needed protecting. When he'd first brought it up I'd snapped at him that managing to bring up Dominic in spite of the odds that were stacked against me was anything but a sign of weakness. But what was the point? Whatever he said I had to put up with because he could destroy me and my son with a few words in the right ear. All I could do was try and brush it off until I could get him to understand it was over between us – without him taking his revenge by turning Dominic in – so that I could get well away from him before my bump began to show.

'Let's go out tonight,' he suggested. 'We can go on a proper date.'

'I don't want to go on a date.'

'Right. So it's just TV and bed by nine p.m. again for you, is it?'

'I get tired, Max. Everything that's happened... it's been a lot for me.'

We lapsed into silence. A flock of birds landed en masse in the bare branches of a tree opposite, only to then take flight again in a dark, fluttering cloud, their actions synchronised by some force beyond my perception. The waistband of my work skirt was beginning to dig into my stomach and I fiddled with it to try and make myself more comfortable.

'I wish you would just be happy,' Max said wistfully. 'Our life isn't so bad, is it? Why don't we start looking at wedding venues? I think Dominic would like it if he knew you were really settled.'

'What makes you say that?'

'He's called me a few times, after you've gone to bed. He worries about you.'

'He does?'

'Yes,' Max said, without elaborating.

I closed my eyes briefly, heart heavy. Was Max telling the truth? Did Dominic really phone him and say he was worried about me?

'Does he talk about… about what he did?'

'No, not about that.'

I got to my feet. 'I need to get back to work,' I said.

'Poppy, just go home. You're clearly unwell. Have a rest, and then we'll get a takeaway later, okay?'

'I'm all right. I should keep busy.'

'Poppy,' he said, voice stern.

'Fine, okay, whatever,' I said. Truthfully, I was worn out. Being pregnant was taking it out of me, and perhaps going home and having a nap was what I needed.

…

Max and I carried on in what felt like a strange parallel universe. He didn't mention the knife or his threats and neither did I, but it hung between us; the rotten core of our relationship. Not that we still had a relationship from my point of view. I was essentially Max's prisoner, but he didn't see it that way.

'I thought perhaps here,' Max said, showing me his phone screen where there was a photo of a hotel. 'We can do it when Dominic is back over Easter.'

'What are you talking about?' I asked him.

'The wedding!' he said. 'We need to set a date and get everything organised. That gives a little bit of time to make all the preparations. Having something to focus on will be good for you. Perhaps it will give you a reason to look after yourself a bit better.'

'What do you mean?'

'Well, you're a bit of a mess, Poppy. You could make *some* effort. Why are you dressed like that at eight o' clock on a Saturday night?'

I snuggled further into my baggy jogging bottoms and cosy hoodie. 'Because it's comfortable.'

He moved closer to me on the sofa. 'Sweetheart, you're not in a good way,' he said. 'And I don't know what the problem is. Yes we had that tiff before Dominic went away, but that was weeks ago. And… well, I'm sorry about all of that. I didn't behave very well, and I shouldn't have made threats.'

A "tiff"? Was he being serious? But since he'd brought it up, I would seize the moment. 'Will you get rid of it then?' I asked him.

'Get rid of what?'

'The knife.'

He gave me a long look. 'I will once I'm sure about us. It's so simple Poppy – all you have to do is let me love you and look after you, that's all I want.'

My stomach heaved and I had to run out of the room. Max followed me, standing in the door of the downstairs cloakroom while I was sick, a frown on his face.

'Are you trying to make me feel sorry for you?' he said, once I was done and had finished splashing cold water on my face.

'How can you be talking about planning our wedding?' I said, desperate to change the focus away from my sickness as soon as I possibly could. I took a deep breath. 'I know you don't want to hear this,' I said firmly, 'but our relationship is over. Surely you realise that? Give me the knife and I will get rid of it. We can't make each other happy, and talking about planning a wedding, it's …' I tried to seize on a suitable word, 'it's just wrong,' I ended limply.

'You *can* make me happy!' Max said. 'You're just too selfish to try.'

He was standing in the way of the door, trapping me inside the claustrophobically small room where the glare of the bright ceiling light on the white tiles made my head spin. I needed to sit down. I needed him to get out of my face.

'What more can I do?' I said, placing my hand against the door frame and trying hard to focus on the city skyline picture on the wall to calm me down and quell my rising panic.

'I want you to love me!' he shouted, grabbing my shoulder to make me face him. 'Is that so much to ask? You haven't been fussy about who else you've loved, so why can't you love the one person who actually gives a shit about you?'

'Tell me where the knife is, Max.'

'I'll never tell you,' he spat.

'Five minutes ago you were apologising for how you've treated me, but you're not sorry, are you? You're only sorry that you haven't got what you wanted! Now let me though.'

He stayed stubbornly in my way. 'It's not just what I want. It's what I deserve,' he said darkly. 'I love you, and I've helped you. I've helped your son. Who else was there for you? Nobody. *Nobody* else cares about you, Poppy. Why won't you get that through your head?'

I pushed him aside and escaped out into the hall, but his fingers closed around my wrist. 'How can you say you love me?' I shouted at him. 'If you loved me, you wouldn't torture me with the threat that at any moment you could ruin my son's life!'

'*Liam* ruined your son's life,' he said. 'Liam forced you into the situation with Kevin. Can't you see that? It's not me ruining your life, your life was already ruined. And yet, I bet if Liam walked through that door right now you'd still throw yourself into his arms.'

I shook my arm free, too disgusted to dignify his statement with a response, and made my way towards the stairs. I would lie down until I felt better and deal with Max's meltdown later. But there was no stopping him.

'You won't even deny it?' he said incredulously.

'No, because you're being ridiculous. You know full well that if Liam turned up at the door I would slam it in his face. How can you possibly be jealous of him? I hate him. I've told you I hate him plenty of times before, why won't you believe me?'

'If you hate him so much, why can't you love me?' he said, the fury in his face making me shrink back against the wall.

'I'm sorry,' I said firmly as he loomed in front of me. 'Please, Max, you have to accept that we don't have a relationship. I am staying here because you're threatening my son. That is the *only* reason.'

He glared at me for a long time, weighing me up. Finally, he nodded, as if some brilliant idea had occurred to him. 'Fine,' he said. 'If you liked your life so much before you had me in it, then we'll take you on a trip down memory lane. I'll remind you what I saved you from.'

'What are you talking about?' I said, my voice unsteady. He could hardly get Kevin to come back, but my life had been troubled before I'd turned to a loan shark for help.

'You can leave,' he said.

'I… I can?'

His face twisted into a smile that sent ice through me. 'Yes, you can. Right now. Right this second.'

…

I tried to wriggle out of his grip as he pulled me towards the front door but I couldn't get away, and I cried out as he threw me into the street. I stumbled and the wild autumn night hurled rain at me, plastering my hair to my face. Running back to the door I yanked at the handle, but he'd locked it, so I screamed at him through the letterbox to let me back inside. Realising it was futile, I ran around to the back of the house, but the back door was locked as well. All of my belongings were inside; the only thing I had with me was my phone, tucked in the pocket of my hoodie. But what use was that? Who would I call? Dominic? He couldn't do anything and it would only frighten him. I was shivering now, my teeth chattering so loudly I could hardly think. Hammering on the back door, I caught a glimpse of Max inside the house but

149

he quickly disappeared out of sight. My phone vibrated, and I took it out to read his message:

You wanted to leave. So leave.

Max, please let me get my things I typed back frantically as raindrops fell on the screen. *I don't even have any money.*

You're right about that he typed back.

The rain was still lashing against me, my hands so wet I could barely keep hold of my phone. I desperately tried to dry my fingers on the top I had on underneath my soggy hoodie, until I was finally able to log in to the banking app, heart thudding loud in my ears. The day I'd done the same thing after Liam disappeared filled my mind, the horror, the shock, the helplessness. I knew exactly what I was going to see.

Balance: £0

Cattleford

33

Harriet and Jessica's faces were white with horror. 'How did he know your log in details?' Harriet said, 'surely after what Liam did you were being more careful.'

'Please don't,' I said. 'I know how stupid I was, but I didn't worry so much with Max – we were already stealing from QHM, why would I think he'd steal from me as well? He had plenty of money, and it never crossed my mind he'd take my money out of spite. I'd never *told* him my log in details, but he had it all there in the house with him – my bank card, the notebook where I was stupid enough to write down passwords–'

'Oh, Poppy,' Jessica said, her eyes huge and dark.

'He always went on about how he'd saved me from the nightmare I was living in and he wanted to prove to me how easily he could put me back there again. He knew I couldn't call the police, or tell anyone what he'd done, because he had the knife. And while he had it, he could do whatever he wanted to me.'

'And he has the audacity to claim that he loves you,' Harriet said with disgust. It had got dark and she stood up to close the floral curtains at the window behind us, shutting out the sleepy street beyond. Jessica – who had taken the news about Kevin's demise much more calmly than I had expected – smiled at me suddenly. 'But you survived,' she said. 'You're here now. You survived all of them. Liam, Kevin, and Max.'

I sighed. 'It's not over yet, though, is it?'

'Perhaps not. But he'll get his comeuppance,' Jessica said darkly. 'Everyone does, in the end.'

'Where did you go?' Harriet asked me as she sat back down at the table.

I closed my eyes for a moment. But I'd come this far. And it was helping to say the words out loud, to make what happened real, so that one day maybe I could move on from it.

Habmouth

I had to accept that Max wasn't going to let me back inside, so I made my way down the street, so wet now that more rain falling on me made no difference. Reaching the supermarket at the end of the road I darted inside, pacing up and down the aisles trying to gather my thoughts. Perhaps by morning Max would have calmed down and he'd let me in to collect my things. But on the other hand, if he let me back in, perhaps he'd be reluctant to let me go again.

Coming to a stop in the bakery section, I gazed listlessly at loaves of bread until I had an absurd desire to laugh. How had my life become so utterly ridiculous? I had no home, no money, not even so much as a change of clothes. My son had killed somebody, and yet all I was doing was standing here uselessly, dripping, and staring at baked goods in the harsh white light of the supermarket. How could it be real? It was like some awful joke.

But then it struck me. I might only have the clothes I stood up in, but I also had the jewellery I was wearing. The big, flashy engagement ring Max had given me, it had to have cost thousands! And then I did let out a strange, strangled laugh, because Max had unwittingly given me the means to survive.

...

I closed the front door of the studio flat behind me and sank down to the floor, resting my head on my knees, nearly crying with relief. It wasn't much, but this shabby little space with its worn out furniture and mouldy bathroom was mine. I'd managed to find a landlord who wasn't too fussy about doing checks and selling the engagement ring had covered the deposit and the first month's rent, still leaving me with enough money left over to buy some clothes, a few household items and a week's food shopping. Once I got my pay at the end of the month I would be okay. I'd secured my bank account – Max wouldn't be able to get into it again – and breaking the news to Dominic about my split from Max hadn't been too difficult, after all, it was him who had tried to make me see our relationship wasn't right.

I couldn't keep calling in sick to work though. It's what I'd done initially, while I'd flitted between cheap bed and breakfasts trying desperately to find a place to call home, but tomorrow it had to stop. Yes, Max would be there and the idea of facing him made my stomach flip-flop, but leaving it any longer would only make it worse. He was the one being unreasonable, why should I hide away? I'd have to look for a different job soon anyway, since my expanding waistline would draw his attention before long, but for the moment what I needed was normality and stability, and I wasn't about to let Max get in my way.

'Poppy,' he said, catching my arm the next day at work. After managing to avoid him for the whole morning, he'd cornered me in a quiet corridor where nobody else was around.

'I've got a lot to catch up on today,' I said calmly, pulling my arm away from his grip.

'I only want to know if you're okay. You've been off sick for four days.'

'I had to find myself a place to live.'

'And did you?'

'Yes,' I said.

'Then you need to tell HR your new address.'

He gave me a smile, but if it was meant to put me at ease it did anything but. 'Max–'

'Your contact details need to be up to date.'

'I will do it when I get a chance,' I told him, in clipped tones. *He wants my address. He's not going to let it drop. He wants to know where I live.*

'Dominic called me last night,' he continued. He was standing too close to me, and I backed away a step. 'He was seeing if I was okay after our breakup.'

'Are you?' I asked him, though I wasn't interested in his answer. I didn't care how he felt. As far as I was concerned he could go to hell.

'I told him I was upset but that I respected your decision.'

'Well, that's good,' I told him, smoothing down my new blouse.

'You look good,' he said, his eyes cold. 'The money from the ring has set you up nicely. Went on a little shopping spree, did you?'

'You didn't leave me with any choice but to sell it. I had nothing but the clothes I was standing up in.' It was clear he'd not intended for me to have any way of supporting myself and the ring had been an oversight. Had he hoped I'd stay outside his house banging on the door all night in the rain until he finally let me in? Well, he'd discover I was made of sterner stuff than that.

'I'm not sure this is going to work,' he said at length. 'Me and you here together at the office. It's… awkward.'

'I'll stay out of your way as much as I can,' I said, refusing to let fear creep into my voice at his threatening tone. This job was my lifeline. Until I'd found another I couldn't let anything jeopardise it.

'Yes. I think you will,' he said, before turning on his heel and walking away. I stared after him. I wouldn't read too much into it and get wound up. He was hurting from the break-up, but he'd come to terms with it soon enough, wouldn't he? He hadn't made any mention of the knife – not that he was likely to bring that up directly while we were at work – perhaps he would let me get on with my life while he got on with his. This unpleasantness surely wasn't much fun for him either, and I knew instinctively that his threat to turn Dominic in wasn't one he would be keen to follow through on. No matter how he treated me, he cared about Dominic, in his way, and it would only be the most extreme circumstances that would push him to do anything to cause him harm. I had to believe that now he had some space to think he'd see reason.

34

Sitting silently on the sofa-bed in my depressing flat, I stared blankly across the room to the insipid blue-grey wall. Words floated around in my head. *You can't really work here any more now, can you Poppy? I think it would be best if you left.* Tears prickled my eyes. Why hadn't I taken it more seriously when Max had confronted me in the corridor and said both of us working in the same place didn't work? Why hadn't I guessed he would do something?

The thought of the obscene email he'd sent from my account, written as if it was from me to him, but sent by "accident" to everyone in the company, sickened me. I'd never written anything like that to him when we were together, and even if I had, I wouldn't have sent it using my work email.

My phone chimed and I picked it up.

Enjoy being unemployed. Hope it was worth it.

I threw my phone down in disgust, but found myself picking it up again when another message came through.

You could have had everything. I don't know how you can think you're better than me.

Leave me alone! I typed back, and hit send before I could think it through. I shouldn't have responded to him. Now he'd got a reaction, he'd keep coming back for more.

I made my way across to the window and peeked out from behind the curtain, trying to do it as inconspicuously as possible. He was still there! It had been hours – all evening, in fact – his car parked outside my flat, with him inside. What the hell was he trying to achieve? Anger flared inside me. I wanted to call the police, but what could I say? All he'd done was park on the street and sit in his car. And besides, how could I talk to the police with the thought at the back on my mind of the money I'd stolen and of what Dominic had done to Kevin? Surely Max would get fed up soon. Sitting out there was pointless; he must know that he would never get me back now. I let the curtain fall. What was the point in deceiving myself? He wouldn't get fed up. I'd crossed him, and he'd told me himself he wasn't going to let anyone walk all over him again after what his ex-wife had done to him. He was going to make me pay for her betrayal as well as my own. His pent up anger had a focus now and I was it. Never mind that I'd never set out to hurt him, that I'd wanted our relationship to work – at least I had before he changed into this man I barely recognised.

My phone rang and I nearly jumped out of my skin. Voice shaking, I answered it and Dominic's voice filled my ear.

'Mum, are you okay?' he asked, 'you sound kind of breathless–'

'I'm fine. Just had to run for the phone,' I lied. 'How are you? Are you okay? I'm so happy to hear your voice.'

'I'm fine,' he said, though his voice was subdued. 'But Max said he thought you were struggling on your own, so…'

Max said. How dare he? How dare Max try to worry Dominic?

'I'm not struggling,' I said. 'I've got a little flat, you'll see it when you come for Christmas. Well, it's a studio – we'll be a bit cramped, but it's okay.'

'Mum…' Dominic's voice was strained. 'I'm finding it hard at the moment. I keep thinking about…' he paused, not wanting to say the words. 'And I dream about it. I feel like I'm going mad–'

'Then come home at the end of the week,' I said quickly, alarmed. 'Or I'll come and see you.' It was the first time he'd admitted to struggling, and the idea of him feeling that way without me there to comfort him was tearing my heart in two.

He sighed. 'I need to try and deal with it on my own.'

'You don't need to deal with anything on your own,' I told him, panicky now. I peeked out from the curtain again, and sure enough Max's car was still outside. 'Dom, I'll come and see you, okay?'

I dug my fingers into the windowsill, furious with Max. I'd be paid at the end of this month, but then what? Who knew how long it would be before I found another job? Expensive train journeys to visit Dominic would become impossible now I wasn't working. I had to stifle a sob. Dominic was hurting, and he needed me, and Max had made it so I couldn't even be there for my son.

'I'm all right,' Dom said. 'I feel better now. I think I just needed to say I was struggling. I couldn't keep pretending it didn't happen. Don't feel you need to visit me.'

'I wish I could give you a hug. Dom, you *are* coping, aren't you? And you haven't ever mentioned it to anybody there?'

'Of course I haven't! I don't even drink alcohol, to make sure I don't start talking about it by mistake. But, please look after yourself Mum. Max said you were ill after I left, that you were always really exhausted, or something? He said you weren't coping.'

'I was just worried about you,' I said. 'I missed you, but I'll be all right now. I really don't want you worrying about me, it's you you need to focus on.'

'I should leave uni.' His voice was decisive. 'This is all wrong, I shouldn't have left.'

'No!' I said. 'You like it there, don't you? You like your course, and you've got friends.'

'Yes, but I feel like I don't deserve it.'

'You *do* deserve it. Don't ever think otherwise. How is giving up on your future going to help anything?'

There was a long silence, and then he said, 'Okay,' and I breathed a sigh of relief.

I was about to tell him that I could still come to see him if he wanted me to, but he hung up before I could say the words. Then my phone immediately started ringing again, but seeing it was Max I declined the call.

You won't get rid of me that easily Poppy, Max messaged me. *You'll come crawling back to me one way or another.*

Cattleford

Footsteps on the stairs made the three of us turn towards the kitchen door. 'Oh, Reef must have woken up,' Jessica said. 'He's still not completely better.'

She hurried out into the hall, and Harriet shook her head. 'So Dominic really didn't suspect any of what Max was doing?'

I waited until I was sure that Reef was upstairs before I spoke. 'No. Max was always the picture of kindness and devotion towards me whenever Dominic was around, and since what happened with Kevin, Dominic has had such a strong bond with Max. After what they had to do that night, it was like it made an unbreakable link between them. A terrible secret that only the two of them were involved in.'

'You were involved too.'

'Yes, but I wasn't *there*. I think that's the thing. I never saw Kevin's body. The worst I saw were Dominic and Max's clothes that I washed, and I barely looked at those.'

I glanced at the time on my phone. We'd been talking for hours. 'Get some rest,' Harri said. 'You've got a midwife appointment tomorrow; you don't want to turn up looking like you've barely slept.'

I trudged up the stairs, meeting Jessica in the hall. 'Is Reef okay?'

She nodded, though there was something odd in her manner, as if she was excited or had had good news. 'Jess?'

'Oh, he's fine,' she said breezily. 'I've given him some medicine and he's asleep again.' As she spoke she glanced at her phone screen, her eyes bright, and I left her to it. Jessica's mysteries would have to wait. I had enough problems of my own.

35

'Are you feeling okay?' Harriet asked me for about the fifth time. I'd had to call her to come and collect me after the midwife was concerned about the baby's heart rate being fast, and I needed her to give me a lift to the hospital to get it checked out. 'Does the baby seem okay? Can you feel him moving about?'

'I'm sure he's fine,' I said, as we left the surgery and made our way out into the car park, where cheerful clumps of daffodils nodded their heads in the breeze. 'It's just a precaution.'

'People don't go to hospital when they are okay,' Harriet insisted as we reached her car, parked in the corner under a tree coated lavishly in powder pink blossom. A sudden gust of wind caused some loose flowers to cascade over us and I brushed fallen petals from my coat. 'It's just to be on the safe side,' I reassured her. Somehow, despite it being my pregnancy, I was in the position of having to calm *her* nerves. 'I'm sure there's nothing wrong. I think I just got a bit out of breath and tired from walking here and maybe that's affected the baby.'

'Then you should have let me drive you!' Harriet burst out.

'You had to be at the shop.'

She lowered her voice. 'Apart from anything else, we don't want everyone seeing you in the village. You can't hide your bump any more.'

'There was hardly anybody about. And it's a nice day, I wanted some exercise. I'm going crazy cooped up in the house.'

I got into the car beside Harriet, whose lips were pursed with unvoiced reprimands. Her face softened as we approached the hospital, and I was glad to have her with me. It had taken me a long time to get to sleep after we'd finished our conversation the night before, and I was drained. Harriet navigated the hospital corridors for me, and sat beside me in the maternity unit once the heart rate monitor had been set up for the baby, but she was clearly on edge.

'Was Jessica okay to take over in the shop for you?' I asked her.

'Yeah, she was fine,' Harriet said. Then she turned to me, a frown creasing her forehead. 'She's acting a bit weird though.'

I nodded. 'I think she got a message last night, after we'd been talking. I was worried she'd be upset after… what we talked about, but she was quite happy, if anything.'

'That's what worries me.'

'Well, if she's happy that can only be a good thing.'

'You'd think so,' Harriet said, 'but with Jess, you can never be too sure.'

…

By the time we left the hospital with the all clear, Harriet had calmed down a little, though she couldn't resist imploring me to look after myself, until, in frustration I snapped, 'I *have* been pregnant before!'

She recoiled as if I'd given her a slap, and guilt flooded me. 'I didn't mean it to come out like that,' I said.

'I'm going to tell Jessica to stay at the shop for a bit longer. You need a proper, healthy lunch and to put your feet up. And I'm not taking no for an answer.'

I opened my mouth to argue, but held my tongue. It wasn't worth the aggravation.

By the time Harriet had left to take over in the shop again and Jessica arrived home having picked Reef up from school, I was relieved to get some respite. Harriet had got carried away babbling on about how excited she was for the baby to arrive, and when she said we should start researching baby yoga classes I'd wanted to scream. Couldn't she see what a mess my life was? I couldn't focus on making plans like that. I couldn't imagine myself going to baby yoga or baby massage or any of these things with my new baby. I wasn't like the other mums. My life was a disaster, and the secrets I kept couldn't be shared. It was bad enough that Harriet and Jessica knew any of it.

She's not looking at the classes for me. She's looking for her. She's planning how she'll spend time with my baby if I'm in prison. I shook myself. Perhaps she was, but then I *had* agreed to the plan. If I was given a prison sentence for the fraud, Harriet and Jessica would be the ones doing activities with the baby, not me.

'Is the baby okay now, Poppy?' Jessica asked. 'Harriet told me what happened.'

'Yes, he's fine. It was just a precaution I think.'

She nodded distractedly. 'I don't suppose you could do Reef's reading book with him, could you? I need to make a phone call.'

She dashed off upstairs without waiting for me to reply. I patted the sofa beside me and Reef obediently sat down. 'I don't like reading books,' he told me matter-of-factly.

'My little boy – Dominic – didn't always like his reading books,' I said. 'But if you practise reading them, it will help you read the things you're really interested in, won't it?'

If he was with Jessica I'm sure Reef would have argued further, but since he was with me he nodded and read his book happily enough. The baby kicked a few times, and I put my hand on my tummy.

'When will it be born?' Reef asked me.

'In a couple of months.'

'How does it get out?' he pressed me.

'That's a question to ask your mummy later.'

He frowned at me intensely. 'Is your baby going on holiday?' he asked.

I stared at him. What a bizarre question. 'What do you mean?' I said.

'Auntie Harri was reading about getting a baby passport on her laptop yesterday. She didn't want me to see, but I could read what it said. I said passports are for going on holiday so why does a baby need one? She got cross and told me not to sneak up behind her.'

I sat completely rigid and Reef looked at me in alarm. I forced myself to smile at him. 'It's all right,' I told him. 'It was just a misunderstanding. Go and play for a bit, your mummy will be down soon.'

He trotted off, and horror washed over me in waves. A baby passport. Harriet wasn't planning to just look after the baby for a few months *if* I got a prison sentence. As soon as he was born, she was going to take him away from me completely. What other explanation could there be?

Habmouth

36

I stared at the blonde strands in my hairbrush, uncomprehending. I brushed my hair again, and more hairs came away in the brush and in my hands – far more than there should be. What was happening to me? I got up and went to the window. Max was outside in his car and a new wave of fear and dread swept through me. Why wouldn't he stop? Why wouldn't he just fucking stop? I ran my hands through my hair and more strands came away, making me cry out in dismay. What had he done to me? After weeks of stress, fear and anxiety, my body was beginning to fall apart. I nearly always felt ill; there were the blinding headaches, the sore throats, and then on top of that the morning sickness. I was either so stressed and terrified I couldn't stay still, or so exhausted I couldn't move. I tried to take care of myself, but my mind was so addled I constantly made stupid mistakes, forgot things, and struggled to concentrate.

This morning it was more important than ever that he left me alone. I needed to go to the doctor's surgery for my initial appointment with a midwife, and on my way home I planned to do a big shop at the discount supermarket as my cupboards were virtually bare. But how could I leave with Max there? I tried to time my trips out of the house carefully and keep them to a minimum – mainly the supermarket or the job centre – but I was painfully aware that if he wanted to, he could find some pretext to leave the office at a different time of day and turn up unexpectedly. Early mornings and lunchtimes had already been added to his schedule of watching me, and there was no telling when or where he would spring up next.

I glared down at his car. Surely, *surely* he would leave in a minute to go to work and I would be able to escape.

...

'Poppy?'

I turned, already knowing exactly who I would see. How long had he been following me for? His appearance briefly stopped me in my tracks – he hadn't shaved for days, his eyes were dark and his face had an unhealthy pallor to it. But then of course he'd be letting things slide. All his spare time was taken up tormenting me, not looking after his appearance.

'Why don't you let me carry your bags?'

I clutched my shopping bags close to me, acutely aware of the information from the midwife nestled near the top of one of them. I glanced down as discretely as I could to check whether I needed to worry – yes, I could see a leaflet, with its title clearly visible. If he looked down into the bag…

'I can carry them myself,' I said stiffly. I continued walking, and he continued following, his footsteps echoing mine.

'Poppy, this is silly,' he said. 'It's a horrible day; let me help you so you can get back home sooner.'

He was right – the December morning was bleak and grey, the clouds seeming to reach right down to the pavement and envelop me in a chilling mist of rain. But it could have been the middle of a blizzard – I still wouldn't let him help me.

I carried on walking. *Leave me alone. Leave me alone. Leave me alone!*

'Come home,' he said. 'Please. Let's forget all about this madness. I know you're not happy. I can see you're not. I'll help you find a new job, and Dominic will have a proper home to come back to over the Christmas holidays. It would be so good, all you need to do is stop being stubborn.'

I gritted my teeth. Of course he could see I wasn't happy. He spent enough time watching.

'Poppy!' he called after me as I sped up. He increased his pace to catch up with me, and I turned to face him. 'Listen to me,' I said, 'I know you're finding it hard to move on, but I will never come back and live with you again. You threw me out on the street, you forced me out of my job, and you've left me with nothing. Please, *please* just let me go. Let me move on with my life, and perhaps you'll get some closure.'

'I still have the knife,' he hissed.

I stopped and examined his face closely. Was it an empty threat? His eyes were unreadable. I had to take him seriously, the stakes were too high for me to dismiss his words as a bluff. 'You care about Dominic,' I said carefully, 'I know you do.'

'Yes, and so do you. But you've got a funny way of showing it.'

'Well, are you going to go to the police?' I asked him directly. 'Is that what you're telling me?'

'No. Not yet. I want to give you time to see sense. But I will. Believe that I will, if I have to.'

For a brief moment his eyes moved downwards, and I was so sure he would see the leaflet about antenatal classes in my shopping bag that my legs turned to jelly and I had to reach out and steady myself on the bus shelter we were passing.

'You're not well,' he said. 'Let me take you home.'

Thank God, he hadn't spotted it. I would have seen it in his face. 'I'm just a little light-headed,' I told him. 'I'm okay now.' I continued walking, and to my relief he didn't follow me, but his next words stopped me in my tracks.

'I'll kill myself,' he said.

I turned and stared at him in astonishment. 'Don't say that.'

'You and Dominic are the only things that matter to me. If I don't have you, I might as well be dead.'

The words flashed through my mind, accompanied by a pang of guilt. *And it would be easier for me if you were.*

'I'm not joking Poppy. I'll do it.'

I put one of my heavy bags down on the pavement, but kept hold of the one I didn't want him looking at too closely. Did I really make him feel *that* bad? No matter how much I hated him, I didn't want him dead, and certainly not like that. I just wanted him to get out of my life and leave me alone. 'I know you're not joking,' I said. I had no idea if he really was serious or not, but he wanted me to believe him, and I wanted him to calm down. I was starting to shake.

'Why won't you even have a conversation with me?' he said. 'You don't answer my messages, and you keep trying to walk away from me.'

'I don't know what I can say that will help you.'

'Meet me tomorrow night. I'll take you out for dinner. We'll talk properly and I can give you some of the things you left at mine. I found your passport, and Dominic's. There is a whole folder of documents, Dominic's birth certificate, all that kind of stuff.'

I watched him warily.

'Well, okay,' I said, with great reluctance. 'I would appreciate having my things back.'

'That's settled then,' he said, cheerful all of a sudden, while a deep sense of dread settled around my heart. I didn't want to meet him. But I did need my belongings – especially stuff like my passport – which I'd forgotten he still had. I didn't want him keeping important things like that in his house. And maybe I *could* talk some sense into him, though I seriously doubted it.

I practically ran back to my flat once he'd walked away, slamming the door behind me and yanking the security chain across. What the hell had I got myself into? The only tiny silver lining was that it was clear he didn't want to give the knife to the police and accuse Dominic. Whatever his feelings towards me, he didn't seem in a rush to do Dominic any harm. But perhaps if his patience with me reached its limit, even that would be a line he would cross.

Cattleford

37

I couldn't give Harriet any sign that I knew what she was planning. I carried on as normal – not that much about my existence hidden away in their cottage was normal – while I tried to plot my next move. There had to be somewhere I could go, something I could do. But I was damned if I could figure out what it was. I lay curled up on the sofa in the living room one evening watching TV and trying to switch my mind off from it all, when I was startled by a burst of angry voices upstairs.

I crept halfway up the staircase and paused, trying not to make a sound. Harriet was standing in the doorway of Jessica's room, blocking her sister's exit.

'Have you lost your mind?' Harriet was saying. 'That man does not love you! He barely even knows you.'

'You can't stop me again!' Jessica shouted. 'He wants to be with me. And I want to be with him. I'm going to go and live with him and nothing you say will make me change my mind.'

Tyler. He must have got in touch with Jessica at last.

'And how long have you been planning this?'

'He messaged me a couple of days ago, and we've been talking all the time since then. We're soul mates, he said so himself.'

I could barely imagine what expression was on Harriet's face at this statement, and there was no mistaking the derision in her voice. 'Soul mates? I think he means *bed* mates. For God's sake Jessica, he doesn't want *you*, not really. This is just like it was with Ben – he filled your head with nonsense, and in the end he was the first to admit that your relationship was meaningless. He *laughed* at you for believing a word he said.'

'Just because you're miserable and cynical, it doesn't mean everybody else is! Why is it so impossible for you to believe somebody could love me?' Jessica cried, trying to wrestle her way past her sister, without success.

'I don't think it's impossible,' Harriet said, her voice softer. 'But the men you pick are all wrong. I only needed five seconds with Tyler and I knew exactly what his game was.'

'You mean you only needed five seconds with Tyler to judge him. Like you judge everybody. Me, Reef, even Poppy. You said horrible things to me about her when she got pregnant as a teenager.'

I shifted uncomfortably. The sisters hadn't realised I was halfway up the stairs, and now I wasn't sure what to do. Should I go back to the lounge and pretend I'd not heard any of it? Why had I decided to eavesdrop in the first place? Now that Harriet's plans for my baby had come to light I just needed to get as far away as I could, as soon as I could, and the sisters would have to work through their problems without me around to referee.

'I didn't mean any of what I said about Poppy!' Harriet protested, and I paused, placing the foot I had raised back down again softly. 'I was just worried about her, and I was being selfish, thinking about how I'd lose her as a friend once she had a baby to take care of.'

'You called her a stupid slag.'

'How the hell can you still remember that?' Harriet burst out. 'I was sixteen, and I was angry I was going to lose my best friend. I knew everything would be different once the baby came, and I was lashing out. Of course that's not really what I thought of her.'

'But it is what you think of me, isn't it?'

'Well, you did sleep with my husband,' Harriet shot back.

'Yes, I did,' Jessica said, 'and you will never, ever let me forget it, will you? That's why you don't want me to leave, because you don't want me to ever move on and be happy.'

Jessica shoved her way past Harriet onto the landing and towards the door to Reef's bedroom, so I quickly dashed down to hide in the kitchen. 'You don't get to run away!' Harriet shouted from upstairs. 'You don't get to leave me here, surrounded by the memories of what you did to me!'

There was a thundering of feet running down the stairs and Jessica's voice was loud from just the other side of the kitchen door. 'I can't stay here! I'm not like you. I can't carry on like everything is okay. I'm suffocated here. I can feel it, I can feel *him–*'

I clutched the worktop with trembling fingers at the sound of a slap from the hallway, and Jessica stopped talking.

'After everything I did for you,' Harriet said, 'after what you've put me through! You're just going to walk out and leave me? You're supposed to be running a business here, Jess. Your son goes to school here. Have you even–'

The front door slammed and I let my breath out shakily. Jessica and Reef had gone. Harriet and I were alone.

Habmouth

I'd known meeting him wouldn't help, but as I arrived home after the awful evening I'd spent with Max I had to admit it had been even worse than I'd imagined. The only positive was the carrier bag in my hand, stuffed with some of mine and Dominic's more important possessions. 'To show I'm being reasonable,' he said as he handed it over. 'I'm not trying to hurt you. I want you to be okay.'

That set the tone for the whole of the meal we shared – his over-the-top generosity, the excruciating way he picked apart my life, explaining how he could make things better for me in a voice so patronising it set my teeth on edge. It was crystal clear by the end of the night that he was, if anything, even more deluded than I had feared, and that there was no chance of him moving on and leaving me alone. It was as if he truly believed that the sheer force of his persistence could make me fall in love with him.

The messages started when I'd been back only fifteen minutes. If I'd thought he messaged me a lot before, it was nothing compared to the tidal wave he unleashed now.

I can't live without you. Do you understand what I'm saying? I CAN'T LIVE WITHOUT YOU.

Do you really prefer living in that shithole to the life you had with me? You've made your point Poppy

You tell me what more I could possibly have done tonight. You don't know how lucky you are.

For God's sake, I love you.

Why are you being such a bitch? You let me buy you dinner then you won't even talk to me?

I could make yours and Dominic's life hell if I wanted to. Don't tempt me.

I'm sorry. I didn't mean that. The last thing I want to do is hurt you.

Even though you constantly hurt me.

What do you want Poppy? Just tell me WHAT DO YOU FUCKING WANT?

I paced back and forth in my flat, eyes prickling with unshed tears. I didn't want him to make me cry, but at three a.m., when I cautiously turned my phone back on after turning it off to try to get some sleep, the flood of messages that had been going on all night finally broke me. I buried my face in the pillow and cried huge, heavy, useless tears. What was I supposed to do? I'd already tried blocking his number a couple of times, but he just changed it and it would all start again. And blocking him a third time, or changing my own number, was risky. Antagonising him was dangerous and the thing that seemed to infuriate him the most was not being able to communicate with me. I couldn't carry on living like this – my life was unbearable – but what choice did I have? Nobody could help me, and even if I thought going to the police would get him to stop, it was out of the question. I had plenty of secrets myself. It was clear to me now that if I provoked Max sufficiently, he would be crazy enough to incriminate himself and Dominic just to get to me. Even worse, if he persisted in watching me, in a few months time he'd notice that I was pregnant and then he'd step things up to a whole new level. He'd told me about his ex-wife deserting him while she was pregnant and hiding his child from him, so what on earth would he do if he knew I was going to have a baby?

When I woke up in the morning after finally getting a brief couple of hours of sleep, a dreadful, hopeless feeling overwhelmed me. Even if I could find a job, going out to work meant being out of the house, and when I was out of the house Max could get to me. But my final month's pay from QHM wouldn't last me for much longer.

Dominic messaged asking how I was, saying he was looking forward to coming back for Christmas at the end of the week, and it took all my strength to message back saying I was okay. Finally, by the evening, my mind fell into a slightly calmer state. I had to look after myself. I'd cook a proper dinner, and then I would have a shower. I did feel soothed as I put a couple of sausages in the oven, and peeled potatoes to make some mash. I could do this. I *had* to do this. I couldn't just give up.

The entryphone buzzed. Picking it up tentatively, I fought the urge to immediately slam it back down again to stop myself having to hear his voice – because surely that's who it would be.

'Poppy, come on, just let me in.'

'I talked to you yesterday,' I told him. 'I've got nothing else to say.'

He rang several more times, and I hovered helplessly by the door, listening for any sound in the corridor. If somebody who lived in one of the other flats in the block went out, or came home, Max would be able to slip into the building when they opened the main door. A fact he was clearly well aware of, as twenty minutes later the front door slammed closed, soon followed by loud thumping on my own door.

My blood froze. He hammered on the door again. 'Poppy!' He was trying the door handle, and a small sound of fear escaped me. *Go away, go away, go away.* He stayed out there a little longer, five minutes, maybe a bit less, though it felt like forever. Then there was a second voice in the hall, a neighbour, saying they would call the police. I ran across to the window where I could look out over the street outside, and after a few moments Max darted out across the road to his car, and sped away.

Propping my elbows on the windowsill I put my head in my hands, leaning forward until the top of my head rested on the cool glass. I had to get away from here. And I had to do it soon.

38

'Two days?' I said to Dominic. 'Is that really all you will be able stay for?'

'I'm sorry,' he said. 'I wanted it to be longer, but the restaurant is really busy over Christmas and they want me to do extra shifts.'

I sighed and switched the phone to my other hand as I knelt down to investigate the contents of my kitchen cupboard. I rarely went out to get food now, not with the threat of Max lurking around, and I couldn't afford to get deliveries with my dwindling finances. Besides, Max would probably take the opportunity to get into the building if he saw I was getting a grocery delivery. I had a few tins of vegetables, and if I risked dashing out to the corner shop close to the flat perhaps I could cobble together a Christmas dinner of sorts for me and Dominic. Hopefully I'd be able to avoid having to tell him I'd lost my job. I couldn't have him thinking he needed to send me money, or worse, leave university. He didn't need any more upheaval. Perhaps it was just as well he was only staying for two days over Christmas – any more than that and he might start to realise how dire my situation truly was.

'You're not short of money though, are you?' I asked him as I shut the cupboard and got to my feet. 'I don't want you working so much that you can't study.'

'No, it's fine. I just... I don't want to rely only on loans, and gifts from Max,' he told me. 'I want to stand on my own two feet.'

I smiled sadly. Of course he would feel that way. He'd had my example to learn from and earning his own money would be reassuring for him. But the fact he would only be with me so briefly over Christmas meant the respite from Max's stalking that I'd been hoping to get wouldn't happen. Yes, I'd get two days off from him hounding me when Dominic was with me, but as soon as he was gone I'd be stuck. Max would watch me every day over the Christmas period when he wasn't going into the office.

When he finally arrived at the door two days later, I hugged Dominic so tight that he laughed and said I was crushing him. 'Mum?' he said, his eyes full of concern as he looked at me properly. 'Are you sure you're all right?'

'*Yes*,' I insisted. 'Come and see the flat. Not that the tour will take long.'

He tried to hide his shock, but his eyes roamed over the grotty furniture with growing horror and came to rest on me again, full of vague questions.

'It's not like I need a lot of space,' I said. 'We don't exactly have many possessions between us, do we?'

He sat down on the sofa bed. One of his trains had been de-layed, nearly doubling the length of his journey, and he was visibly drooping.

'You can sleep in the bed,' I told him. 'I'm okay on the floor.'

'I'm not going to make you sleep on the floor,' he said, 'why would you even suggest that?'

'You just look really tired, that's all.'

'So do you.' He sighed. 'Actually, I told Max I'd go and see him. Just for half an hour or so. But it's so late now that I'd rather stay here.'

I turned away so Dominic wouldn't see the flash of anger on my face. 'I'm sure he would understand if you couldn't make it,' I said at length, trying to keep my voice neutral.

'I told him I would, though, and he – I think he's lonely.'

I could almost have laughed. 'Well, we can't have Max feeling lonely,' I said, barely keeping the sarcasm from my voice. 'You go ahead. We've got the next two days to spend together.'

…

I fell asleep while Dominic was out, but at the sound of the front door opening my eyes snapped open. What the hell was going on? Had Max got inside? I sat up with my pulse thundering in my ears until the light turned on and Dominic filled my vision.

'You gave me your key, remember?' he said, looking at me with concern. 'You said you'd probably go to bed so I should let myself in.'

'Yes,' I said, 'oh, yes. I remember.'

My eyes fell on the enormous bunch of flowers he was carrying. 'These are from Max,' he said. 'I told him I wasn't sure how you'd react, but he said they were just a gesture of friendship. And, well... you don't have any Christmas decorations, so I thought you might–'

'Yes,' I said. 'Okay. I'll sort them out in the morning. Just put them in the sink with some water.'

He thrust a fancy gift bag towards me. 'He gave us a few other things,' he said as I peered into the bag, 'some chocolates, and biscuits. And a Christmas pudding. He thought you might not have managed to get to the shops.'

'Why would he think that?' I couldn't stop myself from asking. As if the bastard would admit it was him who made it impossible.

'I don't know. He seemed really worried about you.'

I picked up my phone, and spotted some messages from him.

You might have turned your back on me, but Dominic hasn't.

If I can't have you, at least I have a son who wants to spend time with me.

It's me he talks to about stuff. He knows you're weak. You can't give him what he needs. It's a miracle he turned out as well as he has

Dominic was watching me so I quickly put my phone aside. 'It was kind of him to think of me,' I said, the words like acid on my tongue. 'But he really doesn't need to worry. I'm not his responsibility.'

'I know, but... maybe I was wrong to say you shouldn't stay with him. I know you don't love him, but you can't really live like this forever, can you? I don't want to go back to uni and leave you in this place on your own.' He took a deep breath. 'This flat… it's horrible. And the street you're on doesn't feel safe. I thought our previous flat was a dump – sorry, Mum – but this place… You know there's blood on the wall in the stairwell?'

'Yes, I know. It's been there a week or so.'

'And that doesn't bother you? Mum, when I got here and saw it I thought maybe it was yours! I thought perhaps one of Kevin's gang–'

'Oh, Dom,' I said, my heart breaking for him. 'Look, I know it's not ideal, but this flat is a stepping stone, that's all. I know it's not much to look at after we got used to Max's house, but no one has given me any trouble. Besides, this time next year I won't still be here.' As I said the words, I realised how much I believed them. But not because I thought I would have moved on to somewhere nicer, it was because I couldn't see any way I could survive for that long.

39

Be reasonable Poppy. Come home and everything will be ok again

No one ever has to find out what Dom did

I know he's leaving today, you'll be lonely again.

I hugged my knees close to me. It was bad enough that Dominic was going in a few short hours, but the knowledge that I would soon have no barrier between me and Max was putting me on the verge of panic. Once Dominic was gone, Max could come and bang on my door again. He could phone me over and over – not that I ever answered. Even the messages had decreased substantially while he knew Dominic was with me, but once my son had left the floodgates would open. I ran my hands through my hair and blonde strands came away, so I quickly leapt to my feet to throw them in the bin before Dominic saw. Sure enough, he frowned at the guilty expression on my face when he came into the room in fresh clothes, a waft of minty shower gel following him.

'I don't have to go back today,' he said at length.

'I thought you have a shift at the restaurant tonight?'

'I do, but I could call in sick.'

I shook my head. 'It's not your job to look after me. It's your job to live *your* life. That's what I want you to do.'

'It's not as easy as that!' he said, with sudden feeling filling his face. 'I try to make it so I'm busy all the time, so that I don't have to think, but it's impossible to stop! How do I make myself forget about it? About Kevin? It's like living inside a nightmare, and I want to wake up but I can't, and when I close my eyes half the time I can't sleep.'

I took a step back in shock. 'Dom–'

'I don't want my life to be like this forever. Sometimes I think it would be a relief to get caught.'

I took both of his hands in mine. 'Dominic,' I said softly. 'Do you think a bad person would feel like you are feeling? The kind of person who *really* deserved to be caught?'

'I don't know,' he said moodily.

'You feel guilty because you're *good*. Somebody who cares about other people, even scumbags like Kevin.'

'Mum–'

I lowered my voice. 'You did what you did to protect me. To protect somebody you love.'

'Are you saying you're glad it happened?'

'How can I possibly answer that? No, of course I'm not glad that you're having to go through this. I wish it had all been solved a different way. But on the other hand, what might have happened that night if Kevin hadn't died? He'd found out where we lived and he would have come for us. We could both be dead now. You knew full well what would happen if he turned up at Max's house, and because you had a knife with you–'

'Which I shouldn't have done.'

'No, you shouldn't, but "should" doesn't matter now. I *should* have gone to the police about Kevin ages ago. I should never have let it get this far. But I didn't, and I can't change it now no matter how much I wish I could. Kevin was a nasty piece of work, and he didn't care about anyone. If there's one thing I know it's that you don't deserve punishment. You don't deserve to suffer. You have to hold on to that. Not only did you save me, but you've helped other families that Kevin would still be terrorising otherwise.'

Dominic picked up his bag and started packing the few things he'd brought with him. 'Someone else will take over the loans,' he said. 'There were a whole load of them involved.'

'You don't know what will happen. Maybe without Kevin the whole operation will fall apart.'

Dominic threw his bag down in frustration, and I struggled desperately to find the words to get through to him. Telling him the whole thing was my fault wouldn't help – it would just antagonise him because he'd insist it was all down to Liam, and thinking about his dad never did him any good. All I could do was try to change the narrative, to stop him from seeing himself as a person who took someone's life to a person who saved the lives of others. It was true, after all. 'Look, Dom, I'm just trying to get you to see it clearly,' I said gently. 'Kevin hurt people out of nothing but greed. You did what you did out of love for your family. There is world of difference between those two things, and I'm proud of you for everything you do, for how you've kept going, for how hard you try. Just carry on putting one foot in front of the other, and one day, Kevin won't be at the front of your mind any more. I promise.' I felt sick as I said these last words, hoping like hell that my promise would come true. How on earth could I possibly know when or if he would move on from stabbing Kevin? I could tell him until I was blue in the face that he didn't need to feel guilty about protecting me from a monster, but I couldn't change how he felt with the sheer force of my words. He had to find his own way. He had to believe it himself.

Dominic looked as though he would argue further, but eventually, he nodded.

...

Just as I feared, Max cornered me the second I left the station after waving Dominic off, and for a moment I wanted to turn and scream in his face in rage. Was nothing sacred to him? Couldn't he give me some brief respite when he knew how much I hated saying goodbye to Dominic?

He fell into step one pace behind me. He didn't speak, not straight away, and somehow that was worse. Just his footsteps echoing mine, one after another on the pavement, occasionally splashing in the shallow puddles that dotted the street. It was another bleak December day, the kind that feels like dawn never really arrives.

'He's gone then,' Max said as we both stopped to cross a busy road.

'Please stop following me.'

'He told me he was shocked at the state of that studio flat you're living in.'

'He'd be shocked by a lot more than that if he knew the truth.'

The traffic lights changed and I hurried over the crossing. Could I make a run for it and take a different route home? No – there was no point. He knew where I lived, and any other route I took would be less direct and take longer so he could simply wait on my street for me to arrive. And besides, at least the road we were on was busy. There were plenty of other people around, taking the opportunity to walk off their Christmas indulgences during a break in the rain. Max couldn't grab me or start saying anything too extreme with so many people to witness it.

'Poppy, you could make life so much easier if you'd just have a proper conversation with me,' he said as we reached the other side of the road.

I didn't reply. I'd already tried having a proper conversation with him when I'd let him buy me dinner and I might as well have been talking to a brick wall. He simply couldn't see beyond his own fantasy. I darted along the pavement, zig-zagging through the people, and Max tried his best to follow me. There were a couple of families up ahead with small children wobbling along on new bikes, and I quickly managed to skirt around the nearest family, but Max was forced to pause for a moment.

I seized the opportunity and ran, not stopping until I reached the door to my block. I almost screamed in frustration when my fumbling fingers dropped the keys on the ground, but there was no sign of Max behind me. I snatched up the keys, unlocked the door and slammed it closed behind me, my feet pounding up the stairs to my floor until finally I was back inside my little studio taking great rasping breaths of air. I put my hand on my stomach, where a tiny new life was growing. What chance did it have if I stayed here in this nightmare?

I've got to get out of here. I've got to escape from Max .

Cattleford

40

'Harri,' I said gently, 'maybe you've had enough.'

She put down her wine glass and eyed me warily, as if she thought I was about to get up and run away like her sister. She'd started drinking soon after Jessica left, and having polished off most of a bottle she was looking worse for wear.

'Drinking yourself into a stupor isn't going to change anything. Talk to me. Tell me what was going on earlier. Why is Jessica so desperate to leave this house?'

'Probably to get away from her bitch sister,' Harriet said and gave a hollow laugh.

'That wasn't the only thing though, was it?' I said. In all honesty, knowing what Harriet was plotting for my baby I had zero sympathy for her. But until I had somewhere else to go, I needed to keep up the pretence of being her friend and carrying on with our "plan". I didn't want to alert her to my suspicions and trigger her to do anything desperate.

'Jessica will be back soon enough,' Harriet said. 'Tyler will get fed up with her. Her so called boyfriends always do.' She reached for her wine glass and I didn't stop her. Let her drink herself into oblivion if that's what she wanted. She clearly cared little enough for me or her sister. *But she did support Jessica all these years. Even after what Jessica did, she helped with Reef. She was there for her.*

Reef. Maybe that's what it was all about. Perhaps being close to Reef was really all she wanted, and she put up with Jessica as part of the package.

'Maybe this time it will be different,' I said. 'Maybe Tyler really is right for her.' Not that I'd been especially taken with him when I'd met him briefly, though he had been friendly enough and Reef liked him.

'Tyler *isn't* right for her. She will come back, you mark my words. I'm the only person who really understands her.'

I shook my head. The pair of them were impossible. They couldn't live with or without each other.

Abruptly, Harriet put the wine glass down and sat up straight. 'What am I doing?' she said. 'Poppy, I'm sorry. I shouldn't be doing this in front of you, getting drunk and whingeing on.'

'It's not like the baby can see,' I said.

She looked at me intently, her gaze surprisingly sharp and lucid considering how much wine she'd put away. 'I'll do a good job,' Harriet said. 'With the baby, if you do end up having to go away for a bit.' Her face brightened. 'You know what, I'm being stupid. The baby is all that matters.' She picked the near empty wine bottle up and got to her feet. 'I'm getting rid of the rest of this.'

I smiled uncomfortably. *The baby is all that matters.* Coming from her, those words could not have been any less reassuring.

...

'Harri, what is all this?' I asked her when she arrived back from Bits and Bobbins a couple of days after Jessica left us.

Her face broke into a smile. 'Oh, it arrived!' she said, 'I'm so glad. I thought it might have got delayed – it's mayhem down the road, some cows got out from Willow Farm and they were all over the street.'

'Cows?'

'Yes,' she said, her hands clutching at the small pile of cardboard boxes. 'A section of fence was broken and the whole lot of them made a run for it.'

She carried the boxes through to the kitchen and started cutting tape with a pair of kitchen scissors. Eventually, an overnight bag emerged, along with an array of other bits and bobs – toiletries, maternity pads and breast pads and a pack of newborn nappies.

'So you can pack your hospital bag,' Harriet said enthusiastically.

For a moment I stared at the heap of items in stunned silence. *This is actually real. I really am having a baby.* I put my hand on my bump and tried to calm down. Why had Harriet done this? This was my job. To do it herself, when *I* was the one giving birth – it left me lost for words.

'I just feel bad for you stuck here all the time, and I thought getting this ready would give you something to do.'

'It won't take me very long to pack a bag.'

'No, I know that.' Concern crept into her voice. 'I– I'm sorry. Did I overstep the mark?'

I looked around at her. There was nothing other than kindness in her face, but Reef's words kept echoing in my head.

Auntie Harri was reading about getting a baby passport.

For a moment I was overwhelmed by the desire to confront her and just get it over with. Let her admit what she was trying to do and we could stop this ridiculous pretence. She'd bought a hospital bag because she was excited for me to give birth to the baby she wanted to steal. That's all I was to her – a walking incubator. She didn't care about me, and she didn't care about Jessica. I felt a pang. Her marriage with Ben had ended horribly, and to find out the husband you so badly wanted to start a family with was having a baby with your own sister was bound to have affected her deeply. But that didn't change what she was planning. And it was unforgiveable.

'It's okay,' I lied. 'It needs sorting out and I must admit I hadn't started thinking about it.'

'I know you're worried,' Harriet said. 'It's okay if you feel daunted or overwhelmed, doing it on your own. Not that you are on your own, of course, you've got me, but I just mean–'

'I know what you mean. But for most of Dominic's life I was a single mum and I made it through. I suppose for *all* of this baby's life I will be a single mum.'

'You don't know that.'

'I can't ever risk having a relationship again.' I laughed without much humour. 'And you think *Jessica* has poor taste in men.'

'Well, me and her were both wrong about Ben.'

I was about to try and ask again about whether Ben might be interested in getting to know Reef, but Harriet quickly changed the subject. 'What do you want for dinner?' she asked, as she went over to the fridge to investigate its contents. She started muttering about needing to go and do a big shop, and my eyes rested on the smiling baby on the front of the pack of newborn nappies. I would find a way out of this mess. No matter what it took, I'd keep Dominic and my baby safe. Nothing else mattered.

...

'Jessica?' I said, as I answered the door. Her face was streaked with tears as she stepped inside, Reef trudging along behind her, and I was lost for words at the tragic state of them. Could things really have gone so wrong, so quickly?

Harriet immediately appeared in the kitchen doorway, and Reef ran across to her and threw himself into her arms.

'Congratulations, you were right,' Jessica snapped at Harriet while she pulled off her bright yellow raincoat and threw it towards the banister, but it missed and fell on the floor. 'He doesn't love me, and he doesn't want me.'

'Jess, I'm not *happy* to hear that–'

Jessica waved her sister's words away with an angry swipe of her hand, before shoving her suitcase towards the bottom of the stairs so that she could step further inside. 'Yes you are. Another one of Jessica's daft fantasies.'

'Here, Reef,' I said, holding out my hand. 'Why don't I put the TV on for you?' He eyed me uncertainly, and I gave him a smile. 'It's okay,' I said.

Eventually he broke free from Harriet and came into the lounge with me. 'Mummy says we're not living with Tyler,' he said. 'They shouted a lot and then we left.' He screwed his face up and said with feeling, 'We were only there for literally three nights! Or a week maybe. Mummy said we'd stay forever.'

'You were there for four nights,' I told him. 'I know it must be confusing, but you can go back to school tomorrow and see all of your friends. That will be nice.'

He threw himself onto the sofa, and I put the TV on. 'I expect Mummy or Auntie Harri will be in in a minute,' I told him, 'will you be okay for a second?'

He nodded moodily, and I rejoined the sisters, closing the door softly behind me. Hopefully Harriet and Jessica would keep their voices down, or take their argument somewhere else, because Reef didn't look in a good way to me.

'Just tell me exactly what happened,' Harriet said calmly. Jessica started crying again, so I encouraged them both into the kitchen to be further from Reef's hearing.

'Tyler said he thought I'd only go and stay with him for a week or so – he didn't think I was serious about us starting a new life together. But that's what we'd been talking about. He'd *said* it was what he wanted!'

'I knew he was dodgy,' Harriet muttered.

'I'm an idiot!' Jessica cried, 'I'm a complete idiot. Why do I ever believe what anyone tells me?'

She fled upstairs, and Harriet disappeared into the living room. The low murmur of her and Reef talking drifted out to me, and with little else to do I made my way upstairs to check on Jessica.

'He lied to me,' she said, as I stepped inside her room. She'd closed her curtains, even though it was still light outside, and she was sitting on the colourful rag rug covering the floorboards in her room, leaning back against her bed. 'We'd made all these plans, and it wasn't real.'

'Maybe it was when he said it,' I tried to reassure her.

'You mean, he wanted to be with me until he spent a few days with me?' she said. 'You think I'm *that* awful to be around–'

'That's not what I meant.'

'I'd prefer to think he was just lying,' she said. 'Like Ben.'

I shifted awkwardly from one foot to the other. 'Jess, listen, about Ben–'

She turned her head and gave me a warning look, which I ignored. 'I know I'm not exactly a good advertisement for what happens when you bring dads back into kid's lives,' I continued, 'but maybe it would be good to get in touch with him. Let Reef get to know him, maybe it will give you and Harriet a bit of space to move on from things and build bridges.'

'By bringing back the very person who caused the problem?'

I sighed, and Jessica buried her face in her knees. I wished I could sit beside her and put my arms around her, but I was getting to the stage where if I sat down on the floor I wasn't sure I'd be able to get back up again.

'I don't know how I can get up tomorrow and act like everything is normal,' she said. 'And… I've left everything in such chaos; the sewing room, all my appointments, I've been so distracted I let myself get way behind. I didn't think I'd ever come back here, so I didn't think it mattered. And Reef's school… oh my God, Reef's school—'

'It's okay,' I said. 'I think Harriet has been cancelling your dress fittings and appointments each day, and we can make a start on getting your sewing room tidy once Reef is in bed – then you won't have to face a mess tomorrow. And the school, well, had you officially told them that Reef was leaving?'

She shook her head.

'Well, then, the worst it'll be is that you get a bit of a ticking off for taking Reef out of school again. It will be all right.'

She let out a sob and buried her face in her hands again. 'I am sorry, Jess,' I said softly. 'I know it probably doesn't help to hear me say it, but it's his loss. If he can't see how wonderful you and Reef are, he doesn't deserve you anyway.'

She lifted her head a little. 'Thank you,' she said. 'At least I know you're not secretly glad.'

'Harriet isn't glad,' I said gently, though I wasn't too sure myself how Harriet felt about anything. 'I think she would have liked to be proved wrong.'

'You don't believe that any more than I do,' she said.

41

Harriet's face pinched as she switched on the light in the conservatory to be confronted with the disorganisation within. I hadn't set foot in Jessica's sewing room for a while, and my heart sank at the thought of trying to tidy up the chaos the room had got into. And doing it with Harriet certainly wasn't appealing. I didn't want to spend any longer with her than I possibly had to. 'You don't have to help with this,' she said. 'You should try and get some sleep.'

'I don't think I'll be getting to sleep any time soon,' I said. 'And I told Jessica we'd try and clear up for her – she's really worried about how far behind she's got with everything. I think if she walks in here tomorrow and it looks like this she might walk straight out again and give up.'

Harriet rolled her eyes as she pushed the sleeves of her black jumper up to her elbows. 'She should have thought about that before she let things get in such a state. I don't know what she thought was going to happen. You can't just walk out on your own business and leave someone else to pick up the pieces.'

'She hasn't really been thinking, I guess.' I surveyed the room again. 'How do we tackle this, though? I have no idea what's going on in here.' Fabric and half-finished garments were piled haphazardly, and open boxes of various sewing supplies were strewn about.

'She has a system, of sorts,' Harriet said, moving the ironing board out of the way to get to the table. 'You start putting things back in these boxes and I–'

'It's all right, I can help.' Jessica's voice in the doorway startled us, but when I turned to her she gave a weak smile. 'I'm a little better now,' she said.

'We'll all do it together,' Harriet said, 'and we'll try and see where you are with some of these clients. I've been having to phone people and cancel appointments this week–'

'I'm sorry, Harri,' Jessica said shakily. 'I should have been doing that… it all just got on top of me.'

She slumped down onto the rattan armchair and I put my hand on her shoulder. 'You don't have to help us,' I said, 'me and Harri can do it.'

'No, I – pass me my diary,' she said to Harriet, 'I'll try and figure this out.'

Harriet passed her a large flowery book along with a pen that had a pink pom-pom on the end, while I sat down at Jessica's work table and turned towards her. 'Are you really feeling better?' I asked her.

She shrugged. 'I've realised you're right,' she said, astonishingly dismissive all of a sudden. 'He doesn't deserve me, and I'm not going to waste any more time crying over him.'

'I should hope not,' Harriet agreed, as she busily started picking up scraps of fabric from the table and floor. 'And I have to say, although I did want you to be happy – even if you don't believe me when I say that – I did miss you when you weren't here. And Reef, of course.'

'I think perhaps I didn't really love Tyler,' Jessica said, with that surprising indifference again, as she traced her finger through the diary before snapping it shut. 'No appointments for a couple of days,' she said. 'It'll give me a chance to catch up on some of the dresses I got behind on.'

My phone rang, and I answered quickly when I saw Dominic's name on the screen. 'Mum?' he said, 'you still haven't said whether you will meet Max! The audit starts next Monday.'

'Dom,' I said patiently, as the two sisters turned to me, no doubt curious what new drama could emerge in my life. 'I cannot see Max.'

'But you could get caught!'

I pressed my eyes closed for a second. Yes, I could. *If* this audit was even real. It was an incredibly convenient way for Max to get Dominic to badger me for a meeting.

'Mum, Max is…' he took a breath. 'He's really upset that you won't speak to him. And it's making life hard for me as well. I keep making excuses for you, but you won't even tell me what's going on. Sometimes... sometimes I wonder why I'm covering for you when you don't even trust me enough to tell me the truth.'

'It's not that I don't trust you,' I said desperately, reeling at switching straight from dealing with Jessica's meltdown to handling Dominic's. 'I'm waiting for the right time.'

'What does that mean? I need to know now!'

I sighed helplessly, while Jessica and Harriet's eyes filled with questions. 'Dom, is Max upsetting you?' I asked eventually.

'No! *You're* upsetting me. I know you don't want to see him, but he says speaking to you one more time will give him closure. He said you left so suddenly that he feels like he can't make sense of what happened.'

I rubbed at my forehead with my hand. Harriet had gone back to half-heartedly picking up the fabric scraps, while Jessica toyed with a fat pincushion on the edge of the table, rearranging the pins into neat lines organised by their brightly coloured heads.

'I'm going to change my surname this week,' Dominic said. 'I can't have my name reminding me of Liam any more.'

'To Dorsett?' I asked him. 'Like Max?'

'Yes,' he replied, but there was a challenge in the way he said the word, as if he wanted me to give him a reason not to, and I seized on it.

'I *am* going to explain everything to you,' I said, and Harriet gave me a warning look. 'I know my behaviour is hard to understand but there is a reason for it.'

'No there isn't!' Dominic said. 'You just don't trust me. Max says you don't trust anybody–'

'I don't care what Max says,' I snapped. 'Me and you, Dom, we're a team. We always have been, haven't we? Whatever I do, I do it because I'm trying to do the best thing for both of us. I know I made a lot of mistakes after Liam left and I'm sorry for what I put you through. You should never have had to go through what you did. I wasn't thinking straight back then, but you *can* trust me now.'

'Except *you* don't trust *me*. Please, just agree to meet Max. For me. I don't want you getting in trouble over the fraud for the sake of not wanting to speak to him.'

'If Max cared about you, or me, he'd do what he could to protect me during this audit regardless of whether I agree to see him,' I said, my voice rising. 'Is this really the man you look up to – someone who is using threats to make me see him?'

'Poppy, calm down,' Harriet said quietly, hovering by my side. 'Think of the–' she waved at my stomach.

'He's just desperate,' Dom said, before pausing. 'Is someone else there, Mum? I thought I heard somebody.'

'Never mind about that. Max is manipulative. Please, can't you see it? He's saying he wants to see me one more time to give him closure, but I've already met with him since we split. I went for dinner with him, but it didn't help at all. It didn't give him closure, if anything it gave him false hope. He needs to understand that there is no me and him, and making threats is certainly not going to change that.'

His voice was angry now. 'At least he tells me the truth.'

'No he doesn't!' I said. I took a deep breath, trying to calm down. 'Come and stay with me,' I said. Harriet began frantically shaking her head, and I ignored her. 'I'll explain everything, I promise.'

'I can't just leave,' he said. 'I've got lectures, and shifts at the restaurant. If you want to tell me something, just tell me now.'

'It's too much for a phone call. Come and see me. I'll message you the address and we can talk properly. You'll understand everything then.'

He was silent for a while, and eventually he mumbled his agreement.

I ended the call and Harriet fixed her eyes on me. 'He can't come here.'

'Not when you look like you've got a beach ball up your top,' Jessica said.

'Yes, well, obviously I will have to tell him about the baby.'

'Poppy, no one needs *telling*,' Jessica said, warming to her theme of discussing my current size. She seemed positively cheerful. Was it really just an hour or so earlier that she was crying inconsolably?

'This will ruin our plan,' Harriet said. 'You can't be sure that Dominic won't tell Max you're pregnant. It's a huge risk.'

'He's my son. I trust him.'

'Then why have you kept it secret for this long?'

'You know why!' I cried. 'Telling him about how Max has been behaving, about the threats he was making to turn me and Dominic in to the police, it would have terrified him! I wanted to give him a chance to get settled at university and have a normal life. I wanted to wait until I could make sure we were all safe, but... well, Max has forced my hand. I am not letting him turn my own son against me. If I wait until I've had the baby, it might already be too late to salvage things.'

'You're making a big mistake,' Harriet said darkly.

'Dominic needs to be wherever is safest,' I said, growing angry with her. How dare she question me? Acting as if it was for my sake that she cared about our plan, when I knew all she cared about was my baby! 'For a while that was at university away from everything, but now he needs to be with me and hear the truth.'

'Poppy, you should call him back. Explain that if he can hang on just a little longer–'

'No!' I exploded. 'Dominic is *my* son, I know what's best. And the baby is mine too!'

The words hung in the air. 'And what is that supposed to mean?' Harriet said, her voice brittle. 'Is this about the hospital bag? I knew you weren't happy about it.'

I was so angry that I lost all reason and blurted it out. 'No, it's about you looking up how to get a passport for a baby!'

42

'She won't come out,' Jessica said, finding me in the kitchen having spent the last twenty minutes knocking on Harriet's door.

'She's not even going to try and deny that she wants to take my baby out of the country then?'

'I don't know,' Jessica said. 'The only thing she said was "after everything I've done for her."'

'I'm more than happy to hear her out,' I said angrily as I shoved the things Harriet had bought for me into the hospital bag. Much as her actions in buying this stuff for the birth sickened me, I wasn't going to let things I needed go to waste. 'But the fact she has nothing to say just shows I was right. Jess, she was going to take the baby and run. There's no other explanation. If there was, she would have just told me.'

Jessica looked miserable. 'I never thought she would really do something like this.'

'You tried to warn me, remember.'

'I didn't mean it. I was just angry.'

I sighed as I zipped the bag closed. 'I'm going to have to leave.'

'When is Dominic coming?'

'He's getting the train tomorrow morning. So it should be early afternoon that he arrives. I'll have the rest of my bags packed ready to go.'

'But where will you go? What will you do?'

'I don't know. But it's not the first time I've had to run away.'

'Poppy, how *did* you get away from Max? And didn't he still have the knife that Dominic used? Wasn't it a big risk to leave while he had that? Isn't it still a risk now?'

The baby kicked vigorously a few times and I let out a little gasp.

'He's an active one isn't he?' Jessica said, gesturing at my bump. 'Always up to something.'

'Max never had the knife,' I said wearily, steadying myself against the kitchen worktop. 'I found that out, eventually. But not before he'd brought me to the brink of insanity.'

Habmouth

I've given you enough chances Poppy.

How do you think it felt for me, sat on my own over Christmas, knowing you and Dom chose to be cooped up in that disgusting little flat when you could have been with me?

What have I got to lose? I could destroy your life, and Dominic's. It's only love for you both that's stopping me, but if you don't want me then why should I keep either of you safe?

I swear to God Poppy I will do it. I will send Dominic down. And you too.

I had to reply to that one, and with shaking fingers I typed back, *What do you want me to do?*

His reply was predictable enough. *Come back home.*

I started to tremble all over. I had to take his threat seriously; I couldn't possibly risk him turning Dominic in. But I couldn't go back to Max's house either. When would it end? I'd have to stay with him forever because he'd always have this threat to use against me.

I began to pace back and forth in my flat, my footsteps punctuating my thoughts. The knife. That was the key. After all, without that he couldn't prove anything. Yes, he could still tell the police that Dominic had killed Kevin, but with no evidence, what would they really do? Kevin's body was in the river, as far as I knew it hadn't been found. Without that knife, he really didn't have a lot to link Dominic to Kevin's death, and as my ex the police would surely be suspicious of anything he said against my son that he couldn't prove.

I paused at the window and glared down at Max's car, sat in its usual spot just in front of the graffitied railway bridge down the road. Could I go back to his house and try to find the knife? Was there any chance that would work?

If I come home with you, you need to stop all of this, I replied.

I will! he typed back quickly, and I could sense the joy in his words. *It will be so good Poppy. We'll be happy like we were to start with. We'll put it all behind us.*

I picked up a bag, acting quickly before I changed my mind, but soon my body began to disobey me. I opened the drawer containing my socks and underwear, ready to scoop it all up and shove it in the bag, but my hands wouldn't move. It didn't matter what my mind said, I couldn't bring myself to pack, not when Max's house was the destination. I slumped down onto the sofa bed, staring listlessly across the room. *If I go back to him, I'll never be free.*

I must have sat there for a long time, because my phone chimed and I picked it up.

Are you leaving yet? I'm outside waiting for you.

My skin started to crawl. As if I didn't already know he was sat outside waiting for me. He was always sat outside waiting for me.

I'm still packing, I told him.

Are you sure you haven't changed your mind?

Of course I haven't changed my mind, I replied desperately.

Because you know what's at stake

My emotions overwhelmed me and I picked up my pillow and screamed into it. I couldn't go to him. I couldn't let him take over my life, and the life of the baby growing inside me. I just couldn't. But I couldn't not, either.

I'm sick of this Poppy. You've got twenty minutes.

I fidgeted around with my bag, my mind screaming. Twenty minutes. How could I solve this in twenty minutes? I stood and started pacing again, and soon my phoned chimed.

19 minutes

I covered my face with my hands. Think! There had to be some other option. Could I call the police and tell them *I* had killed Kevin to protect Dominic? No, that wasn't the answer. All it would do is draw attention to Kevin's death. Right now, as far as I knew, they weren't even investigating it.

18

This was a nightmare. If I got in that car, I might as well be saying my life was over. But if it was my life for Dominic's, there was no question. His would always come first. *But there is another life. There's a baby.* I wouldn't bring up a baby in Max's house. Not when I knew how he treated the people he claimed to love.

17 Come on Poppy. This is stupid. Just come with me and all your worries will be over.

I tugged at my hair in frustration, and strands came away in my fingers. In a desperate fit of emotion, I attacked my hair in a vicious fury, more strands coming away in my hands until I finally stopped and ran to the bathroom mirror. I barely recognised the face staring back at me. I was pale and my cheeks had lost the last of the fullness which had returned during my time in Max's house eating proper meals. My eyes were wild, hair a birds' nest –

though thankfully it was not visibly obvious that it had started coming out over the past few weeks. I placed my hands on the edge of the basin, staring at that face. I'd ruined my life. I'd ruined my son's life. I'd ruined my baby's life. *What do I do?* I asked the mirror – or maybe not just the mirror. I was asking the world. Perhaps I was asking God. Whoever I was asking, no answer came.

I darted back out of the bathroom and picked up my phone. I'd missed the last three messages from Max, and my stomach lurched when I saw the number in the most recent message.

14 minutes Poppy.

Think, think, think! There had to be something I could say to him to make him stop this. Some way to get him to see sense. He didn't really want to do this – I knew in my heart that he cared about Dominic in his own twisted way.

Max, please, I typed to him. *Dominic looks up to you. You said yourself that if you don't have me at least you have a son. Why destroy that as well?*

I don't really have him, do I? He's not going to come and stay with me in the holidays. He's always going to go to you. He's always going to worry about you. We should be a proper family, together. Why make him choose?

Do you really want to be the person that destroys his life? I asked him.

If I have to. I don't want to, but I will. It's down to 11 minutes Poppy and I swear on Dominic's life, if you don't get down here before I get to 0, I will go straight to the police and turn him in.

I threw my phone down. There was no getting around it. I couldn't talk any sense into him. I tried to think logically. If he was saying he would go straight to the police, did that mean he had the knife in the car with him? Perhaps he did – maybe he didn't want to give himself a chance to change his mind. If I was right and he had it with him, could I grab it somehow? Maybe if I finished packing a bag and went downstairs I could give the impression I was cooperating, but at the last minute, rather than go with him I could grab the knife and get rid of his means to torment me. Yes, he could still threaten to expose the fraud, but at least that didn't involve Dominic.

10 minutes. There's no way out of this except my way.

I picked up my bag. How the hell was I going to grab the knife from the car without him stopping me? It would be hard even if I knew exactly where it was, but he was hardly going to have it sat right there on the seat beside him. He probably didn't even have it with him anyway. I was just clutching at straws.

9 minutes. Tick tock.

I let out a cry of frustration.

I am not messing around Poppy. Don't test me.

8

With a sudden flash of inspiration I grabbed my phone, and almost cried out with relief when Dominic answered my call straight away.

'The knife,' I gasped. 'What happened to it?'

43

'Mum?' he said, his voice betraying his fear. 'Why are you asking me that? We can't talk about this on the phone–'

'Just tell me!' I virtually screamed.

'It's… it's in the river,' he said.

I gasped. Could it be true? All this time, had Max been bluffing? 'Are you sure?' I asked.

'You're scaring me,' he said, 'why are you asking about it? Has something happened? Have the police–'

'No. I'm sorry, I didn't mean to frighten you.' It took everything I had to keep my voice calm, especially when another message from Max came through.

7 minutes

I pressed the phone back against my ear. 'Could you tell me exactly how you know it's in the river? Did you see Max throw it in?'

'Why do you want to know?' Dominic asked me yet again. 'Something must have happened.'

'Nothing has happened. I'm probably being silly, I just started worrying and I want to put my mind at rest. Do you remember exactly what happened to it? Did you see Max get rid of it?'

'No,' he said, and I had to dig my nails into my palms to stop myself crying out in dismay. '*I* threw it in,' he continued, and hope surged inside me.

'You – you did? You're sure?'

'Yes, I'm sure. A lot of it is a blur, but I remember that clearly. I wanted it away from me; it was a relief to hear it hit the water.'

'So there's no doubt at all? You kept hold of it the whole time until you got rid of it? Please just tell me!'

My phone vibrated. *6 minutes*

'Yes, sort of. It was in my jacket pocket – the big, deep pocket on the inside – I had to put it somewhere when I helped Max carry the – you know – he was heavy–'

'I understand.'

'Then once we'd got rid of… him, I took the knife out of my pocket and threw it in the river.'

5 minutes

'Thank you,' I said, 'I'm so sorry I frightened you. It's just being here on my own, it was making me think weird things.'

'I'll come and see you again soon.'

'It's okay, Dom, don't worry. You've only been back a week after visiting me at Christmas.'

'Mum–'

'I love you,' I said, 'I'll call you again soon.'

I know you don't have it, I messaged Max, *so please leave me alone now.*

I waited, barely breathing, for his reply. It took a while, but finally he did respond.

I have these messages.

Hundreds and hundreds of messages where you harass me and make vague threats? I replied. I hurriedly scrolled through the messages he'd sent me that evening. There was nothing concrete in them. He'd not said specifically what he was going to turn Dominic in for, or what evidence he supposedly had, and neither had I. Showing these messages to the police would prove nothing except that he was stalking me and making my life a misery.

I'll ask you one more time Max. Leave me alone.

For once, he was silent, and I dropped to my knees on the floor, tears streaming down my cheeks as I laughed and cried simultaneously with pure relief.

Cattleford

'Was that really it?' Jessica asked me, her blue eyes wide. 'Did he really just leave you alone after that?'

'No,' I said. 'Of course he didn't. I was naive to think it would make any difference. Not having the knife meant he had less leverage, and I didn't have to worry about him going to the police over Dominic, but I still had to find a way to escape. Max knew he couldn't get me to go and live with him again, but he didn't want to let me go. He still doesn't. But when Dominic comes here tomorrow I'll tell him the truth and we'll decide together what to do.'

'What about Harriet?'

'What about her?' I said, my voice rising. 'I don't want to see her. I don't want to speak to her. She made out that she wanted to help me, concocting this mad plan for me to turn myself in, but she doesn't care about me! She wanted me gone. I… she was going to kidnap my baby Jess. *My* baby. I don't even want to be in the same house as her. In fact, I can't be. I'm going to go and get a room somewhere. The pub has rooms, doesn't it?'

Jessica took my arm gently as I tried to leave the kitchen. 'Poppy, stop,' she said. 'It's gone midnight, you can't possibly go anywhere now. Harriet can't do anything to you tonight, can she? Get some rest, and Dominic will be here tomorrow.' She put her arms around me and her hair tickled my face. I closed my eyes. *Dominic.* I needed him. We needed to be together.

Jessica let go of me and looked at me closely. 'You're probably not going to be able to get to sleep are you?'

'Probably not.'

She looked thoughtful. 'Max told you he had a wife once, didn't he?'

'Yes. She was called Caitlyn. It was years and years ago.'

'Come with me,' Jess said, and I followed her as she grabbed Harriet's laptop from the living room and went through to the conservatory. Sweeping some fabric aside she put the laptop down on the table. 'Let's try and find Caitlyn,' she said.

'I don't know anything about her. And what could she tell me now, after all these years?'

'You won't know until you ask, will you?'

I sat down beside her, watching her face light up with animation as she got to work.

'What are you doing?' I asked her, as her fingers moved across the keyboard.

'Well, not a lot is coming up for Caitlyn Dorsett. You can try as well if you want.'

She pushed the laptop over to me and after fifteen minutes I accepted defeat. If that was her name, she certainly didn't have much of an online presence.

'They're divorced though, right?' Jessica said.

'That's what Max told me.'

'So she could have gone back to her maiden name?'

'Yes, I suppose so, but I don't know what her maiden name was and I don't know how we would find out.'

Jessica pulled the laptop back towards her and started working away busily again. 'Right,' she said. 'I've found somewhere I can search for historical marriage records online. He was married a while ago, wasn't he? It might be long enough ago to be on this site.'

I thought about it. 'He said he got married when he was twenty, and she was twenty-two. He's forty-five now, so twenty-five years ago.'

'Any idea where?'

'He's always lived in Habmouth as far as I know. Perhaps that's where he got married too – or somewhere nearby.'

Jessica filled in a few details while I pulled my cardigan more tightly around myself. It was draughty in the conservatory, and the blinds weren't down, the black expanse of glass making me feel oddly exposed.

'Here!' she said triumphantly. 'Simple as that, look.' She pointed to the screen and I leaned forward to see what she had found. 'Max Dorsett,' I read, and my eyes travelled across the screen. 'Spouse's surname, Riddock.'

'Caitlyn Riddock,' Jessica said. 'That doesn't sound like a particularly common name; we might be able to find her.'

'She'll be keeping a low profile, surely, if Max might still be interested in her.'

'Maybe,' Jessica said, as she tried searching for Caitlyn Riddock. Sure enough, there was little to be found, the search results showing women too old or too young to have been the woman Max had married.

'He said she had a daughter,' I said. 'He thought she was his. Would that help?'

Jessica paused for a second, 'Look at this,' she said, gesturing towards one of the search results – an old news article about a car accident. She opened it and we both quickly scanned through it. 'Caitlyn Riddock, 38, was hit by a car and killed late on a Saturday evening, nine years ago,' I said.

'And she had her thirteen year old niece Grace Riddock staying with her and her family at the time,' Jessica said.

I sat back in my chair with a sigh, trying to process what it could all mean.

'It's probably not her,' I said. 'Max never said she was dead.'

'But Max saw a photo of Caitlyn with a thirteen year old girl, isn't that what he said? And this woman is exactly the right age to be the woman he married.'

'Yes, but–'

'Why was she out late on a Saturday night when she had a teenager staying with her as well as two younger kids of her own?' Jessica asked.

'Well, it says she lived with a fiancé, Tariq. He would have been at home with the kids.'

'Even so. I think it's odd.'

'People get hit by cars sometimes, Jess. You can't read more into this than there is.'

'No, but think about it!' she said insistently. 'Don't you think that photo he saw could have been a picture of Grace staying with her aunt Caitlyn? Max sees it, gets completely the wrong idea and goes and confronts his ex wife, thinking that Grace is his daughter that she's been keeping secret?'

'And, what, gets a stranger to run her over? It wasn't Max driving the car. It was a tragic accident.'

'Sometimes accidents aren't accidents. Maybe he confronted her and she was running away from him, or so upset by him that she wasn't looking where she was going. Who knows, maybe he pushed her into the road but the driver didn't see him. It was dark – not long before midnight.'

'That's a lot of conclusions to draw from very little evidence.'

'It sounds like something he'd do, though, doesn't it?'

I put my hand up to my forehead, where an ache was starting. 'Yes,' I said, 'I suppose it does.'

Habmouth

44

The banging broke through into my dreams until I woke with a start. 'Poppy!' Max's voice called out. 'Poppy, you can't ignore me forever!'

He hammered on the door again. 'Poppy!' He was trying the door handle and I started to shake. Sitting up in bed, I hugged my knees and willed him to go away. Before long there was silence and I crept out to the hall. The little security window in my door revealed an empty hallway, but at my feet was a folded sheet of paper he'd pushed under the door, and I picked it up with trembling fingers.

You might have won this time. But I will never leave you alone. You don't get to ruin my life and move on.

I tore the paper in half in rage. After discovering Max didn't have the knife, I'd slept the best I had for a long while, until he'd woken me by banging on my door. What an idiot I had been to think I would get even one night of respite! I ran over to the window, and when I pulled the curtain aside he was getting into his car. *Drive away. Please, just drive away. Leave me alone.*

He didn't drive away. His car was there for the rest of the night, and it was still there the next morning.

The new year could be a fresh start for us, Max messaged me. *I'm feeling forgiving. Let's put all the unpleasantness behind us. I know you must be getting tired of this.*

Yes, I was tired of it. I was sick to death of it. My life had no meaning or purpose any more, not when I was too scared to go outside and face the risk of feeling his hand on my shoulder, or hearing his footsteps a pace behind me. But I wouldn't give up.

I'd conserve my strength, and then I would pick a moment that seemed safe, and make a run for it. Max would be starting back at the office after the Christmas break soon, I was sure of it – perhaps even the very next day – and I would have to seize my chance.

Later that day, I packed my bag carefully, and settled down in bed to get an early night. I'd made my decision now, and though to begin with I'd been at a loss over where to run to, a face had drifted up hazily from the back of my mind – a face from a time when I had been safe, when the future had been something full of excitement and promise. It hadn't taken me too long to track Harriet down online, and I'd quickly received a reply to my message asking for her address. I had just about enough money left to do what I needed to do. The sequence of events was simple enough. I only needed to get onto a bus without Max seeing me, and then before I knew it I'd be at the train station, boarding a train that would have me speeding away from Habmouth. I would change my phone number and email address, freeing myself from Max's constant communications without the possibility that he would turn up at my door in a fit of rage. Harriet and Jessica would no doubt be surprised to have me arrive on their doorstep, but I would cross that bridge when I came to it. I had to go to somebody Max would never suspect. Somebody he wouldn't even know about.

I set an alarm, but woke well before it. Had I managed to get any real sleep at all? It didn't feel much like it, though at the thought that this might be the day I escaped restless energy filled my body. Every time I had looked out of the window during the night Max's car was still there, but if he was supposed to be starting back at the office today he would surely have gone back home to sleep – or at the very least to have a shower. I ran over to the window, but paused before I moved the curtain. What if he *was* still out there? I couldn't bear it. Taking a deep breath, I yanked the curtain aside before I could talk myself out of looking, and I gawped at the bare spot in the road in front of the railway bridge. I blinked several times, but the spot remained empty.

Neither was there any sign of him when I looked down my street in the other direction. He'd gone.

I pulled on some clothes, doing everything as quickly as I could. It was possible Max might decide to drop by before he started work, but as he'd still been outside when I'd last checked out of the window at two a.m., I suspected he wouldn't turn up at my flat this early in the morning. I had a last quick glance around the studio flat before I left. *Please let it be the last time I see this place.* If I had to come back here in five or ten minutes after having abandoned my plan to escape, I wouldn't be able to bear it.

The January morning was icy cold as I took the first step outside the door. Snow was forecast, and I pulled my coat tightly around me. Eyes darting all around, I sought out any sign of Max's face, Max's car, but there was nothing. Reaching the corner of the street, I rounded it quickly. The roads were quiet, and my nerves jangled alarmingly. Should I have tried at some other time of day? Maybe when there were crowds? But that wouldn't help; Max could turn up at any time. Before Christmas he must have been working from home some days, or inventing some excuse to leave the office. There was no time of day that I could truly know I would be safe.

The bus stop was deserted. I was five minutes early, and I stood impatiently under the shelter, unable to stop myself turning my head to check up the road, down the road. *Just calm down. Any second now, it will all be over.*

'Poppy.'

Jumping out of my skin at the voice behind me, I froze in horror. He'd crept up on me from the path behind the bus stop, and now he was standing beside me, so close I could feel the heat of his breath when he spoke. 'Are you going somewhere?' he asked, his eyes on my bag.

'Max, please,' I said, almost hysterical. 'Just leave me alone! Please.'

The bus was supposed to get here in just a few minutes. There were other people about now, some of them walking determinedly towards the stop. Max couldn't make a scene, not with witnesses. If I could just get on the bus, I'd be safe, wouldn't I? But he was standing right next to me. Even if, by some miracle, I did manage to get on the bus without him following, he'd seen the bag. He'd guess I was heading for the train station.

Other people came and stood beside us, and Max stayed silently by my side. He would get on the bus with me, there was no doubt about that. I tried to think. If I could run away from him somehow there would be another train that went to Cattleford an hour later, I could just walk to the station. *But he'll wait for me at the train station.* The station was big, but everyone had to go through the ticket barriers to get onto the platforms. He would wait for me in the foyer, and I'd be in no better situation than I was right now.

The bus arrived, and once the doors hissed open I got on, and he got on behind me. It was busy this morning, and in the crush of people getting on to the bus I managed to seat myself near the door, while he was forced to sit a few rows back from me. All at once, a plan formed in my mind. It was mad, and it probably wouldn't work, but what else did I have?

45

I fidgeted constantly, drumming my fingers on my knee. We were getting closer to the train station, but there was still one stop to go before we reached it. When we stopped there I'd wait until the last second, and then leap off the bus before Max even knew what was happening. He'd get off at the station, I knew that, but I would find somewhere to hide, take off my coat and change my appearance as much as I was able. I had an old hoodie of Dominic's in my bag – I could put that on with the hood up. If he was fixated on looking for a woman with blonde hair in a plum coloured coat, he wouldn't pay too much attention to a slim figure in a baggy grey hoodie, especially not when there was likely to be a crowd of people there at this time in the morning.

The bus stopped and I slowed my breathing. A few people filed off, and some started getting on. I watched the queue, my pulse racing. The last person stepped on, and I grabbed my bag from beside my feet. This was my chance. Exploding out of my seat, I nearly stumbled and fell flat on my face in the aisle, but I steadied myself and raced to the doors just before they closed and the bus pulled away. I caught sight of Max's face staring at me through the window, and I took a deep breath and ran.

...

Less than half an hour later, I nearly laughed out loud as the last of Habmouth disappeared and the train sped out into the countryside. My plan had worked – better than I could ever have expected. Despite spotting Max straight away at the station, with my hair tucked away and the hood close around my face he didn't give me a second glance. I melted into the other crowds at the ticket machines, and when I risked sneaking a look back as I stepped out onto the platform, there he was hanging around the entrance, looking puzzled and lost. How long would he stand there for? Just a few more minutes? Or would he wait for hours, searching in vain for the woman in the purple coat who would never arrive? I took great gulps of air. God knows what I was going to say to Harriet and Jessica. And Dominic, for that matter. But right now that didn't matter. Right now all that mattered was that I was safe. My phone beeped:

I don't know how you did it Poppy, but I will find you. I don't care what it takes. I will find you.

I blocked his number. Yes, it would infuriate him, but now I'd escaped and I knew he didn't have the knife, I didn't care about making him angry. His words couldn't hurt me any more.

Cattleford

I barely slept. I lay on my bed, trying to rest, though the knowledge that Harriet was in the house made my skin crawl. But Jessica had been right. It was too late at night to go anywhere else, and Dominic was coming here, it would freak him out if I suddenly gave him a different address.

I got up early, thankful that there was no sign of Harriet, and after showering I set to work packing up my belongings, mind whirring. If I left with Dominic, perhaps we could get a flat together. He had his student loan and his job at the restaurant. Maybe once I'd had the baby I could find some childcare and get a job. *But what if there really is an audit at QHM? What if I get caught?*

I heard Jessica and Reef go out, and then a short time later the front door slammed shut as Harriet left for the shop. I spent the morning drifting listlessly around the house, exchanging a few words with Jessica once she returned after dropping Reef at school, but her mood was heavy too, and the house was oppressive with misery. The thought of Max's ex-wife Caitlyn kept turning over in my mind. Was Jessica right? Was the Caitlyn we'd found online really the Caitlyn Max had been married to? And if so, had Max been involved in her death somehow? It was a bit of a coincidence that he mentioned seeing a photo of her with a teenager right around the time that she died, when the Caitlyn we'd discovered had had a teenage niece staying with her.

I had to stop dwelling on it. It wasn't helping me. I tried to focus all my energy on imagining the moment when Dominic arrived. How I would feel when I caught sight of his face – his hair that would have grown too long while he was away – his warm brown eyes that still took me back to the days he'd turn his little heart-shaped face up to me as a child, the days when I had been his whole world. I had to forget Max, and Harriet. I had to put them in the past where they belonged. Hopefully I wouldn't even have to lay eyes on Harriet again since she'd hidden away at the shop, no doubt too ashamed to face me.

I messaged Dominic, saying that I was happy to come and meet him at the station, but he insisted it was fine and that when his train got in he'd make his own way to Harriet's house. The time passed excruciatingly slowly, and once it was mid afternoon and I knew it wasn't too much longer until I would finally hold Dominic in my arms, the front door slammed and I dashed downstairs.

'Harriet,' I said flatly. Of course it was Harriet. It was hardly like Dominic had a key to the house.

'Poppy,' she said, her voice like glass.

I was so shocked to suddenly be presented with her that my mind went completely blank. 'Dominic will be here soon,' I said, since no other words came to me.

'How nice for you.'

She made her way through to the kitchen and started filling the kettle, and I followed her. 'Are you still not going to even try and explain yourself?' I said, my voice rising.

'I have nothing to explain.'

'Nothing to…' I stared at her in astonishment. 'Harriet–'

'I thought we were friends!' she said. 'I thought you trusted me.'

'And I thought the same.'

She pointed her finger at me. 'No, you thought I was going to steal your baby!'

'You *were* going to steal my baby!' I said, although my voice faltered. She wasn't acting how I expected her to. She didn't seem guilty. She seemed hurt, if anything. 'You've given no other explanation for what you were up to,' I continued. 'And all this so-called looking after me, all these gifts, the hospital bag, the plan you hatched to get me out of the way–'

'Yes, that's right,' Harriet said, her voice scathing. 'Just because you know I can't have a baby of my own and I've shown an interest in yours, of course that makes me some sort of child abductor.'

'Then prove that I'm wrong! Why did you find out about getting a passport for a baby behind my back if it wasn't because you wanted to take him out of the country without my knowledge?'

'I don't want to tell you why I was doing it. Why should I explain myself to somebody who makes such vile accusations about me? You don't want my help? Fine. Go off with Dominic and throw everything I've been trying to do for you back in my face.'

'What are you talking about?' I said. 'What are you trying to do for me? It seems to me like the only person you've been thinking about is yourself!'

Harriet scooped up her phone from the work top and started jabbing angrily at the screen. 'Here,' she said, holding it out to me. 'Read it.'

I took the phone from her, though the words swam in front of my eyes for a moment. 'Plane tickets,' I said.

'Yes. For all of us. Even Dominic.'

'I don't understand.'

She took her phone back from me and opened another email, which was about the purchase of a villa.

'Harri, you're going to have to tell me what this means.'

'It was after you told me about Kevin's death that I started all of it. You're in such a bloody mess, Poppy. Our plan for you to turn yourself in, that was when I thought this was just about fraud! You can't go to the police and risk them finding out that

Dominic stabbed Kevin. You need to run. And then I thought, well, I don't want to stay here. Jessica isn't happy either. Why don't we all go?'

'And the baby—'

'We were supposed to be going in a couple of weeks, before the baby is due. I was only looking up passports for babies in case you had the baby early and we needed to change our plans last minute.'

'And the villa?'

'I'm buying it. I have all the money from the house I owned with Ben just sat there in the bank. We can rent out this cottage once we're gone and get some income from that as well.'

'Harri—'

'A whole new life in the sun was what I was offering you. But no. You had to believe the worst of me.'

I reached out for her arm and she shook me away. 'I know I seem cold sometimes, but is it any wonder? Look how I'm treated. My husband, my sister, and my best friend. None of you care about me. You just suspect me of all sorts and don't even try and understand how *I* might feel.'

'That's not true! Harriet, I'm so sorry. I didn't want to believe it—'

'And yet you did.'

'I honestly couldn't see any other explanation. And you didn't offer one! You just went and hid, what was I supposed to think?'

'I don't care what you think any more. You've made it perfectly clear what a low opinion you have of me, so that's the end of it.'

I stood beside her helplessly as she made herself a mug of tea and then sat down at the kitchen table. She slid a newspaper across to her and made a show of looking at it, though I knew she wasn't really reading it.

'What can I say?' I asked her. 'How can I make it right?'

'You can't,' she said simply. 'I don't want anything to do with you any more. Once Dominic gets here I want you to leave, and you'll never hear from me again. You've hurt me too much, and there's no coming back from it.'

We were both startled by a knock on the door. Dominic! He was finally here!

I flung open the front door, my nervousness at him noticing my bump pushed to one side in my desperation to see his face, but my excitement fell dead immediately. Dominic was there, but standing just a pace behind him was someone else. A face that stopped me in my tracks and made me stagger backwards, clutching at the door frame. Max.

46

Following some desperate survival instinct, I grabbed Dominic and tried to pull him inside in time to shut the door in Max's face, but it didn't work. Max shoved the door open, and I found myself face to face with him in the hall. He closed the front door gently behind him, and stood staring at my stomach.

'Mum,' Dominic said, once he'd finished doing the same, 'you just need to hear him out. He wants to help–'

'No.'

'He said if I bring him to you and you can have a proper conversation, that it will be the end of it. He just wants closure.'

I crossed my arms protectively across the top of my bump.

'Were you ever going to tell me?' Max asked. His voice may have sounded soft and kind, but the caring expression didn't reach his eyes. In fact, the only thing I could see in his eyes was fury. 'You must be due soon.'

'What's going on?' Harriet said, emerging from the kitchen. 'Is this him?' she asked me, stopping in her tracks at the sight of the man next to Dominic. 'Is this Max?'

For a moment we all stared at each other in a tense standoff, and then Max spoke. 'You were going to stop me from ever knowing my own child,' he said. 'When I *told* you what my ex-wife did to me?'

'Your ex-wife didn't have a daughter with you,' I said, taking a chance on the findings from my detective work with Jessica being true. 'You saw a photo of her with her niece.'

Max's eyes narrowed. 'You've been busy.'

'And you are living in a fantasy world. You know it's over between us. And if you didn't get closure the hundreds of times I've told you that, I don't know what more I can possibly do.'

'Except it isn't over, is it? You're pregnant.'

My mind raced. What could I say? How could I possibly salvage this? He knew the baby was his and even if I tried to persuade him otherwise he was never going to believe me.

My eyes slipped uneasily over to Harriet's. But while I was practically incoherent with shock and worry, her eyes were dark and glittering as she calculated how to manage the situation. 'I think we all need to calm down,' she said.

Max turned to her. 'You… whoever you are, just keep out of it. This is between me, Dominic and Poppy.'

'*She* is the woman who has sheltered me all these months after you kept me a prisoner in my own home and forced me to run away!' I said. Dominic was staring at me in bewilderment, but there would be time to explain it to him later. 'I was struggling to even go out and get food because I didn't want any more confrontations with you. The stress was making me ill! You lost me my job, and I couldn't get another one, not when I couldn't leave my flat without worrying you would be there waiting for me.'

'This is nonsense!' he said. 'All I've ever wanted is for you to just hear me out—'

'Go on, then!' I said, my voice rising, 'Tell me whatever it is you haven't been able to say to me in the thousands of texts, and emails, and answer phone messages. Not to mention all the times you've cornered me in the street or banged on my door. It must really be something big to have not been able to get the words out when you've had so *many* opportunities.'

'Not in front of everyone,' Max said.

'Mum,' Dominic said, 'what are you talking about? You lost your job? And Max was—'

'I wasn't doing anything!' Max snapped at him. 'Your mum is exaggerating. I just wanted to talk to her, that's all.'

'Well, you heard her,' Harriet said. 'You want to talk, then talk. We're all fascinated to hear it.'

At a sound on the stairs, we all looked round as Jessica made her way down.

'How many people are there in this house?' Max asked, as if he'd been confronted with an army, not just the two sisters.

'Anything you want to say to me, you can say in front of them,' I told him.

Max reached out for my hand and I moved away from him.

'Poppy, come on. We were going to get married. If our time together meant anything to you–'

'Stop it,' I said, 'stop doing this. Stop trying to twist everything. *You* started making threats.'

'Because you were going to leave me!'

'Tell Dom the truth,' I said, gesturing at my son. 'Tell him exactly what you were threatening to do.'

Fear flashed in Max's eyes, and he turned to Dominic. 'Don't listen to her,' he said. 'I told you how worried I am about her. How erratic her behaviour has been.'

'You didn't tell me she'd lost her job,' Dominic said.

'Well, she… it's not my place,' he blustered. 'And she was the one trying to hide the fact she was pregnant! Denying a baby the chance to know its father – how is that right? Before you listen to her ridiculous accusations you should ask yourself what kind of woman your mother really is!'

'Just stop,' Dominic said, watching Max warily. 'You said you were coming here to help.'

'Dom,' I said, 'he doesn't want to help me. He only cares about himself. He's been stalking me, and threatening to turn you in to the police. That phone call I made, asking about the knife–'

'Mum, no!' Dominic said, his eyes on Harriet and Jessica. 'You can't talk about that.'

'They know.'

'They *know*?' he breathed.

'Max said he had the knife,' I explained, 'he told me he would turn you in if I didn't go back to him. That's why I called you that night, to see if he really had it.'

Dominic stared at me for a long moment, his face drained of colour. For a second I thought he would faint, he looked so shocked. 'I think you should go,' he said to Max eventually.

'Oh, I'll go,' Max said. 'I'll go straight to the police and tell them exactly what you *and* your mum have been up to.'

'Go on then!' I cried. 'Do it! What's keeping you?'

'Poppy,' Harriet said, taking my arm, 'there's no need for it to come to that.'

I felt light-headed, and my knees started to buckle. Dominic and Harriet supported me between them and led me into the living room where I slumped down on the sofa. Max watched, his eyes narrowed. 'That's it, Poppy, play the victim.'

'She is pregnant,' Harriet hissed at him. 'You should have some respect for her.'

'Just leave me alone!' I screamed at him, rising from the sofa, even though my legs were still shaky. 'I have asked you hundreds, *hundreds* of times to just leave me alone!'

He grabbed me, and I fought him like a wildcat while Dominic tried to pull him off.

'You had nothing when I found you,' Max spat at me as Dominic succeeded in pulling him away. 'It was me that finally got you to make something of your life. You're *nothing* without me, Poppy. And if you think I'm just going to walk away when you're having my baby…'

'Yes, you are,' Harriet said, fixing him with a glare. 'I can see you for exactly what you are. And I've dealt with men like you before.'

Max burst out laughing. 'Oh, really?' he said. 'Come on then. Deal with me.'

47

'Max, you need to leave,' Dominic said, as calmly as he was able. 'You can't talk to Mum like this.'

'I'll talk to her however I want. You said once you were proud of her. What do you think about what she's done? Stealing money, involving herself and you with that psycho Kevin? She's a great example. I'm sure she would love it if you followed in *her* footsteps.'

Tears pricked my eyes. 'That's why I want to do the right thing now,' I said quietly. 'After having the baby, I wanted to clear my name. I was going to turn myself in for the fraud and take whatever punishment was given to me.'

'Oh I see,' Max said. 'You were going to go and say how sorry you were, how *I* was the person who got you into it…'

'You *were* the person who got me into it.'

'It's all very convenient for you.'

'Right,' Harriet said, 'this has gone on long enough. Poppy needs to rest. And you need to leave.'

'I'm not leaving. Not until this is sorted out.'

'We'll both leave,' Dominic said. 'We'll take a walk and calm down for a minute.'

'Dom, no–'

'Mum, it'll be okay. We'll sort this out.'

'Perhaps you should let him,' Harriet said quietly. 'You and Max can both gather your thoughts and work through this when you've had a few moments to take a breath.'

I stared at her. 'I am not letting Dominic go anywhere with Max on his own.'

'Then Jessica will go too,' Harriet said. 'I'll stay here with you.'

Jessica looked as startled by this suggestion as I was, and was about to protest but Harriet fixed her with a look. 'Does that sound okay, Poppy?'

All of them were looking at me. It didn't sound okay. None of it sounded okay. But I was desperate for Max to go away, and with Jessica going along with them Max wouldn't be able to do anything to Dominic. Not that I was really sure if he would *do* anything anyway, but I knew how he could twist things with his words, how manipulative he could be.

'Mum, I'm on your side,' Dominic said reassuringly. 'Stay here and rest.'

Reluctantly, I nodded. I wasn't feeling good, and right now I'd agree to virtually anything to just get Max out of my face. The three of them filed out of the house, and as soon as the door closed Harriet turned to me urgently. 'Right,' she said, 'let's go upstairs and get our things. You've already been packing, anyway, haven't you?'

'What are you talking about?'

'You know as well as I do that you can't trust a word that comes out of that man's mouth. He'll talk Dominic and Jessica round with some bullshit and before you know it he'll take over your life again.'

'You want to run away right now? Where would we go?'

'To the same place we were supposed to be going in a couple of weeks. The sale on the villa hasn't all gone through yet but we'll find somewhere near to it to stay in the meantime.'

'It's too sudden…' I said, my mind racing.

'Well, what's your plan? Sit here and wait to have your future dictated to you by some scumbag? Poppy, you can't stay here and hope it'll be okay. He knows you're pregnant now, and your life will never be your own again.'

I wanted to argue. I wanted to say that I wasn't some push-over who would let that happen, but I had to face facts. Max would be relentless now he knew I was pregnant. He'd been bad enough already, but now he would never give me a moment's peace. 'Harri,' I said slowly, 'me and Jessica were doing some research on Max's ex-wife last night. She died when she got hit by a car. Jessica thinks Max confronted her and that he was involved somehow.'

Harriet's face softened and she put her hand on my arm. 'It just shows even more clearly that you have to get away. There is no way of salvaging this. I know it's overwhelming, but you have to run, while running is still an option.'

'I thought you hated me now,' I said. 'After what I accused you of, you said I'd hurt you so much that there was no way back from it.'

'Oh, forget about that,' she said dismissively. 'We're friends, Poppy. If I washed my hands of Jessica every time she made me lose my rag I'd have stopped talking to her when we were toddlers. We'll pretend it never happened. Now go upstairs and get your things.'

'I don't know…'

She went over to a drawer in the living room and took out her passport. 'Make sure you've got your passport. And Dominic's.'

'I don't know if Dominic will come.'

'I think he should. For the moment, anyway.'

When I didn't move she took my face in both of her hands. 'Poppy, this is happening. We need to go. I know it's hard, but just focus, okay? I can help you, but you need to keep it together. Don't think about anything except getting what you need and being ready to leave.'

…

'Okay,' Harriet said when I met her on the landing. She was holding a big suitcase. 'I've got enough to last me, Jessica and Reef for the moment. We'll need to get him from school and then we'll leave for Spain straight away. I'll message Jessica and tell her to join us, and you message Dominic.'

I followed her down the stairs. Perhaps her idea made sense. But running and leaving Dominic while he was out with Max felt cowardly, even if I was going to message him and tell him to go with Jessica to the airport. I should explain everything to him face to face, but how could I when Max was with him?

I was about to try and say all of this to Harriet when the door burst open, and Max, Jessica and Dominic nearly collided with us in the hallway. Max immediately spotted our bags.

'Nice try,' he said. 'You know, I was prepared to be reasonable about this. To sort something out that would be best for us both. But *you* – you were going to run away!'

'Mum?' Dominic said. 'You weren't, were you?'

'No,' I lied. 'I mean… look at me! The baby's due any day now. I can't go anywhere.'

'Of course she was!' Max exploded. 'She has a bag in her hand.' He grabbed it from me and opened it, picking up my passport, which was at the top. 'Look at this!' he waved it at Dominic.

Dominic's face was filled with pain. 'How could you do this to me?' he asked quietly. 'Were you even going to tell me?'

'Of course I was!'

'You wouldn't tell me you were here. You hadn't even told me you were going to have a baby.'

'Because of–' I stopped short of saying Max. The tide was already turning against me, and in fact Max was smiling, enjoying the fact Dominic was so angry with me.

'Dom, you know how worried I've been about you. I just haven't known what to do for the best.'

But he was too hurt to listen. 'Me and you against the world, that's what you used to say. I wanted to give you another chance to explain everything. But you were going to leave without another word to me!'

'Dom–' I reached out to him, and he pushed my hand away. 'I was going to tell you where I was going. Please…' I said. My eyes were filling with tears, but he wrenched the front door open and slammed it behind him, leaving me facing Max, who smiled nastily. 'Looks like you've burnt your last bridge, Poppy,' he said. 'Come on. Just come home with me. You've made your point. I'll smooth things over between you and Dominic.'

'I am never going anywhere with you.'

He grabbed my arm and I tried to shake it free of his grip. 'Don't be stupid,' he said. 'Realise when you've been beaten.'

'Is this what you did to Caitlyn?' I spat at him. 'You confronted her, didn't you? You thought Grace was your daughter, and you went after her. That's why she was out in the middle of the night. And that's why she got run over and killed!'

Max shoved me away from him, and I stumbled. After rushing to steady me, Harriet slapped Max across the face. 'Don't you *dare* push her about!' she said. 'Do the decent thing, and leave Poppy alone.'

'You know why that bitch Caitlyn got herself killed?' he yelled at me. 'It's because she did exactly what *you* are doing. She wouldn't talk to me! That's all I wanted, and what did she do? She got a fucking restraining order against me because I broke into her house once or twice, just to try and talk to her. What else was I supposed to do? She went off and started a new little family, as if what she'd had with me meant nothing to her at all! Her brother posted that picture of her with Grace. I didn't realise she was *his* daughter and Caitlyn was only her aunt. Yes, I went and confronted her. I waited outside the house and she came out, I heard her telling her fiancé she was going to get some milk for breakfast in the morning. I followed her down the road and she didn't see me, but when we were in a quiet corner I stopped her and asked straight out what the hell she was doing hiding my daughter from me. Yes, she started saying Grace was her niece, and I said it was bullshit, and she tried to run. She stumbled, and then she got to her feet and ran through some bushes. I followed her, but it was too late. There was a main road the other side of the hedge and she'd run straight out in front of a car.'

'It was your fault she died,' I breathed. 'She must have been terrified to not even look where she was going.'

'No. It was *her* fault that she shut me out and let me get the wrong idea about everything! Would I have had to confront her if she had kept in touch with me? She ran out into that road all on her own, because she didn't want to have a straightforward, adult conversation.'

'No one can have a straightforward conversation with you Max! You're not living in the real world.'

He grabbed my chin in his hands, 'No,' he said, '*I'm* living in the real world. It's you who won't be, if you try and take my baby away from me.'

I was about to yell at him, scream at him that he'd made my life a living hell, but before I could speak, he dropped like a stone.

48

I gazed down at him, crumpled on the floor. What on earth? Then I looked up, and Jessica stood there, shaking. In her hands was a heavy vase from the living room. 'Jessica?' I said, 'What have you...'

Harriet quickly took charge. She knelt down next to Max, her fingers against his wrist. 'He's dead,' she said flatly.

Then my knees really did buckle, and Harriet caught me as I fell. 'Jessica, go and collect Reef from school,' Harriet said calmly.

Jessica gently put down the vase and backed away from us.

'How long do you think Dominic will be?' Harriet asked me, as I stared at Jessica, who was slowly edging towards the front door.

'I don't...' my eyes slid down to Max and I knelt beside him. A strange moaning, wailing noise escaped from me. 'Oh God,' I said, 'oh God. What do we do? What do we do, Harri? He's dead! He's dead, he's–'

Harriet grabbed me and gave me a gentle shake. 'Poppy, calm down,' she said quietly.

'We need to call the police,' I said, scrabbling to my feet to go and find my phone. 'We can say that Max tried to attack me – it's not that far from the truth. Jessica was just protecting me. They'll understand.'

'You're not injured,' Harriet said. 'None of us are. You haven't been attacked.'

'What are you saying? We have to call the police. An ambulance. Maybe he's not really – maybe he's okay.' I gave him a shake. 'Max!' I said, 'Max. Wake up. Wake up! For God's sake–'

'He is dead, Poppy.'

'I just wanted it to stop,' Jessica said, her voice startling us. 'It was like Ben. How he kept going on and on at me, shouting. I couldn't think. I just had to make him stop.'

Anxiously, I felt for Max's pulse myself. I hadn't fully taken in what Jessica had said, but the words gradually filtered through. *It was like Ben. I just had to make him stop.*

'Harri?' I said, as I felt her stiffen beside me. 'What is she talking about? Where is Ben?'

Harriet's eyes glittered darkly. 'Poppy, whether you like it or not, you're involved now. Why did you think we weren't that shocked when we found out what Dominic did to Kevin? We know what it's like. When you've been backed into a corner and you just lash out.'

'I didn't mean to do it,' Jessica said, 'I'm sorry, I don't know what happened, I just–'

'Jess, stop it,' Harriet said. 'You know what Max has been doing to Poppy. He had it coming to him. Just like Ben did.'

'Did you kill Ben?' I asked Jessica directly.

'He was shouting at me. Saying how stupid I was, that of course he'd never really wanted to be with me, that the whole thing was just some sort of game to him. I tried to ignore him, but he just wouldn't stop.' Her voice rose. 'He just wouldn't *stop!*'

'Don't upset yourself,' Harriet said.

'Where is he? What did you–'

'The same as what we're going to do with Max,' Harriet said.

'No. We have to call the police.'

'We're not calling anyone,' Harriet said, stepping into my path. 'We can still make this okay. We'll bury him, and then we'll leave. All of us. Me, you, Jessica, Reef, and Dominic.'

'Ben's here somewhere, isn't he?' I said. 'That's why you both find it so hard in this house.'

Harriet doesn't really like coming out into the garden. I recalled Jessica's words as she worked on the raised beds that day in early spring. The garden. That's where Ben was buried.

We all jumped out of our skin as the front door opened. 'Dominic!' I cried out in horror. 'This… this isn't what it looks like.'

'Yes, it is,' Harriet said, closing the door quickly behind him. 'It's exactly what it looks like. Max is dead. The only thing we need to worry about is what happens next.'

49

'He was a bad man, Mum,' Dominic said simply, as he reached down to pick up his brother, baby Freddie, who was crawling a bit too close to the edge of the pool outside our villa. 'Just like Kevin was bad.'

'Dom–'

'You deserve this,' he said, gesturing vaguely at the villa behind us, and the beautiful sun drenched hills. 'And besides,' he continued, 'you didn't do any of it. Jessica was the one holding the vase and *I* was the one who drained Max's bank account to give you some extra spending money.'

'And you really think no one will realise?'

'It's just going to look like he emptied the account himself and ran away. Once the fraud is discovered, people will assume he got scared of being caught and that's why he disappeared.'

'But, Dom–'

I paused as the door behind us opened, and Harriet, Jessica and Reef joined us on the terrace. 'Oh, look at Freddie,' Harriet cooed as Dominic put the little boy back down a bit further from the water, and he set off at a rapid crawl. After the horrible argument I'd had with Harriet before Max showed up at the cottage, I'd worried that her anger towards me would resurface, but my anxiety had been misplaced. We'd all lived together in the villa for several months – Dom visiting during his holidays from university – and now she was away from the suffocating house and reminders of her old life, Harriet had mellowed. She was always ready with a smile, and sometimes I felt like we were girls again. In fact, I seemed to recall we'd dreamed of living in a villa just like this once.

'So, not only did Jessica have an affair with your husband, she also killed him,' I had said to Harriet one night, not long after we ran away.

'Like I've told you before, I felt angry with Jessica sometimes, but it was always him I really blamed. And he made it easy to cover up what had happened. It turned out he'd quit his job, and he was planning to leave me and start a new life anyway. People weren't so surprised when he disappeared. I managed to forge his signature on the documents for selling our old house, and I don't think anyone ever reported him missing.'

'It shows what everyone really felt about him then,' I told her. 'He might have thought he could take whatever he wanted, but in the end he didn't have anyone who cared enough to notice he was gone.'

I recalled that conversation as I lay in the sun and Dominic sat down to play with his baby brother. Harriet looked happy enough now, and for the most part the same could be said of her sister, but occasionally a haunted look flickered across Jessica's face, and I found myself wondering, not for the first time, what had really happened to Tyler.

'That was all in the past,' she said, when I broached the subject later that day, as the sun dipped down below the hills and we savoured the last of its rays over a glass of wine. 'That was part of a different life. Do we really have to think about what we did before, or how we came to be in this place?'

'I don't know.' To be honest, my life before was becoming hazier and hazier. It was surprisingly easy to forget, sometimes, the trail of crimes that had led us here.

'I think,' Jessica said, 'that we got what *we* deserve, don't you?'

I smiled slightly, as the tranquil pool glittered in the fading evening light.

If you liked No Safe Haven and you're keen to read more of my books in the future, I invite you to subscribe to the LK Chapman newsletter. I send only occasional emails with information about new releases and offers – no spam. You will also be able to download a free short story when you sign up!

Visit my website, **www.lkchapman.com**, or any of my social media pages to sign up to the reading group.

Thank you so much for supporting me by buying my book, it means a lot to me, and I hope you enjoyed reading No Safe Haven. Please consider leaving a rating and review to help other readers to discover my book – it really does make a huge difference, and is much appreciated.

Twitter: **@LK_Chapman**
Facebook: **facebook.com/lkchapmanbooks**
Subscribe to the LK Chapman newsletter at **lkchapman.com**

Other books by LK Chapman

No Escape psychological thriller series:

Worth Pursuing (short story)

Anything For Him

Found You

Never Let Her Go

Psychological thrillers/suspense

The Stories She Tells

Into The Lake

Sci-fi thrillers

Networked

Too Good for This World (short story)

Acknowledgements

As always, thank you to my family for your unwavering support while I worked on No Safe Haven. I know living with an author isn't always the easiest thing!

For my beautiful cover thank you to Dissect Designs.

And of course a big thank you to my lovely readers, who make all this worthwhile.

About the author

LK Chapman writes books about relationships, family drama, secrets and lies – from dark and disturbing tales of obsession and jealousy, to twisty thrillers with a dash of romance – her passion is creating characters that get under your skin and stories that keep you gripped.

Chapman's books are inspired by her studies in psychology, and she has always been fascinated by the strength, peculiarities and extremes of human nature. As well as working as a psychologist, Chapman volunteered for mental health charity Mind before starting her journey as an author. It has been an incredibly exciting journey and she is so grateful for the support of her readers.

When she is not writing, Chapman will usually be found in her garden or getting out and enjoying the outdoors – immersing herself in nature and giving her mind a chance to work on her next story!

You can find out more about LK Chapman by visiting her website **www.lkchapman.com**.

Into The Lake

A dark, gripping and twisty thriller with a dash of romance
A whirlwind romance. A drowned girl. And somebody wants vengeance.

When ex-model turned wedding planner Natalie receives an invitation to her school reunion, she isn't sure if she should go. A life-changing injury has altered her appearance, and she worries about the stares, and the questions. But to her surprise the reunion could hardly work out better for her – after hitting it off with troubled former classmate Josh, Natalie is swept up in a whirlwind romance and finds herself engaged to him.

But the excitement of planning her own wedding is short lived, as she receives the messages:

Josh Sparkes is a murderer.

Why don't you ask him what happened all those years ago?

Ask him about Mikayla.

Ask him about the lake.

As abusive messages keep on coming and Josh gets caught in a downward spiral – consumed by memories of his unhappy adolescence and filled with questions and self-doubt about Mikayla's death – Natalie has to put herself in the path of a killer to get to the truth. Can she prove Josh's innocence and get her own happy-ever-after, or will she be next?

Into The Lake is a twisty, thoughtful and compelling read where dark and difficult pasts are laid bare as an eighteen year old mystery refuses to stay buried.

The Stories She Tells

A dark psychological page-turner
A heartbreaking secret. A lifetime of lies.

When Michael decides to track down ex-girlfriend Rae, who disappeared ten years ago while pregnant with his baby, he knows it could change his life forever. His search for her takes unexpected turns as he unearths multiple changes of identity and a childhood she tried to pretend never happened, but nothing could prepare him for what awaits when he finally finds her.

Rae appears to be happily married with a brand new baby daughter. But she is cagey about what happened to Michael's child, and starts to say alarming things: that her husband is trying to force her to give up her new baby for adoption, that he's attempting to undermine the bond between her and her child, and deliberately making her doubt her own sanity.

As Michael is drawn in deeper to her disturbing claims, he begins to doubt the truth of what she is saying. But is she really making it all up, or is there a shocking and heartbreaking secret at the root of the stories she tells?

The Stories She Tells is a powerful psychological novel exploring the lifelong impact of a traumatic childhood.

No Escape Series

Anything For Him (Book 1)

Vulnerable and alone after the tragic loss of her parents, Felicity finds herself in a relationship with volatile and troubled Jay.

Against her better judgement, Felicity allows Jay to draw her in to a twisted revenge plan against his former best friend. Soon Felicity becomes trapped, and as Jay turns increasingly controlling and abusive, she questions everything he has told her about his past and his former girlfriend, Sammie. But when she tries to expose the truth, she comes up against an even greater threat. Someone obsessed and dangerous. Someone who has always been in the background of Jay's life. Someone who will do anything for him.

Anything For Him is the first book in the chilling NO ESCAPE psychological thriller trilogy. It can also be read as a standalone psychological thriller.

Found You (Book 2)

She escaped. But he's coming to get her.

After her imprisonment at the brutal hands of her ex, Jay, Felicity is slowly putting her life back together. She's got a new name, a new hairstyle, and even a new partner: strong, supportive Scott, whose down-to-earth nature makes him the perfect stepfather to little Leo. Though the nightmares still haunt her, she's starting to feel that her struggles are over; that she may, finally, be safe.
But Jay is still out there somewhere.
And Felicity can't shake the feeling she's being watched.

Never Let Her Go (Book 3)

All he wants is his family…

After escaping her ordeal at the hands of her obsessive ex, Jay, Felicity thought she was safe, building a new life with Scott and son Leo in a seaside town. Little does she know that Jay has tracked her down and wormed his way into the confidence of Vicky, a woman from Scott's past who has her own very sharp axe to grind…

In the gripping final book of the No Escape trilogy, Jay's obsession with Felicity pushes him to ever more desperate lengths to get her back. Felicity soon discovers that he'll stop at nothing, and history begins to repeat itself as she finds herself terrified, alone, and at Jay's mercy once again. Can she escape him before it's too late, or will she be destroyed by his determination to never let her go?

Printed in Great Britain
by Amazon

30765882R00138